WASTED * PRETTY

JAMIE * BETH * COHEN

Black Rose Writing | Texas

ISBN: 978-1-68433-253-3
PUBLISHED BY BLACK ROSE WRITING
www.blackrosewriting.com

Printed in the United States of America
Suggested Retail Price (SRP) $18.95

Wasted Pretty is printed in Palatino Linotype
Author photo courtesy of Michelle Johnsen

PRAISE FOR WASTED PRETTY

"Every girl's dream and every girl's nightmare rolled into one. You won't be able to put it down."
–Aimee L. Salter, author of *Love Out Loud* and *Every Ugly Word*

"Relatable if you're in your teens and enjoyable if you're looking back on that time, *Wasted Pretty* is an important and satisfying must-read novel for all ages."
–Lindsay Jill Roth, author of *What Pretty Girls Are Made Of*

"I lost a weekend to this book in the best possible way. I just could not put it down. Every time I thought I knew where it was headed, I was delighted to discover I was wrong."
–Gemma Baker, Co-creator and Executive Producer of the television show *MOM*

"*Wasted Pretty*, a chillingly real roller coaster of a read, left me breathless. Jamie Beth Cohen didn't waste a word in this beautiful and complicated story about the challenges of being a teenage girl filled with equal parts suspense, love, and music. The story is so well-told that I felt each of Alice's hopes and heartbreaks down to the bone."
–Caren Lissner, author of *Carrie Pilby*

For Egg and The Hopweisers
From Bean

*   *   *   *   *

Lyrics used courtesy of Kate Beck

WASTED*PRETTY

PART 1

CHAPTER 1

Every Pittsburgh summer starts like this. Hundreds of people swarm Flagstaff Hill in Schenley Park and wait for the sun to go down so the movie can start. But every summer is a little bit different.

This summer, instead of hanging out on blankets with girls from the lacrosse team, Meredith and I sit at a table under the movie screen facing all the people. A very official looking walkie-talkie makes staticky noises between us. A breeze moves through the ring of trees at the back of the crowd. Everything looks lush and green and though it's warm, it's not muggy the way it will be in August. King Freddie, the Queen cover band playing on the stage behind us, entertains the crowd while it's still light out.

Meredith's bored. She pulls a *Sassy* magazine out of my bag. It's a cute boho-chic, over-the-shoulder thing that holds way more stuff than it looks like it should. Meredith got it for me on her last trip to Aspen. The cover of the magazine advertises articles on "The Perfect Boy" and "Bathing Suits that Fit You."

"Do you see this shit?" Meredith is a master of the full-body eye roll.

"Not cool."

Last month Kurt and Courtney were on the cover. I mean, it's not like they're the most functional couple or anything, but I doubt they give a crap about the perfect bathing suit. *Sassy's* going downhill.

Meredith lights a cigarette, and I make her put it out.

"Alice, it's not like the picture of your father's disembodied head can see me!"

Above the stage behind us there's a banner with my father's image on it. His bald head and dark, Hulk Hogan-style mustache are blown up to massive proportions. "WQEV's Dennis Burton – Pittsburgh's Favorite DJ – 1991&1992" is written in what's supposed to look like pink spray paint. 1992 isn't even over yet, so I'm pretty sure my dad made up the poll that earned him that honor.

"Just please don't smoke at the table," I beg her.

She produces Twizzlers from her own boho bag and chomps on them instead.

When I was really little, I came to Flagstaff with my parents and my brother, Nate. My mom would pack an elaborate picnic basket full of health food that she and Nate would devour. My father would hide potato chips and Slim Jims under the blanket he carried. When my mom wasn't looking, he'd sneak me some. Back then my dad was a teacher, so the beginning of my summer vacation was the beginning of his, too. I think he looked forward to it more than I did. I've always loved school.

Meredith doesn't offer me Twizzlers. She knows my mom has me on a strict food plan. "Don't call it a diet," my mom says. "It's a lifestyle!"

In middle school, back when I still ate whatever I wanted, I'd sit on blankets at Flagstaff with my friends, passing M&Ms and cans of pop back and forth, giggling about the boys on the next blanket. When you go to a fancy, all-girls school, you don't really know boys as people, just as objects of your burgeoning desire, although, in my case, none of them ever desired me back. I was too tall, too thick, too much of a jock to be desirable. The only thing that even got me a seat on the cool-girls' blanket was Meredith. We're the youngest in our grade, but she's always been the Queen Bee. Apparently an overabundance of self-confidence comes standard with a multi-million-dollar trust fund.

I take a baggie full of cut veggies out of my boho and offer Meredith some, but she shakes her head.

I lost more than twenty pounds junior year by eating my mom's homemade meal bars and protein shakes, plus a well-balanced dinner and lots of celery. I'm my mom's guinea pig, and I've finally shown some results. Most of the year it was hard to see the weight loss because our school uniforms are designed to hide the fact we're actually female, but now that school's out, it's hard to miss. The four inches I've grown since last summer add to the overall effect.

"What's the movie tonight?" Meredith has given up on *Sassy* and is flipping through one of my *Rolling Stones*.

"*E.T.*" The movies they play at Flagstaff are always ten years old.

She pantomimes sticking her finger down her throat. "Didn't your dad have to carry you out when we saw that in the theatre?"

"You really never miss a chance to bring that up, do you?"

A few of my dad's radio station interns come by to pick up more stacks of bumper stickers to pass out, and Meredith bats her eyelashes at them and does that stupid hair-flip-thing girls do in movies.

"You have a boyfriend," I remind her when the interns are out of earshot.

"You really never miss a chance to bring that up, do you?" Now she's batting her eyelashes at me.

After my freshman year, my dad turned a side gig in sports reporting for the local paper into an on-air job at WQEV. His outsized personality doesn't jibe with the Top 40 music they play, but his no-nonsense nature – also known as abrasiveness – clicked with the drive-time listeners, and he quickly became the station's largest draw.

It was his idea for QEV to sponsor the movies at Flagstaff, so after freshman year, I went from hanging out on blankets with my lacrosse team to walking up and down the hill with the station interns handing out bumper stickers. My brother used to be in charge of the intern crew, but when he decided to stay at Penn State for summer classes this year, my dad put me, a sixteen-year-old, almost-high-school-senior, in charge of a bunch of college guys. It doesn't make any sense, but a lot of what my dad does is like that. People think he's either a visionary or unstable. People don't seem to realize how often those things go together.

I'm fishing one of my mom's meal replacement bars out of my bag when the walkie-talkie on the table starts to crackle.

"I talked to her at the station this morning. She's doesn't look sixteen."

I'm the only sixteen-year-old at the station and practically the only "her." I reach for the walkie-talkie, but Meredith puts her hand on mine, "Let's listen."

"I'd do her," another voice says.

"Ooooohhhh," Meredith whispers. "Do you think it's one of the cute ones?"

Here's hoping.

"Burton would kill you," the first voice says. "But did you see that rack?"

I hate it when guys call girls' boobs a 'rack.' I hate it more when they call *my* boobs a 'rack.' It's the only place I didn't lose weight, and while the girls at school seem to think this is some amazing gift, I'm starting to think it's not.

"I heard she's fucking Johnny," a third voice says.

I try to take the radio away from Meredith, but she holds me off.

"No way," the second voice says. "Burton would kill him."

"She's probably a virgin," the initial voice says.

"He's not wrong," Meredith says to me with a shrug.

"Meredith!"

At some point last summer Meredith got it in her head that we had agreed to lose our virginities on the same night, she to her boyfriend, Richard, and me to his younger brother, Dylan, but I never actually agreed to that. Dylan's fine, but the only reason he even looked at me was because I was Meredith's friend. And the only reason I looked at him was that I was tired of being someone who hadn't been kissed. We only hooked up a few times and never had sex.

Meredith picks up the walkie, pushes her hair back like she's serious and says to me: "I got this." Then she presses the button. "Hey assholes, we can hear you. Alice can hear you, and she's your boss! Your dicks are probably as small as her boobs are big and you wouldn't know what to do with either!"

"Stop!" I grab the walkie-talkie out of her hands.

"Too much?" She grins.

"Too much!"

"Come on. That was fun."

It would have been fine if they were just some assholes at the mall – she has lots of creative responses when people yell things about my boobs – but this is different.

"I have to work with them the rest of the summer!"

"They won't bring it up. I'm sure they're shitting themselves right now. You know I got your back."

Meredith does always have my back, but she's just unpredictable enough for that to be scary. She's a little like my dad that way.

She pulls binoculars out of the crate next to her and tries to find the interns on the hill. "You'd tell me if you slept with Johnny, right?"

"Meredith!"

"Well?" She takes the binoculars down from her face and side-eyes me.

"No, I wouldn't tell you, because then I'd miss all your virgin jokes too much."

"Alice?!"

"Come on, of course I'd tell you. Don't worry, I have not, nor will I ever, sleep with Johnny."

"That's a shame. He's hot."

"He's also, sort of, like, my brother."

"Like you never had a crush on him."

"Yeah – when I was thirteen! I had a crush on everyone when I was thirteen!"

Johnny interned at the station the whole time he was at the University of Pittsburgh, and when he graduated last month, my dad created the position of chief-lackey to keep him around. Johnny's like a member of our family except he has a much higher tolerance for my dad's shit than the rest of us do.

"Uh, Alice –" Meredith has the binoculars up to her face again.

"Seriously, I'm not sleeping with him. I'm still a virgin, you can keep making fun of me."

"No, not that." She hands me the binoculars. "Look at the other table."

Johnny's staffing the station table at the top of the hill. When I find him in the binoculars, I expect him to be surrounded by interns, but instead, he's standing alone with one other guy. One very particular guy. I make a strange sound that can only be described as an audible swoon.

"That's him, right?" Meredith is trying to grab the binoculars back, but I slap her hand away.

"That's him."

The Hottest Guy Ever.

Meredith and I keep seeing him at the Pitt Field House. We're going to be co-captains of the lacrosse team at school next year, so between the varsity season and tryouts for the Regional Developmental Summer Team that start tomorrow, we've been working out there. Her family has donated so much money to the school that two buildings on campus are named for them, and we're allowed to go wherever we want. The Hottest Guy Ever works out at the Field House. The first time I saw him I forgot I was supposed to be spotting Meredith and she almost dropped a barbell on herself. That wasn't cool of me, but my brain sort of shorted out. Last week, The Hottest Guy Ever asked me about my shirt, and I was just barely able to eke out that it was my brother's. It was probably not a great idea to wear Penn State gear to a Pitt workout facility, but all my clothes are too big, so I've been living in what's left in Nate's closet.

And now The Hottest Guy Ever is talking to Johnny.

"If Johnny knows the Hottest Guy Ever, then it's sort of like I know The Hottest Guy Ever." I'm in a daze of possibility.

"That's not how the transitive property works, genius. And I saw him first."

"You have a boyfriend!" I fake-yell at her through gritted teeth. "And I saw him first at the Field House and, that's not how it works anyway!"

"Oh, I'm sorry, how does it work? You, the sixteen-year-old-virgin, ride off into the sunset with The Hottest Guy Ever? Yeah, that sounds totally plausible."

"Why are you such a bitch?" *But she has a point.*

"Because I'm good at it." She winks at me, something so creepy only Meredith May would attempt and subsequently get away with. "You're not going to have time for a new guy this summer, not with the Summer Team."

"If I make the Summer Team."

The Regional Developmental Summer Lacrosse Team pulls girls from the tri-state area to play in tournaments for scouts. A few colleges were interested in me after junior year, but I don't have an offer for college yet.

"You'll make it." Her voice is kind now, because she knows I'm super-nervous about the tryouts. "We'll both make it. Anyway, you should probably just hook up with Dylan again this summer."

"Not that again."

"I just want what's best for you." Her tone is mock-maternal.

"You just want me to get laid."

"And that." Meredith adds a devious smile to her wink.

"You gotta stop winking!"

The walkie-talkie crackles again, and I brace myself, but this time it's Johnny.

"Wonderland, Wonderland, come in, Wonderland."

"What's up, Johnny?"

"Didn't copy, Wonderland. Come in?"

Johnny insists on using nicknames and trucker lingo when we're on the radios.

"This is Wonderland, come in Johnny-Five."

"You getting ready to wrap this up?"

"Yes indeed, good buddy." My tone is deadpan. He can make me say the words, but he can't make me like it.

"You holding any T-shirts?"

"Yes."

Silence.

"Sorry," I correct myself. "Affirmative."

"Ok, pull a small for my friend. I'll send him down."

Meredith mouths "Oh. My. God." at me.

"I thought the shirts were only for interns." Is this a test? I'm supposed to be in charge, and I know Johnny will report everything back to my dad.

"Can you break a rule for once, Wonderland?"

I'd probably break a lot of rules for The Hottest Guy Ever, but at the moment I've forgotten how to breathe.

Meredith grabs the walkie out of my hand and says, "Affirmative. 10-4, good buddy."

CHAPTER 2

The Hottest Guy Ever is standing in front of our table. He's tall and broad, clearly all muscle, and he has shaggy blond hair that falls over his forehead. He has a sweet face that I suspect makes him look younger than he is, and light, sparkling eyes. There's a strap across his chest that holds an acoustic guitar on his back. He's like a clean-cut Kurt Cobain, and the orange light of the setting sun makes it look like there's a spotlight illuminating him from behind.

"Johnny said I could get a shirt?"

I can't speak, so I nod.

I'm leaning back in my chair because his presence is too much, but Meredith looks like she's about to crawl across the table and lick his face. She has stripped off her station shirt to reveal a salmon colored tank, and her upper arms are pushing her boobs together. She's so damn pretty. She has the same brown hair and eyes I do, and she's almost as tall as I am, but there's just something special about Meredith May. If she hadn't been my best friend since kindergarten, I'd probably hate her. I'm just as surface and petty as the other girls at school even though I pretend I'm not.

Meredith finally speaks because The Hottest Guy Ever and I are just staring at each other. "You look more like a large than a small."

"Oh, yeah, it's not for me." He points towards a blanket where a petite light-skinned Black girl with spiky, fuchsia hair is playing the guitar. "Someone spilled wine on Tess, so Johnny said she could have a shirt."

"Of course." I can finally breathe again.

Of course, he has a girlfriend. Of course, she's a fabulously punk pixie chick. If I didn't hate her with a burning passion, she could be a total fashion inspiration – not that my parents would let me dye my hair. I will forever have boring, long brown hair to match my boring brown eyes. Maybe the guys who think my rack is the only thing I have going for me are right.

I hand The Hottest Guy Ever a shirt.

He's about to turn away, but then he says, "Haven't I seen you on campus?"

I kick Meredith under the table.

"Yeah, at the Field House? You asked me about my shirt last week?" My voice goes up at the end of each sentence. It's like it didn't really happen unless he remembers it, like I don't exist if he's not seeing me.

"Oh, you're the Penn State fan."

"Not exactly, but yeah."

"I'm Chris Thompson." He extends his hand, and I can't bring myself to take it until Meredith nudges me. His grip is strong, and I can feel callouses against my palm. Things rearrange themselves inside me.

"Alice." My name has never sounded so plain.

He waits a minute before he drops my hand. When he finally does, Meredith tries to steal his attention. "You play music?"

"Yeah. I'm in a band. Wasted Pretty – have you heard of us?" He asks me, not her.

Unfortunately, all I can do is shake my head slightly. I don't understand how it can feel so heartbreaking to let him down when I don't even know him.

"Tess is the lead singer."

Of course she is.

"I've heard of you," Meredith pipes up.

I turn and glare at her. She's lying. I can tell because her voice is a touch too high. Also, she only listens to the crap they play at the station. She can sing every lyric in every song on Wilson Phillips' first album.

"Yeah?" he asks.

"Sure." Meredith bats her eyelashes and pushes her boobs in and up. This normally works for her. It's how she snagged Richard, golden boy at our brother school, Aiken, a year ahead of us and off to Bucknell in the fall.

The Hottest Guy Ever looks her over as if he doesn't believe her, but might be flattered she's bothering to lie. "Cool."

"What kind of stuff do you play?" I ask.

He faces twists, creating all sorts of dimples. "I hate that question."

"Oh … yeah … sorry, dumb question." Maybe it was better when I couldn't breathe and therefore couldn't talk.

"No, it's not a dumb question. Everyone asks it. I get it. It's just that Tess is much better at explaining it than I am. It's really her band." The Hottest Guy Ever speaks softly, but I can hear every word he says, like there's some magical connection between his lips and my ears. *I wish.* "I don't know," he continues. "Imagine a little bit of The Pixies mixed with PJ Harvey and then throw in some Smiths?"

"Oh my god, I love The Smiths!"

"Don't get her started on The Smiths." Meredith interrupts our moment with a pronounced sigh. "She has yet to recover from their break-up. I actually made her cookies to try to cheer her up. And I don't bake. All her favorite music is from 1987."

"Not a bad year to be stuck in, musically." The Hottest Guy Ever is smiling right at me. It's not the way other people look at me. It doesn't make me feel weird or self-conscious. The way he looks at me makes me feel special. "We do a cool cover of 'William, It Was Really Nothing.'"

"I looooove that song."

"Tess writes all of our original stuff. You know, dark, black-eyeliner lyrics with heavy guitar, but also a little poppy, in a tongue-in-cheek kinda way – but people always think we're ska because, you know, Tess is Black and from England, and one of the guys sometimes plays a horn." Of course Tess is from England. I'm sure her accent is absolutely amazing. "We're really more rock 'n' roll than that, you know, grungy? I don't know. It just sounds stupid when I talk about it." He pauses, but he isn't done talking. "You should just come hear us some time."

Meredith kicks me under the table.

"Oh … yeah … cool," I stutter. Everything inside me comes alive.

"Alright, see ya," he says. "Thanks for the shirt."

He starts to walk back towards Tess when I inexplicably yell at him, "We have key chains!"

He turns back around and smiles widely. The shape of his face completely changes, and he looks like a different person: still unbelievably hot, but more approachable. I get the sense he doesn't smile like this a lot.

"I'm good," he says with a wave.

Back on his blanket, he and Tess lean against each other with a casual intimacy that drives me crazy.

"'We have key chains?'" Meredith huffs. "What's wrong with you?"

"'I've heard of you?'" I say. "What's wrong with you?"

Some interns come by and ask for more stickers to hand out. Snapped out of my wistful stare, I spin around and see my dad and another guy talking to the band as they come off the stage.

"Crap!"

"He's never here," Meredith says in disbelief.

I turn back to the interns, but I can't look any of them in the eye, and they certainly aren't looking at me. How can we all be embarrassed at the same time?

"We can actually pack up," I bark.

"Do you think he saw you talking to him?" Meredith asks.

"My father sees everything. Unbelievable."

I try to sneak a look back over to The Hottest Guy Ever, but Meredith catches me.

"Seriously?" she asks. "You don't know anything about him except he has the same questionable taste in music you do."

"So?"

"And if you think you're going to be the Courtney Love to his Kurt Cobain, it looks like that role is already taken."

"Thanks."

"I just don't want to see you get hurt. You're not gonna screw him, so really, what's the point?"

She's right, and everything that was feeling pleasantly warm and gooey inside me turns sharp and cold as my dad approaches.

"Alice. Meredith. How'd it go tonight?"

"Fine." I can't look him in the eye either.

And then he says it. "Alice, who were you talking to?"

I look at Meredith, but she's no help. She's either as stunned as I am, or she's enjoying the fact that I got caught.

"Who?" I manage to ask.

"You just gave someone a station shirt, Alice. I couldn't see his face, but he didn't look like an intern."

"He's a friend of Johnny's."

"And he's probably twice your age."

"I'm not ten! And he just needed a shirt for his girlfriend!"

"Burton!" Meredith practically yells. She's an effective distraction. "You're never here! To what do we owe this pleasure?! And where is the Lovely Lois?"

She's being overly dramatic and saccharinely sweet. My father hates it when she calls him Burton, but she doesn't care. It was one thing to watch me get caught by my dad, but she's not going to leave me flailing by myself on the edge of a grounding. She'll sacrifice herself to take the real heat off me.

"Mrs. Burton," my dad says, pointedly correcting Meredith's 'Lovely Lois' comment, "is catering an event, and Karl and I are headed to the South Side, but he wanted to see what was going on here first."

"What?! Karl's in town?" I whip my head back around to the stage. The guy talking to the band is Karl Bell. Major League Baseball player. So Freakin' Hot.

My dad waves him over.

Karl's black hair is slicked back, and his dark eyes gleam. His big smile, which has always reminded me of someone getting away with something, electrifies the air, and I can't help smiling too. I'm sure I'm blushing.

"This can't be little Ally Burton, can it?" He spreads his arms so wide he nearly knocks my dad over.

"It's Alice," I say into his shoulder as he lifts me off the ground and swallows me in a ginormous bear hug. People don't generally lift someone as tall as I am, but Karl, at 6'5", has at least seven inches on me. The biting, sharp smell of his cologne fills my face.

We met Karl when I was in Children's Hospital after I wrecked my bike in fifth grade. He and some other Pittsburgh Pirates were visiting sick kids, and he wandered into my room. I haven't seen him since I was thirteen and the Pirates traded him to a team in Texas. Last I heard he was playing in Asia. Everyone in my family was sad when he left – he was like our own personal celebrity before my dad got "local-famous" – but I was the only one who cried. When I think of myself blubbering at his goodbye party, I tell myself it's just because I was so young, but I know it was because he was my first crush.

"What are you doing here?" I ask when he finally put me back on the ground.

"Burton and I are headed out to some bars."

There's no alcohol in our house, and my dad doesn't drink unless he's trying to impress someone. It's like some weird adult peer-pressure thing.

"No," I clarify. "What are you doing in *Pittsburgh*?"

"Burton didn't tell you I got signed?"

"Here? You're back?" I feel something tingle in my stomach at the thought of having Karl Bell here again. My whole family's happier when he's around.

"No, the Padres."

"Aren't they in … California?"

"You really don't know anything about baseball, do you?"

"Nope." A dumb giggle comes out of my mouth. Someone my size shouldn't giggle.

"The Padres and the Pirates are in the same league. I have a few days off now, but we have three games here this week."

"Oh, cool," I say. "Is Samantha here?"

Karl's wife, Samantha, is almost as cool as he is. I think I might have had a crush on her, too. At our cook-outs, everyone would be in the backyard listening to my dad and Karl trade ridiculous stories while she would sit in our living room nursing a ginger ale and letting me braid her long blond hair. She only talked when I asked her a direct question, but she didn't seem to mind me sitting very close to her. No one ever uses our living room, so it felt special to be in there with her.

"Nah," he says, shaking his head. "She's back in San Diego getting stuff set up. She says hi." He adds this with an edge in his voice, and I don't know if I believe him.

I'm unsure of what to say next. As a thirteen-year-old, I used to talk Karl's ear off about who-knows-what, but now it's just awkward. And I don't like the way he's looking at me.

"Didn't you used to be … chubby?"

There it is. That didn't take long.

"My mom has this new health food thing she's doing. I lost some weight." I'm supposed to be selling the product to everyone who notices, but I always sound apologetic when I talk about it.

"Nice going."

A group of girls come up to the table to get an autograph. Karl isn't really famous, but he's a hometown boy, something Pittsburgh takes very seriously. My dad doesn't like when people pull focus from him, so he says goodbye to us, and ushers Karl out of the crowd.

"Midnight?" my dad asks. As if I could forget my curfew, which I unsuccessfully tried to renegotiate last weekend.

"I'll probably stay at Meredith's." I don't know why I say it. We don't have plans, but at least if I stay there, I don't have to worry about a curfew.

"Don't forget to leave a message if you're sleeping there."

Meredith does an excellent job of a fake beauty pageant smile and a regal wave (elbow-elbow-wrist-wrist-wrist) as Karl and my dad leave.

"Ugh! I can't believe my dad saw me talking to The Hottest Guy Ever! That guy is so hot my brain gets scrambled when I look at him."

"Screw Chris Thompson," Meredith says. "Karl Bell is beyond hot."

"Come on, he's like forty and married. And you have a boyfriend!

Plus, he sort of creeped me out."

"I'd do him!" Meredith says with a wink.

"Gross! Not ok! And please stop winking! Is tonight over yet?"

"Not even close." Meredith slings her arm over my shoulder, and we walk up the hill towards Johnny.

CHAPTER 3

Johnny has a blanket in front of his station table. Meredith and I crowd him over to an edge. He and I used to fake wrestle and hip check each other when he first started at the station, but now that I have boobs, he keeps a safe distance.

"How was baby's first Flag?" He talks to me like I'm a puppy.

Technically I'm in charge, but I know my dad made Johnny come to watch over me.

"It's not really my first Flag. When Nate ran things last year, he made me do all the work anyway."

"Are the interns listening to you?"

"They're doing something!" Meredith answers. "Hubba hubba!"

Meredith is not above looking like a dork to get a laugh, which is a good quality to have if you're looking to counter-balance being abrasive most of the time.

"What does that mean?" Johnny asks me.

"You must have given one of them the walkie at some point. We heard them talking ... about me."

"And?"

"They think you're sleeping together!" Meredith announces, like it's an answer on a game show.

"Meredith! Stop! Someone's going to hear you." Johnny looks all around to see who might have heard.

Even though I was mortified when the interns were talking about it, it's sort of funny to watch Meredith give Johnny shit.

"Johnny, you realize we're not sleeping together, right?"

"Can you both stop talking, please?" I think Johnny is sweating.

Meredith cackles, so I push it further to amuse her.

"I'm sorry Johnny, you want me to stop talking about how the interns think we're having sex?"

Meredith laughs with her whole body.

"Seriously Alice. As far as I'm concerned, you're thirteen and always will be, so, please, stop. And don't mess with the interns. You'll get someone fired."

I make kissy faces at him, and he throws a handful of popcorn at me. Popcorn is not allowed on Lois Burton's don't-call-it-a-diet plan.

"I'm not going to mess with anyone. They're assholes. Meredith told them they all had small dicks."

"This conversation is officially over. No more talking," Johnny instructs.

*   *   *   *   *

When the movie ends, the interns and I have to clean up the hill. That's the deal my dad made with the city to let us pass out the station crap before the movie. Meredith makes a big show of begging me to let her leave with some girls from the lacrosse team. She pretends she won't go if I don't want her to, but I know she never had any intention of touching anyone else's garbage.

"Can you come out later?" She offers me a drag of the cigarette she's picked up from a girl on the team.

"I'm gonna be a while, don't worry about it. Pick you up tomorrow?" I look around to see who might catch me, and then I sneak a drag off her cigarette.

She hugs me around my neck. "We're gonna rock tryouts. Love ya, Chickie!"

"That girl is trouble," Johnny says as soon as she's gone.

"That girl has gotten me through 12 years of private school."

"Doesn't mean she's not a bitch."

"People always say that, but what no one understands is that when you spend every day surrounded by girls who are nice to your face but say horrible things behind your back, it's really helpful to have someone who says everything right to your face."

"If you say so, Wonderland."

"Don't call me that."

Johnny says he's not feeling well as soon as we're done with clean up, which leaves me alone with the interns for post-Flagstaff hot dogs and fries at The Original Hot Dog Shop. That's their "payment" for staying until the end of the night.

I can't eat anything at The O, per my mom's instructions, and it feels like I might be putting on weight just by smelling the fries, so I'm grumpy and antsy. I sit at the end of the long table ignoring the interns and willing them to ignore me. But it doesn't work. One of the interns slides his chair down the table towards me.

"You're Burton's daughter, right?"

"Yeah. Alice." I'm still mad at all of them for the walkie-talkie shit. Or maybe I'm just embarrassed. I wish Meredith were here.

"I'm Clay. Sorry about being late tonight. I'll only eat half a hot dog, if it helps."

"It's fine. I didn't even notice."

"Oh yeah? I got there after the movie started. But I cleaned up an entire section by myself, so that should make up for it, right?"

So he wasn't there when the other guys were talking about me. Maybe I don't hate him. But I don't trust him.

"Sure. Enjoy." I pull a baggie of celery out of my bag.

"You're at Frazer, right? I went to Aiken with Nate."

"Really?" Most guys from Aiken don't end up interning at the station. They end up at law firms or on political campaigns.

"Yeah, just for a few years. In middle school. My dad taught there. But when he left my parents couldn't afford it."

"Oh. Sorry?" I can't imagine ever leaving Frazer. I wouldn't know what to do with myself in public school. Or a co-ed one for that matter.

"It's no big deal," Clay says. "I mean, I guess it was a big deal, but it was a long time ago."

"The school wouldn't help you? I get financial aid at Frazer."

"Yeah, it just wasn't enough. How's Nate? Still playing soccer?"

"Yeah, he's at Penn State. He started on varsity his freshman year, so he thinks he's very important."

"I know people think he's hard to get along with, but he was always nice to me. Even when everyone else treated me like a staff brat."

"Yeah, Nate's never cared about money. Just soccer."

"What about you?"

"Excuse me?"

"What do you care about?"

"You ask a lot of questions."

"You don't care about anything?"

"No, of course I do." *I care about The Hottest Guy Ever.*

"Hmmm." Clay takes another bite of his hot dog. "You don't like fries?"

"I'm … I'm on a meal plan." He doesn't seem to be an asshole like the rest of the interns, but I'm not sure I like where this conversation is going.

"A diet?"

"No, it's not like that. My mom's developing a line of health food. I'm sort of her guinea pig."

"You must have a lot of willpower." He waves a fry at me.

"Not really. I just do what I'm told."

"Always?"

"Why do you care?"

"I don't really. Seeing you sitting all by yourself down here sneaking celery reminded me of the lunchroom at Aiken. Just thought I'd make sure you were ok."

"I'm fine. Thanks."

"Well, ok then. My bad. Have a good night."

He slides his chair back towards the rest of the interns, and I get up to pay for their food. Boys are weird.

CHAPTER 4

I pull the van into the spot next to my dad's station wagon, which has temporarily become mine. It's puke green and as big as a boat. Last week my dad brought home a super-cute RX-7 for me, but I can't drive it because it's stick. He thought he could teach me, but that didn't go well, so until I figure it out, I have his Wally Wagon. I don't know where the RX-7 came from. He's always complaining about how much my mom spends developing her business, but then out of nowhere, he has this beat-up old sports car for me. It's totally rad, but it doesn't make any sense. Which is just sort of how things go with my dad.

I drop the walkie-talkies and the crate with the other valuable stuff on Johnny's desk and then put my head in my dad's office because the door is inexplicably open.

Shawn, the Jamaican custodian who introduced me to reggae before anyone in my class knew what it was, is in there.

"Ally-Ally, what are you doing here? It's late!"

"Just dropping off some stuff from Flagstaff."

"You still eating your momma's bars? You're lookin' good!"

"Thanks Shawn." Shawn doesn't look at me like I'm a piece of meat. He looks at me like he's proud of me.

"Your momma gave my momma some of those bars. Stinky! But they filled her right up!"

The bars do smell horrible. I'm used to it now, but I know the girls at school whisper about the weird things my mom puts in my lunch.

Everything's wrapped in Saran Wrap and covered in butterfly stickers. It's all about butterflies and magical transformations with my mom. Despite the plastic wrap, the smell seeps out. If everyone weren't basically afraid of Meredith, I know I'd take shit for it, but no one gives Meredith May's best friend shit, at least not to my face.

"That's great Shawn!"

"Let's get out of here," he says. "Mr. Burton doesn't like people in here when he's not around."

"Shawn, this place is a mess."

He puts his hands up like he doesn't take responsibility for it. "Oh Ally-Ally, Mr. Burton doesn't let me clean up in here anymore. I still have the key and take out the trash, but I don't touch the piles."

Piles is a nice way of saying *Leaning Towers of Crap*.

"Give me a trash bag," I say to Shawn. "This is absurd."

"Ally, I don't think that's a good idea."

"Don't worry about it, Shawn. He won't get mad at me for cleaning up. He might even appreciate it."

"Ok, Ally-Ally. Don't stay too late."

My dad goes to a lot of promo events, like openings of bank branches, car dealerships, and carpet stores. He's constantly being given toasters and coffee mugs. I put a bunch of stuff in an empty drawer in a file cabinet, and I'm getting ready to file some papers when I see a piece of letterhead from Frazer. I hold it under the desk lamp.

May 26, 1992

Dear Mr. Burton,

As we discussed on the phone today, despite our generous financial aid award last year, Alice's tuition account remains severely in arrears. Per our conversation, her 1991-92 tuition balance must be brought to zero and her 1992-93 tuition bill, discounted as it is, must be paid upfront, by August 15, 1992 if she is to return for her senior year.

As you know, Alice is a superb student and an excellent member of our community, but we are not in the habit of allowing families the kind of leeway with bill payment as we have allowed you.

On a personal note, I have enjoyed working with Alice on the yearbook staff and know she will make an excellent Business Editor. She has also been a wonderful babysitter to my boys, and I will certainly stay in touch with her whatever the outcome of this financial matter is.

I appreciated your candor on the phone, and I know you are taking this matter seriously. Please know we are also taking this matter seriously. We do not want to lose Alice from the class of 1993, but we are not at liberty to deviate from our policy.

Sincerely,
Kristine Wilson
Bursar/Yearbook Advisor
Frazer Girls' School

I'm light-headed, like when I drink coffee on an empty stomach, which I'm not supposed to do. I've been at Frazer since Kindergarten. I'm good at it, not the social part (I wouldn't be good at that anywhere), but the actual school part and the sports part, and it's all I've ever known. And Meredith's there, which is the only thing that makes being crap at the social-part tolerable. Plus the high school I'm zoned for in the city doesn't have lacrosse.

This is not happening. It doesn't make sense. My dad just got me a car. I mean, it's not new, but it's still a car. Why would he get me a car if he hadn't paid my tuition? Why wouldn't he have paid my tuition? And why's he out drinking with Karl Bell if everything is falling apart?

Before I even realize what I'm doing, I grab my bag and head to Johnny's. If anyone knows what's going on, it'll be him.

CHAPTER 5

Johnny used to live in a fancy low-rise halfway between the station and Pitt, but that was when his parents were helping him with rent. Now that he's graduated and decided to try to make it for real in radio, he's paying his own way. His parents wanted him to be a cop like his dad, but he has no interest in ever holding a gun. He moved into a studio in a converted house on a tiny dead-end street in South Oakland overlooking the hollow. I haven't been inside, but my dad and I dropped him off after an event last week. It's a red brick building on a corner, with a statue of the Virgin Mary out front. I may have grown up in Jewish summer camps, but you can't live in Pittsburgh and not know the trademark blue of the Virgin's shawl. His place turns out to be easy to find, even in my utter panic.

I'm pressing the buzzer with one hand and pounding on the door with the other before I realize I'm crying. I use the cuff of my flannel, which I've thrown on over my station shirt, to wipe my snot. I'm just about to give up when the door opens, but it's not Johnny. It's The Hottest Guy Ever.

He cocks his head to the left, confused. He can't be more confused than I am. I try to turn and run, but my legs aren't cooperating, instead I just put my hands up to my face and pretend I'm not there. *Smooth.*

"Are you crying?"

"Uhhhh ... I was. I'm fine now. I should go." I still have my face in my hands. "What are you doing here?"

"I live here. What are you doing here?"

I wipe my face again with my cuff and put my hands down.

"I thought Johnny had a studio."

"He does, on the second floor. I have the attic to myself, but I can hear his buzzer. So you're here for Johnny?"

"I just need to talk to him."

"But you're crying."

"I'm not crying. I *was* crying. I'm fine."

"Ok." He puts his hands up showing he won't ask any more questions about my tears. "Do you need to hang out here until he gets back?"

He motions to a grimy couch at the end of the porch, and I manage to shake my head.

"Why don't you just sit down?" He sits on the steps leaving me only a sliver of space to fit next to him.

"Why *were* you crying?"

"It's just … I mean …" I gasp and sniffle like I'm going to cry again, but I manage to hold it together.

"Sorry, you don't have to tell me."

"Why do you care?" It comes out bitchier than I intend it to, a self-protective reflex from a lifetime making my way through Frazer as a scholarship kid. My dad points out my shitty tone frequently, but I never realized how I sounded until now.

"Why wouldn't I care? You showed up on my porch crying. And you like The Smiths. So I feel responsible."

He does that wide smile thing, and I can't help but smile back. It almost feels like he's happy to see me. Thank god he has a girlfriend, or I don't think I could function this close to him. Especially not with that smile.

"That's nice," I say. "But I don't want to talk about it."

"That's fine. What did you think of the movie?"

"*E.T.*?"

"Yeah."

"Why do you want to talk about that?" It's my bitchy voice again.

"I don't know. What do you want to talk about?"

"I don't want to talk about anything!"

"Whoa. Chill." His hands are up again. "I'm just trying to be nice."

But it feels like it's more than that. He's probably one of those guys who flirts with everyone.

"I'm sorry. That was deeply uncool of me." I wipe my eyes. "*E.T.*'s a classic. Instant classic. Excellent film."

"Agreed."

Silence.

It's almost as if I've killed the mood, if there had been a mood to kill, which there can't be, because he has a girlfriend and I'm a bitch and sixteen, and I shouldn't be here.

I'm about to get up and leave when he says, "Why don't you come in for some tea?"

"Tea? I don't like tea." *Grown-ups drink tea, and I am not a grown-up.*

"Come on, my mom says tea makes everything better. You've probably just never had good tea."

He puts his hand on my lower back like he's going to help me stand up and heat radiates out from his palm all along my spine. I use the wall next to me to steady myself.

I imagine this is the kind of thing that might happen when you like someone, and they like you back. Like, really like you, and they're not just checking out your rack. I guess I always hoped that someone's touch could change you, make your atoms vibrate in a new way, but maybe I didn't believe it would actually happen to me. At the station table tonight Chris Thompson looked me in the eye and let his gaze linger longer than it needed to, even when Meredith was trying to make it all about her. And it felt good. I didn't want to think about it then, because it seemed so unbelievable, especially with his hot girlfriend, but it's hard to ignore what it feels like when he's touching my back. I had started to think my life was better when no one was looking, but I didn't know someone looking could feel like this.

"Come upstairs. We'll hear Johnny when he comes in. We can hear everything in this place, the walls are shit."

I want to go upstairs with him, but not to wait for Johnny. I want to go upstairs and pretend none of this is happening. I want to pretend he doesn't have a girlfriend and I'm not sixteen, not a virgin.

I take a very deep breath and try to do the right thing. "I should probably go."

"Listen, I'm not gonna *make* you stay. But you probably shouldn't be driving."

I don't really feel like driving, or going home to an empty house, or worse, running into my dad in the kitchen fixing himself a late-night snack. "Ok. I'll hang out for a bit."

"Good. Let me move your car, though. You can't leave it hanging out of the driveway like that. Parking's a bitch around here, but I know where to find a space. Give me your keys."

Our fingers brush when I hand them to him, and I feel something I've never felt rumble through parts of my body I didn't know were capable of feelings. He looks at me just a touch too long before he goes to the car, and that's when I know for sure this isn't in my head.

CHAPTER 6

Chris Thompson's apartment is surprisingly large for an attic, but it feels cramped, and even with all the lights on, it seems dingy. There are two couches in the living room that look almost as bad as the one on the porch. He leads me into the kitchen. It's brighter – lit by an overhead circular fluorescent bulb, and has a linoleum floor that was probably white once. I sit at the large bare table.

He puts a kettle on the stove. "Who doesn't like tea?"

"I don't know." I shrug. "I've never liked it. It's dirty water."

"You just haven't had good tea." He slides into the chair across from me. "My dad's British; you'll like this tea."

"Ok." It's a good thing he doesn't have a British accent or I probably would have taken off all my clothes by now. That would be bad.

"So you and Johnny are close?" he asks.

"Yeah, I've known him since I was … uh, since he started at the station." I know I should just tell him who I am, how young I am, but then he'd probably stop looking at me the way he's looking at me.

"We grew up together," The Hottest Guy Ever says. "He claims Burton isn't an asshole, but he's totally an asshole, right?"

"He can be. Do you know him?"

"I had a run-in with his son. In Summer Soccer League in high school. It was pretty bad. There was a collision, and his leg got broken. It was this whole big thing. Burton was coaching, so he got me thrown out of the league, because he said I wouldn't take responsibility for my actions, except I really didn't mean to do it. The worst thing was it basically confirmed all of my parents' worst thoughts about me."

Holy Shit. The Hottest Guy Ever is CJ Thompson. CJ Thompson is Chris Thompson.

I wasn't there the day it happened, but everyone knows the story. Nate was playing a year up, so they were on the same team, even though Nate was only fourteen. It was a scrimmage, and they weren't supposed to be playing all out. Nate already had interest from colleges, and after his broken leg, my dad worried he wouldn't be able to play again. It all worked out fine, but by the time Nate was full strength again, CJ had become a mythical character in our family, a synonym for a self-satisfied asshole who valued himself over the team and thought he was better than everyone else. *Don't be a CJ!* my dad would yell whenever my brother gave him attitude.

I knew I had to say something, but what? "That's horrible."

"Yeah, Burton likes to throw his considerable weight around. He did it even before he was Pittsburgh's top DJ of 1992."

"You've seen the billboards, huh?"

I know my dad rubs people the wrong way, but no one has ever been this frank with me. I'm about to come clean, when the teakettle whistles. It startles me, but Chris Thompson doesn't flinch. He doesn't take his eyes off me. For a moment, neither one of us moves, but then the whistle gets really loud, and he gets up to make the tea.

It's too much, sitting alone in Chris Thompson's apartment with only tea between us. It really seems like he likes me, and I have no idea how to act. Or how to tell him he shouldn't like me. Because I really want him to like me, even if he has a girlfriend and nothing could ever happen anyway because how could I tell my dad I was dating CJ?

He's still holding my gaze when I blurt out, "Can I use your bathroom?"

He looks at me like I've ruined another moment. Which I have. If they were actually moments to be ruined.

"It's by the front door."

The bathroom is horrifying. It goes beyond dingy to downright dirty. It looks like decades of dirt have changed the shape of the windowsill next to the sink. With great effort, I try to touch as few surfaces as possible while I splash water on my face. Then I look in the streaked mirror. I try to see myself as Chris Thompson sees me. He doesn't know I'm the "after-picture" in my mom's business plan – a girl transformed from "boxy to babe" in nine short months.

Nothing's going to happen, but I can't help wanting it to. I'm not in control of these thoughts. I should be thinking about how I'm going to approach my dad about my tuition, but when Chris Thompson touched the small of my back on the porch, everything else went away. I stare at myself for a long time. When I'm finally ready to leave, the door, which is actually an accordion style vinyl partition, won't unlatch.

"Ummmm …" I say loudly, simultaneously knocking on the wall next to the doorframe, because knocking on the vinyl doesn't make any noise. "Ummm …"

"You ok?" I hear him call from the kitchen.

"Um, I think I'm stuck?" I yell back.

"Oh … Did you lock the bathroom door?" His voice is getting louder as he comes closer.

"Of course I locked the bathroom door."

"Crap," he says from the other side of the door. "I'm sorry – I should have mentioned it. It's been acting weird lately."

"Are you saying I'm stuck in here?"

"Well, sort of. It does open. Johnny actually knows how to open it. At least he got me out once before, but I haven't locked it since."

"You locked yourself in your own bathroom?"

"Yeah, we don't really have talk about that," he says with a laugh. I can imagine his lips curling into a slight smile. "Sorry about this."

I balance on the edge of the bathtub trying not to touch the soap scum. "You're not some crazy guy who planned to lock me in the bathroom all along are you?"

"Yes, I sit around waiting for random women to show up on my porch and then I entice them into my bathroom with the broken door. You figured me out."

He thinks I'm a woman. This is awkward.

"Listen –" but he interrupts me before I can tell him the truth.

"Hold on! I hear someone downstairs. It's probably Johnny. Don't go anywhere. Ha. Ha."

A minute later they're both outside the door.

"I don't understand," Johnny says. "Who's in there?"

"You know, the chick from the station."

"What chick?" Johnny asks. "There aren't any chicks at the station."

I brace for disaster.

"Her name's Alice. The one who gave me the shirt for Tess." Chris Thompson saying my name is the best and worst thing I've ever heard.

"Alice?! Alice Burton? Burton's daughter is locked in your bathroom?"

"I don't think she's Burton's daughter," Chris Thompson says. "Does Nate have a sister?"

"Yeah, Nate has a sister. Named Alice. Who works at the station in the summer. And she's sixteen."

"No," Chris Thompson speaks almost inaudibly, but I can still hear him. "The chick in the bathroom is not sixteen."

"Alice, is that you?" Johnny asks.

"Can you just get me out of here so I can go home?"

"What the hell are you doing in Chris Thompson's bathroom? Wait, don't answer that."

"Nothing, I'm not doing anything. I came here looking for you. Can you please just get me out of here?"

"Ok, step away from the door."

I climb into the bathtub because there's really no way to get any further from the door. I'm grateful I'm wearing my Doc Martens, because the things growing in the bathtub are scary.

There's some jiggling, and then some shaking, and then the vinyl partition rips away from the wall. I climb out of the bathtub.

"What the hell is going on, Alice?"

CHAPTER 7

I don't know where to begin. On top of that, the sight of Johnny's face forces me to realize he's not going to have any answers. I burst into tears.

"Seriously," Johnny says sternly. "I need one of you to tell me what the hell is going on here, 'cause this doesn't look good."

I can't stop crying long enough to answer. I flop onto the couch by the door. It gives off a puff of dust. Johnny looks at Chris Thompson suspiciously. Chris Thompson doesn't look pleased.

"This isn't my thing." The Hottest Guy Ever puts his hands up to indicate he takes no responsibility for the sixteen-year-old girl crying on his couch. "She came here looking for you. I have no idea what's going on. I had no idea who she was. I'm gonna get out of here. I think I'm out of milk?"

Johnny's tone changes. "Oh, you're going to Eddie's Market? Will you get me some? Whole – not the skim crap you drink." Johnny can do that; he can change gears on a dime, ask you for help while simultaneously making an accusation. I think he learned it from my dad.

"Sure ..." Chris Thompson doesn't look at me.

In the kitchen, I tell Johnny about the letter and public school and how there's no lacrosse and how I won't be able to go to college without a scholarship. I go on and on, and he looks just as clueless as I feared he would. To his credit, he attempts to make things better.

"He's not gonna let that happen. It means too much to him to have you at that school. He doesn't talk about it on the air because he has to do his whole every-man thing, but it's all he talks about around the station. I mean, come on, Nate's smart – frankly, Nate's probably smarter than you, sorry – but Nate doesn't give a shit about anything but soccer. You're smart and you work hard – Burton values that. He's not gonna let you get bounced. He's too damn proud you're going to be captain of the lacrosse team."

"You say that, but – "

"But nothing. I'm sure it's a mistake. Are you sure that's what the letter said?"

I reach into my boho bag and put the letter on the table in front of Johnny.

"Why do you have this?" His eyes are so wide it's like I've just pulled a dead bunny out of my boho.

"I don't know, I panicked?"

"This is not good." I don't understand how the night could get worse, but then he lays it out for me. "Listen, it's one thing for something to be happening. It's another thing for you to know it's happening. But it's a completely different thing for him to know you know it's happening. How did you get into his office? I thought he kept it locked now."

"Shawn was emptying the trash. I told him I would close up."

"Alice! He's going to fire Shawn! And if I'm in any way implicated in this, he's gonna fire me, too, not to mention I'm on the hook with Chris Thompson because a crying thirteen-year-old showed up on his doorstep."

"I'm sixteen, and he didn't really seem to mind – "

"That's another thing, Alice." Johnny sounds like he's impersonating my father. "You will not hook up with Chris Thompson. 'Cause then we're all truly screwed. He's made some shitty decisions in his past, and I will not take the heat for either of your hormones."

I blink my eyes hard to fend off the tears, and also a slightly guilty smile. Even in the state I'm in, I can't help thinking about how it feels when The Hottest Guy Ever looks at me. I don't understand how my head is going in so many directions at once.

Johnny looks at his watch.

"Alice, don't you have a curfew?"

"Yeah," I groan. "What time is it?"

"It's after twelve. Where does Burton think you are?"

"At Meredith's, I guess. I mean, I was supposed to call, but I basically said I was gonna sleep there."

"And you didn't call?"

I shake my head and purse my lips because I know this is another screw-up.

"And where exactly *are* you planning to sleep?"

"I wasn't *planning* to sleep anywhere! I didn't *plan* any of this! It just happened. I thought you'd know what to do!"

"Don't yell at me," he says too calmly.

We're silently staring at each other when Chris Thompson walks in with the milk. He puts a quart in his fridge and a quart on the table between Johnny and me.

"I heard you two yelling from the landing. So, whatever this is, it isn't going well, is it?"

He's trying to break the tension, but Johnny is unmoved.

"We were just gonna recap." This is a thing my dad does on air when he wants to point out how stupid someone is being. "Alice thinks she's getting kicked out of school because her tuition isn't paid; she took a letter from her dad's office, so he's going to know she knows; and she's out past curfew, and no one knows where she is. On top of that, she has nowhere to sleep tonight." I start to laugh, but Johnny shoots me a look. "On the plus side, she can go from laughing to crying without missing a beat, and she seems to have an endless supply of tears, so that's gotta be worth something, right?"

"She can stay here," Chris Thompson says to Johnny.

I stop crying, because you can't cry when you can't breathe.

"She cannot stay here," Johnny responds, as if I'm not sitting at the same table with the two of them.

"Where else is she going to sleep? You have a studio – she's not going to sleep downstairs."

"I'm right here," I say.

"Oh, you're right." Johnny's voice is thick with sarcasm. "You *are* right here. How silly of me. Do you have a solution you'd like to share with us?"

I shake my head.

"Ease up, Johnny. She can stay here, on the couch. It's not a big deal. It's really the least of her problems right now."

"Thanks," I say to Chris Thompson, and our eyes connect, but I look away quickly because I don't want him to look away first.

"Listen, this is what's gonna happen." Johnny's voice is authoritative. "Alice, you're going to call your house and leave a message saying you're at Meredith's. Any chance she called looking for you already tonight?"

"No, she's out partying. And I have my own line. No one picks it up when I'm not there."

"Does your dad have Caller ID?" Chris Thompson asks.

"No," Johnny responds for me. "Burton doesn't trust technology. We don't even have PCs at the station."

"Alice, you're gonna call your dad. Then, you're going to the station to put the letter back. Shawn'll be on 'til four. He'll let you into the building, but he won't want to let you into the office. Tell him you left a nearly full pack of cigarettes in there, and you don't want your dad to find them because he'll be mad."

"I don't smoke," I protest.

"Listen, Alice, I know you don't buy your own cigarettes, but I know you smoke when you're with Meredith, so don't play innocent with me."

Johnny's been paying far more attention to me than I realized, or I'm far less stealthy than I thought.

"Stop at Eddie's on the way to the station. Buy a pack of cigarettes, get rid of three of them and crumble the pack up a bit so it doesn't look brand new. Keep it on you and when you get into the office, put the letter back where you found it, and then pretend you found your cigarettes. Offer the pack to Shawn, as thanks. He won't take them at first, but take one out and then offer it to him again. He'll come out with you to have a smoke, and at that point, he'll hit on you."

"No, he won't. He's practically family. I've known him longer than I've known you. Don't be gross."

"Listen Alice, you've heard the interns talk. And tonight you need to use that. It's for Shawn's own good you get that letter back in there, but you can't tell him that, so just let him hit on you, and roll with it. He won't take it far, he just likes to flirt."

I scowl at Johnny.

"And," he says, "If you come back here, I don't wanna know about it. It's called plausible deniability."

"Listen to you." I'm genuinely impressed with the plan. "You're a regular criminal mastermind."

"There's no perfect crime," Johnny says. "You still driving your dad's wagon?"

I nod.

"You're never going to be able to find a place to park that thing back here. Really, you don't have anywhere else you can stay?"

"I don't think so."

"I'll drive you to the station," Chris Thompson says.

Johnny and I both look at him. I don't know which one of us is more shocked.

"I have a bike. I can park anywhere. I'll run you over and bring you back. You can sleep on the couch. It's really no big deal."

I want to be grateful, but I went from being someone he potentially could have *maybe* been interested in, to someone he has to save, and I hate it.

"I'm outta here," Johnny says, standing up and grabbing his milk. "I don't want to know or hear anything more about any of this. Make sure Shawn doesn't see you," he says to Chris Thompson. "And, Alice, come here."

By the door, Johnny gives me a hug like he used to when I was little, back when he used to take me on missions all over the city. Once we spent a whole week testing strawberry milkshakes at various fast food restaurants to determine which was the best. The thought of eating something that sweet now makes me queasy, but it reminds me of a time when things were so much easier.

Since I started to lose weight, he has kept his distance, and it makes me feel radioactive. Hugging him reminds me why I came here in the first place. He knows how to negotiate around my dad in a way I haven't quite figured out. Hugging Johnny is the first time tonight it feels like things might actually end up ok. Then he takes me by the shoulders and looks me square in the eyes.

"I need you to understand," he says. "Even Meredith can't know you slept here. No one can find out. And please, do not sleep with Chris Thompson. Do you understand me?"

I nod silently, but I feel a small smile creep across my face. I'm sure my cheeks are flushed.

Johnny leaves the apartment shaking his head.

CHAPTER 8

Chris Thompson's motorcycle is parked around the corner from Eddie's Market.

"Have you ever ridden before?"

I shake my head. I haven't even been on a bicycle since the accident that landed me in the hospital when I was ten.

Chris Thompson puts a helmet on me and adjusts it a bit. Then he puts on his own helmet.

I flip open the visor. "Why are you being so nice to me?"

"You mean after you lied to me?"

"I didn't lie. Not exactly."

"Yeah, I was pissed before, but then I realized, it must be really hard to be Burton's kid. I don't know, I guess I just feel bad for you."

"Thanks, I guess."

I don't want him to pity me. I want him to go back to looking at me the way he did before, even if he does have a girlfriend, which makes me a horrible person.

"Don't worry about it. Now get on and hold on, ok?"

It would normally take more than ten minutes to get from Johnny's place to the station, but we make it there in six. I hold Chris Thompson tightly around the waist, quite literally for dear life, and survive. He parks around the corner, so if Shawn wants to have a smoke with me, he won't see Chris Thompson or the bike. Inside I do what Johnny told me to do, and Shawn responds just as Johnny said he would. I put the letter back where I found it, and when I shut the door to my father's office, I notice a visceral sense of relief. I show Shawn the pack of cigarettes I have "recovered" from the office, and he accompanies me to the parking lot. He doesn't hit on me, Johnny was wrong about that, but he does ask where my car is – he calls it a yacht. I tell him I'm staying down the street with a friend. As I walk off into the night, smoking the cigarette Shawn has lit for me, I feel almost good. While I haven't solved the problem of my tuition, Johnny's right – it's not my problem to solve.

"Did it go ok?" Chris Thompson is leaning up against his bike, running his hand through his hair.

"Just like Johnny said."

Up close, it's hard to look at him without blushing, and suddenly I feel ashamed. The adrenaline of the night is wearing off, and I remember he's seen me at my worst, snot-covered and blubbering. A child.

He hands me the helmet. "Do you want to go for a ride?"

"What do you mean? Like, back to your place?"

"No, like a ride, a real ride." The wide smile that changes his whole face reveals itself.

"Ok." I'm exhausted, but I'm not going to say no to riding around the city with my arms around Chris Thompson's waist.

"Do me a favor though. Lean into the turns, not out of them. You could kill us both."

"Sorry."

* * * * *

We go to parts of the city I've never seen before. Most of the traffic lights are blinking yellow, so we barely have to stop, but when we do, Chris Thompson drops his hand down and squeezes my shin. His hand on my leg is more exhilarating than going one hundred miles an hour down an empty city street. It's how I felt right before my bike accident, the feeling of freedom when I first took off from the top of the hill. I never want to get off his bike. I just want to be wrapped around his body, taking the turns too closely.

Back in South Oakland, Chris Thompson pulls the bike into an alley and parks between the front of the Wally Wagon and the back of another car.

"I need to grab some clothes." I walk towards the back of my dad's car.

"This is a beast."

"Tell me about it."

"I'm surprised Burton lets you drive it – what would you do if you got a flat?"

"What do you mean, 'What would I do?'" I say with a snort of a laugh. "Call Triple A! What would you do?"

"You don't know how to change a flat?"

"No. I mean, I know how you use a jack. And I know how a jack works: it's physics. I just haven't ever had to do it. Anyway, this really isn't my car. It's Burton's. He got me my own last week, but it's stick, and I can't drive it, so instead he's driving it, and I have this thing."

"You can't change a flat, and you can't drive a stick? What good are you, Alice?" Chris Thompson teases me, and I like how it feels.

"Seriously, I'm a waste of space." Now I'm flirting, and I really shouldn't be.

"I can teach you how to drive stick."

"Really?"

"Yeah. My parents live in Zelienople – there's a lot of land, and I have an old truck out there. I could teach you in an afternoon. No big deal."

I like the sound of it: me and Chris Thompson driving around a field in Zelienople. It has *Dirty Dancing* written all over it. I stand on the sidewalk with the clothes I'm going to wear to tryouts tomorrow. I've wrapped my shorts around a pair of clean underwear and the necessary two sports bras.

"Did you grow up in Zelie?" I ask.

Chris Thompson doesn't seem like he's from the country.

"No, the 'burbs. I grew up with Johnny. My parents moved out there when I went to college. Do you even know if you have a spare in here?"

"Probably?"

Chris Thompson pulls open the back of the wagon and looks in the way-back.

He issues a challenge. "Show me your spare."

I walk to the back of the car leaving my clothes for the next day in a heap on the sidewalk next to the helmets.

I lift part of the floor of the way-back to reveal the spare and a lot of other things, mostly small stacks of paper that look like half-sized index cards rubber-banded together. They look like smaller versions of the index cards my mom tracks her various recipes and formulas on. I turn to Chris Thompson triumphantly, but he looks shocked.

"What?" I ask.

"Do you know what those are?"

"No." I turn back to the mess of stuff. "What are they?"

Chris Thompson picks up one of the stacks – there must be over a hundred bundles, each one more than two inches thick.

"These are lottery tickets."

And finally the "why" comes into focus, or maybe it's the "how." I'm instantly furious. I stare at the piles of tickets surrounding the spare. I gasp for air, but I don't cry. I've finally run out of tears. Everything inside me goes ice cold – I actually shiver.

I try to take a breath, but I'm having trouble forcing air into my lungs. I take a step back and wobble. Chris Thompson takes my hand in his, and I try to hold on to him, but I can't control my fingers. They feel like they are evaporating as everything becomes shaky: my breath, my vision, my bearings. Still not able to look at Chris Thompson, I try to focus beyond him at the glow of an orange streetlight. It reminds me of the sun setting behind him at Flagstaff. Was that really only a few hours ago? The halo around the light begins to morph into several halos of varying colors and shapes. Again, I try to take a deep breath, but my chest only gets tighter. My nostrils flare. I am keenly aware of all of the negative space in my body.

"I can't breathe," I hear myself say. And then everything is black.

CHAPTER 9

I open my eyes to find myself on the disgusting porch-couch. I close my eyes again and then blink them open. Chris Thompson is next to me with his arm around my shoulders. I close my eyes again and breathe in his smell. I consider pretending to be asleep so I can stay this close to him for a little while longer.

"Alice, can you hear me?"

I nod.

"Are you ok?"

"I think so. I mean, I can breathe now, so I guess I'm ok."

"Alice, do you know who I am?"

I open my eyes, turn towards him, look intently and then say, "No?"

His eyes get wide, and I start laughing.

He jabs me under my ribs. "Not cool."

"Sorry," I manage to say, still laughing. "Did I pass out?"

"Yeah, I think you did. You've only been out a couple minutes. As long as it took me to carry you over here and grab our stuff."

Instinctively, I suck in my stomach, a holdover from when I weighed a lot more.

"I don't think I've ever passed out before."

"I guess there's a first time for everything."

I look down and see he's holding a stack of lottery tickets, and all the horrible feelings rush back. My stomach seizes, and for a minute I think I'm gonna vomit. "Does Johnny know?"

"That you passed out?"

"About the lottery tickets."

"He doesn't know about either. Why?"

"It's just something he said earlier. 'It's one thing for something to happen, it's another thing for people to know it happened.'"

Chris Thompson looks at me like I'm going to say more, but I can't, not out loud. It's becoming clear to me that whatever's going on with my family is larger than me and my tuition and the fewer people who know about it, the better. I put my elbows on my knees and my head in my hands.

"You think you're ok to walk upstairs?" he asks.

"I guess."

Chris Thompson hands me my clothes. "You want to know a secret?"

"Not really." I'm feeling weighed down by far too many already.

"The front door can be opened if you jiggle the handle and then lift up really hard. There's a key to my place above my doorjamb upstairs. If you ever need a place to be, you can be here. The couch is yours."

"Thanks. I promise not to make a habit of coming over crying, locking myself in your bathroom, and passing out."

"Yeah, probably best not to." His smile is kind. It's smaller than the wide one that changes his whole appearance, and I think I like it more.

Upstairs I wander aimlessly around the apartment while Chris Thompson put sheets on one of the couches. There's something about watching him make a bed for me that's too intimate. I step out of the room the way a doctor does when you get undressed, and when I come back in, Chris Thompson's playing guitar on the couch. His feet are up on the steamer trunk/coffee table. He's humming as he plays, as if to himself. I recognize the tune. It's Billy Bragg's "Lovers Town Revisited." I start singing along because every lyric of every song on Billy Bragg's "Back To Basics" collection is seared into my head from heavy rotation on my Walkman. Another 1987 classic I have not retired yet. Chris Thompson stops playing and looks at me with a wry smile – one I haven't seen before. Then he starts laughing, although it is clear he's trying not to.

"What?"

"Nothing…" The corners of his mouth turn upwards.

"No, say it."

"Are you … tone deaf?"

"No, not technically," I say with a proud smile. "I hear quite clearly when other people are singing, but –"

"But you know *you* can't sing, right?"

"Oh yeah! I mean, I've been told that, but I actually can't hear how bad I sound so sometimes I forget. I mean, I sound great to me."

"Seriously? You think you sound good?" It's the half smile, the one that promises more.

"Well, I know I don't sound good because people have told me. But yeah, I can't really hear it."

"And you like to sing?"

"Yeah, why?"

"You're very weird." Now it's the broad smile, the one that looks like it can't be contained.

I'm not smiling. "Weird?"

Weird is not good. There are things you can get away with at Frazer: you can get away with being a bitch, and you can get away with being a jock, and, if you're Meredith May you can get away with being both, but you can't get away with being weird. Weird is the kiss of death.

"Weird-good," he reassures me.

"What does that mean?" I'm not sure anything can take away the sting of Chris Thompson calling me weird.

"Well, let's just say most people who sound like you sound probably wouldn't enjoy singing so much and definitely wouldn't sing in front of other people. Weird-good. Like fearless."

"Oh, I'm not fearless," I assure him. "I just don't embarrass easily. My dad says that's one of the downsides of Frazer. He thinks being surrounded by other girls all day makes us terribly uncouth. We have highly competitive burping contests, and my friend, Lindsay, figured out how to stick a cooked noodle up her nostril and pull it out her mouth –"

"That's disgusting," Chris Thompson interrupts.

"Yeah, but also sort of cool."

"See? Weird."

He plays two R.E.M. songs and then a Smiths song, and I sing along. He laughs the whole way through, but he doesn't seem to want me to stop.

*   *   *   *   *

When I wake up the next morning, Chris Thompson is already at the kitchen table eating a bowl of cereal. A second bowl sits empty at the seat across from him.

"You want some Lucky Charms?" He pushes a bag of cereal towards me, and I inspect it.

"These aren't Lucky Charms." I haven't had sugar cereal in years, but I remember Lucky Charms.

"Wow. That was sort of snotty. You really are a Frazer girl, aren't you?"

"Sorry – are they generic, or something?"

"Yes, Princess, they're generic." He takes them back. "And if they're beneath you, don't have any."

"Sorry, I didn't mean to be rude." I never do. "Thank you, yes, I'd love some … cereal." I can't bring myself to say "Marshmallow Mateys."

He pushes the bag back towards me.

The first spoonful makes my teeth hurt. It tastes like candy and reminds me of what it was like to be a kid visiting my grandmother and not caring about what I ate or what combination of nutrients and carbs make the best metabolic reaction, or whatever the hell kind of science experiment my mom is running on me.

"You feeling better?" he asks.

"Honestly, I don't think so, but thank you for last night."

As soon as it comes out of my mouth, we both laugh at the loaded phrase.

"Did you sleep ok?"

"I don't know. I'm still tired. Your couch is lumpy."

"Oh no! I forgot to take the pea out of it! Apologies, Princess." He pretends to take off a hat and leans forward in a little bow.

"Haha. That was so funny I almost forgot to laugh."

I usually have a Lois Burton Signature Protein Shake for breakfast, so the sugar of the cereal is a shock to my system. It makes my body buzz. Or something does.

"Listen, I was serious about teaching you to drive stick. You wanna give it a try?"

"I'm warning you, it was a disaster when Burton took me out."

"I'm sure anything involving Burton probably has the potential for disaster."

"True."

Chris gets up to look at a calendar on the wall. There's a picture of the Cathedral of Learning from Pitt's campus on it. "I think I'm off work on Friday – wanna do it then?"

"You have a job?"

"Yes, Princess." He's clearly frustrated with me. "Those of us who don't live at home have to have jobs to pay our bills."

He talks to me like a puppy, the same way Johnny does, and I realize this means we're "friends." I know he has a girlfriend, and I'm still in high school, but it's still disappointing. I'm a horrible person for coveting someone else's boyfriend, regardless of how unrealistic it is.

"Stop it." I roll my eyes. "I just didn't know."

"You thought I played music with Tess and waited for crying girls to show up on my porch? And my rent just paid itself?"

"I don't know – you're still in school. I thought maybe your parents paid your rent?"

"Oh, that would be nice. I was cut off when I transferred to Pitt. They pay my tuition, but that's it."

"Oh, well, at least they do that."

We both snort a laugh.

"So Friday? It'll take us longer to get out to Zelie than it'll take me to teach you. Promise."

"I have lacrosse on Friday ... if I make the Summer Team." The thought of not making the Summer Team, and the ramifications that would have on top of no senior year at Frazer, no senior year with Meredith, no chance at a college scholarship and possibly no college at all counteracts the sugar high, and I come down hard.

"We'll find a time," he says, as if he's solving all my problems. As if it were that easy.

CHAPTER 10

Meredith lives in the most gorgeous mansion in Shadyside. It's the neighborhood next to Oakland, but a world away from the dead-end street overlooking the hollow and all the small houses chopped up into smaller apartments.

I let myself into her house through the kitchen door. Meredith's perched on a high stool at the breakfast bar eating a banana. The sun is streaming into the room making it look like a spread in a Pottery Barn catalog. Meredith fits right in; she always looks magazine-perfect. I get supplies out of the pantry to make one of my mom's shakes. I don't even think her parents noticed when I started keeping them here.

"Why didn't you fuel up at home?" She doesn't call what I do "eating."

"I was running late. You ready?" It's not exactly a lie.

"I'm always ready!" She flashes me a smile, and I think she's not going to do it, but then she does it. She winks.

"Stop that!" I whine.

We have a 20-minute drive to Fox Chapel, the suburban high school where the tryouts are being held. Their campus is sprawling whereas Frazer's is compact, but I'd rather be from the city than live out there. The Fox Chapel girls will have a home-field advantage for the tryouts though, which sort of sucks.

In the car, Meredith tunes the radio to QEV, and my dad is on the air talking about the Pirates playing the Padres tonight.

"We going?" she asks.

"Yeah."

"Your box or mine?" she laughs.

God, we really are snobs, although "my box" is really the station's box.

"Doesn't matter."

"Will your box have Karl Bell in it?" She makes a kissy face with her lips.

"Yeah, probably, after the game"

"Your box. Definitely."

"Have you started *Moll Flanders* yet?"

"No, why would I? School ended, like, last week?"

"I started it …"

"Oh my god, you miss it."

"What?"

"School! You already miss school. How is that possible? You complain all the time about how mean everyone is to you, but you actually miss it! You're so weird."

I want to tell Meredith that Chris Thompson called me weird last night, but I know I shouldn't.

"I don't complain about everyone. Just the birth-control-bitches."

"Hey, I'm a birth-control-bitch now!"

"Yeah, but you're my birth-control-bitch."

She winks at me.

The birth-control-bitches meet at the lockers when the one o'clock bell goes off for lunch and pass a bottle of Evian around while they take their pills. I don't have a problem with them being on the pill – I wish I had a reason to be on the pill – but the Evian pisses me off.

I ask Meredith if she's nervous about tryouts. It can be hard to predict her reactions in these situations. Generally, she enjoys competition, but she's rarely up against anyone who challenges her.

"I don't know. I guess it's intense to be competing against all the best girls, but we're good, right?"

"I hope so."

"Do you have any Chapstick?" She fishes around in the glove

compartment, but this is my dad's car.

"In my bag."

She pulls my boho onto her lap, and my stomach twists. Johnny was right to have me put the letter back. If Meredith saw the letter, I don't know what I'd say. She doesn't seem to realize, even though it's plainly obvious, that most people don't have as much money as she does.

She applies my Morello Cherry Body Shop lip balm and throws my bag into the back seat. "You nervous?"

"I guess. A little," I lie. I was less nervous when I thought the Summer Team would just be a cool way for me to spend the summer with Meredith, but now my whole future depends on it, and I'm sort of a wreck.

At the fields, we join a group of girls who are already warming up, including Amanda, the only other girl from our school who was invited to try out. She's going to be a junior, but there's a chance she might be better than I am.

"Hey chicas!" Amanda moves her bag so there's room for Meredith and me next to her in the circle. "I thought I'd be the last one here – you two are always ahead of the game."

Meredith would have preferred to be the first ones here, and it's my fault we're not. But rather than blame me in front of everyone, she uses it as an opportunity to exert her authority over Amanda, and she makes sure the other girls in the circle take notice. "It's not like we're late."

"No, no, I didn't mean it that way."

With my legs out in front of me, and my head to my knees, I ease into the stretch. My body works differently now that I'm taller and I've lost so much weight, and sometimes it takes me by surprise. I was never heavy, just … solid. I'm pretty sure Chris Thompson wouldn't have looked twice at me last summer. I still have my forehead on my knees, thoughts racing in my head, when I realize everyone else is already up and in two lines on the field. I hustle over, but it doesn't go unnoticed that I'm lagging behind.

"What's going on with you?" Meredith hisses in my ear.

"Nothing."

"You worried about a junior from your own school taking your place?"

"I'm fine, I just got caught up stretching."

"You're thinking about that guy, aren't you?"

It's like she can read my mind. Unbelievable.

"That's futile," she continues. "You'll probably never see him again. You need to focus."

I want to tell her I've already seen him again, but I don't.

"Alright. Calm down." I say.

But she's right. I'm a step behind all day.

CHAPTER 11

After tryouts, Meredith doesn't understand why we have to stop at my house before we go out. She insists I can wear whatever I want out of her closet – possibly the greatest benefit to losing weight this year – but she doesn't know I haven't been home in 24 hours. I fill up my boho bag with a fresh supply of meal bars, shake packets, and celery sticks. Because of all her business stuff, my mom's never around, but at least she leaves baggies of pre-cut celery in the fridge.

I grab a pair of Nate's jeans from his closet because they fit me better than my own clothes do. My mom was supposed to take me shopping now that I don't have to wear a uniform every day, but she's been too busy. I pair the jeans with a station tee because it's clean and it fits. It doesn't do much for me, but fashion has never been my thing. I suspect this comes from years of being the scholarship kid at a rich girls' school. It was easier to give up on being fashionable than to try to keep up with the girls in my class.

"You're going like that?" Meredith's head is tilted in judgment.

"I don't want to talk about this. I can't care what I'm wearing when my body is this tired."

"Suit yourself ... Get it?!" Wink.

"You're hilarious."

When we get to the stadium, the station box is full of people who've watched me grow up ... and Chris Thompson. I cannot believe I didn't take Meredith up on her offer to raid her closet.

"You don't look ... horrible," she tells me.

"You are not nice." But this actually constitutes extreme kindness on her part.

"You gonna talk to him?"

This is a disaster. Does he remember he's not supposed to really know me? What if he says something to her about me sleeping over? But why would he say that? And why is he here? Before I've gone through every possible way this night could implode, she shoves me towards him. "Look, he's getting food!"

I meet Chris Thompson by the chicken fingers.

"Hi," I say.

"I thought I might see you tonight."

"What are you doing here?" It sounds bitchy, but I don't mean it to.

"Burton gave Johnny two tickets. Johnny brought me."

"Interesting. Where is Burton?" I ask.

"Haven't seen him yet."

"Lucky you."

"I don't think he'd recognize me. I was sorta scrawny back then."

Chris Thompson is not scrawny now.

He reaches into the pocket of his jeans and hands me a cassette case. "Here, I brought you one of our tapes."

"You want me to see if I can get Burton to play it?"

Chris Thompson's face falls.

"No, it's for you. You said you hadn't heard us."

I'm used to people handing me tapes, but they're never really for me.

"Oh wow, thanks." How is this not flirting? I mean, he didn't make me a mixtape, but this is even better. He's on this tape. And he gave it to me. I know he has a girlfriend. I know I'm still in high school, but I think he likes me anyway.

Johnny walks by on his way to the drinks and flicks me on the forehead. Hard.

"What's up, Wonderland?"

I swat his hand away, and he keeps walking.

Chris Thompson leans in towards me, just slightly, but enough so I can tell he isn't leaning away from me, "How'd lacrosse go?"

"Not great. And I'm totally exhausted."

"I picked up the new Cure disc today. Have you heard it?" He speaks so quietly I'm forced to lean in to hear what he's saying. Now we're both leaning slightly towards each other. This totally feels like flirting.

"Just the single." I smile. "Very pop-y."

"It is, but it's not bad." Chris Thompson looks at me, and it feels like I am the only person in the room. I've never been looked at like this before. I wonder if anyone can look at someone like this or if this is a special gift only he possesses. And if anyone can do it, why hasn't anyone looked at me like this before? And why is he looking at me this way when he has Tess? He doesn't seem like the kind of asshole who would have a perfect girlfriend and flirt with someone else, especially if that someone else is me. "I should dub this Smiths bootleg I have for you. You can only get in England. It's a live show."

"That'd be cool. Thanks."

And then, when neither of us says anything else, my brain shorts out and I blurt, "Where's Tess?"

"You know about that?"

"About what?"

"That Johnny's been trying to date her since he moved into the building? That's where he was when you came by last night. He insisted on walking her home." He pauses with a confused look on his face. "Wait, what did you mean?"

"I just thought ..." I can't bring myself to say it.

"That Tess and I were together?"

"I don't know what I thought."

Chris Thompson is flirting with me, and he's single. I put a hand on the table behind me to prevent myself from keeling over from the weight of this new information.

"Tess is my cousin."

"Oh."

"No one ever thinks we're related, you know, 'cause she's Black, but it's true. Her mom is my dad's sister. Her dad is from Trinidad. She moved here from London to go to Pitt, and we started a band when I moved home. When we were kids, she used to send me all these great tapes of songs we couldn't get here. Anyway, Johnny's really into her. I'm surprised you didn't know – he can't shut up about her."

"Well, he can't shut up about anything. He's perfect for radio."

I hear a bat crack, and it seems like the whole stadium takes a deep breath in unison. I look down toward the field. I don't care what's happening in the game, but everyone seems interested, so I feel like I should seem interested, too. Then the moment passes, and Chris Thompson and I are just looking at each other. He seems quite comfortable standing there silently looking at me. I'm less comfortable, but I sort of like the queasy feeling I'm having. And then Johnny walks by again with a plate full of fried food and flicks my forehead. I slap his hand. Hard. We're both surprised by my force.

"Chill, Wonderland," he says sternly.

"Don't call me that!"

"My bad," Johnny says and gives me a look like I have three heads, or like I'm flirting with someone he told me to stay away from.

Chris Thompson goes with Johnny to the front of the box, and I plop into the seat next to Meredith with a plate full of celery and carrots.

"What was that?" She takes food off my plate.

"What do you mean?"

"The way he was looking at you. Was he flirting with you?"

"I don't think so." I don't know why I lie to her, it just seems like the safe thing to do.

"Are you friends with him or something?"

"I don't know. I guess."

"What does that even mean?"

"He's a friend of Johnny's. Transitive property."

"That's not how the transitive property works!"

"Then I don't know!"

"Ok – so, if you're going to be friends with him, then maybe I'll try to bang him."

"Stop it. You have a boyfriend."

"Right, and you don't. And if you're just gonna be friends with a guy that hot, I have to wonder if you want one."

I can't take my eyes off of the back of Chris Thompson's head and his shaggy blond corn silk hair. He turns around and sees us looking at him. He smiles a wide, knowing smile and though I want to look away, I can't. I smile back.

"Holy crap," Meredith says.

"What?"

"He likes you."

"He doesn't."

"Isn't he with that punk pixie chick?"

"No, she's his cousin."

"Whoa. Ok, I know it seems absurd, but trust me, but I can tell these things. He likes you."

"I don't want to talk about it."

Meredith flips through a *Sassy* magazine, and I monitor Chris Thompson's every move: who he's talking to, what he's eating. I'm watching to see if he's going to turn around again and look at me, but he doesn't.

"I'm gonna go," Meredith says after she's eaten all the veggies off my plate.

"What!?"

"Richard's here with some friends. He told me his section. I'm gonna go find him in the cheap seats. Wanna come?"

"I don't know."

"You wanna hang here with The Hottest Guy Ever?"

I do. But I can't tell her that. The whole thing is so dumb I can barely admit it to myself.

"I should at least wait until my dad shows up. I'm sure he's down in the dugout or doing something in the press box."

"You should come out to Richard's later. He's having a party."

"You didn't tell me Richard was having a party tonight. And what about tryouts tomorrow?"

"Number one, it's the summer, there's basically always a party at Richard's, and number two, tryouts don't start 'til 9am. We'll be fine."

"I thought we were hanging out here tonight." I'm practically whining, and I wish I would shut up.

"Yeah, but … this is boring. I can't even sneak a drink here. I thought I would last long enough to see Hot Karl Bell, but there's no way …" she trails off. "Come with?"

"No, it's fine, just go."

"I don't want you to be mad at me."

"Whatever."

It's just like Meredith to do whatever she wants and then get offended when I have a reaction to it.

"Hey look, here comes Chris Thompson." Before I can say anything, she has me up on my feet and is pushing me towards him.

"Hey," she says. "I gotta take off, will you entertain Alice, please?"

He looks confused. I smile awkwardly.

"See you, lady!" she calls as she makes her way to the door. "Come out later if you want!"

"You need to be entertained?" Chris Thompson asks with a wry smile, like he's almost making fun of me. I saw this smile last night, when he told me I couldn't sing.

"She just feels guilty because she's deserting me."

"You know there's a baseball game happening right now? Like, right over there. Most people consider that entertainment."

"I know. Meredith's just being weird."

"Where'd she go?" He cannot possibly care where a sixteen-year-old girl is going on a Friday night, but it almost sounds like he does. I suspect it's part of his gift of quiet charm.

"A party. Her boyfriend's."

"You gonna meet up with her?"

"I doubt it. I'm gonna stay and see Karl."

"Johnny says he's a real dick."

"Really?" I ask. "He's not."

I don't know why I'm defending Karl Bell, especially after the way he looked at me at Flagstaff, but I guess I'm defending the Karl Bell I knew when I was thirteen.

Chris Thompson shrugs. He puts veggies and some dip on his plate and grabs a Coke.

"Want one?" He holds the can out to me.

Coke is not allowed on Lois' non-diet plan, but I can't say no to Chris Thompson.

"Sure, thanks." As he hands me the can, our fingers brush, and things inside me do that thing they do when he's around; they rearrange themselves.

"Come down front," he says. "We can make room for you since your friend ditched you."

I'm about to follow him to his seat when the door to the box flies open, and my dad and Doug from the station's business office make their entrance.

"The tunnels aren't the problem! It's the drivers. There's no need to slow down in a tunnel – people just don't know how to drive!" My father is always complaining about the Liberty Tunnels.

Doug nods along as each person in the box tries to get my dad's attention. Everyone but Chris Thompson: he's disappeared into the crowd.

CHAPTER 12

The Pirates lose to the Padres. The reaction in the box is mixed. I've noticed people tend to be loyal to the celebrities they know, even if it means rooting against their home team. Not long after the game ends, a group of freshly showered baseball players bursts into the box. They look so much larger than they had on the field. My dad and Karl hug in a big, manly way. My dad is thick and tall, but Karl's taller. Karl turns to me and picks me up in a huge bear hug. It's disorienting, and the yelp I let out attracts the attention of everyone in the box. I'm super-embarrassed when I make brief eye contact with Chris Thompson. He gives me a look I can't decipher, but it makes me want to apologize to him, which is absurd considering he's ignored me since my dad arrived. It's as if knowing I am Dennis Burton's daughter and seeing me *be* Dennis Burton's daughter are two different things.

"Ally! I just can't get over how grown up you are!" Karl says this while he has me in the air and then he puts me down. "Wow! Look at you."

Karl's aftershave is overpowering, and he doesn't even try to hide the fact that his eyes are lingering on my chest.

"Sooooo," he drags the word out expectantly. "You must be ... dating?"

Before I can stop myself, I instinctively look for Chris Thompson. He's standing alone down by the seats while Johnny is with my dad.

"Um, no." I look down at my feet. When I look up again, Chris

Thompson is watching Karl and me.

"Everyone too afraid of your dad?" Karl's laugh is sinister.

"Yeah, that must be it." I so don't want to be having this conversation.

"Must be hard."

I shrug. I hadn't really thought of it that way before Chris Thompson.

Another player approaches us. He says, "hey," and looks me over like he's trying to figure out exactly who or what I am. I get that a lot these days. "You going across the river?"

"Yeah, let's do that." Karl turns to me. "You have an ID?"

"Uh, no."

"Too bad," he says. "You could totally pass for 21. One of the guys has a stake in a killer bar on the South Side."

"Cool," I say, even though it's not the least bit interesting to me.

"We're going to take your dad out, get him drunk, and watch him get into an argument with someone about something." Karl lets loose with a mean, self-satisfied laugh.

I've never seen my dad drunk.

Karl gives me a hug that lasts just a bit longer than is comfortable. Talking to him has put me in a bad mood.

I push my way through some fairly large guys to get to my dad. "I'm going to spend the night at Meredith's."

"Two nights in a row? Would your mom say it was alright?" He's clearly annoyed that he needs to parent me while trying to be Dennis Burton, Pittsburgh's Top DJ of 1991 and 1992.

"Yeah," I say, as casually as possible. I'm trying to sell it by not defending myself too vigorously.

"Ok," he acquiesces. "See you in the morning."

He draws me close to him and kisses me on the head. I shake him off.

On my way out of the box, I run into Chris Thompson.

"Hey," he says, a bit sheepishly, like maybe he feels bad for how he stopped talking to me as soon as my dad arrived. It's not my fault I'm Dennis Burton's kid.

"Hey," I say.

"You going out with these guys?"

"No." I laugh at the absurdity of it. "Are you?"

"Yeah."

"You are?! Going to a bar with my dad? I swear to god this night couldn't get any more messed up."

"I'm not going to a bar with your dad. I'm going to a bar with Johnny where your dad is going to be."

"Oh yeah. That makes it sooooo much less weird."

We're nearing the door. It's bottled up with people finalizing plans and saying goodbyes. Chris Thompson and I get crowded close together with a crush of people in front and behind us.

"Was he horrible to you tonight?" I lean in so he can hear me; it feels dangerous and normal at the same time.

"No. I don't think he recognized me. At least he didn't say anything."

"If he recognized you, he would have said something."

"Yeah, I figured. It's really weird he's your dad."

"You have no idea."

We get shoved closer together as we approach the door. I can smell Chris Thompson. Everything around me slows down for a moment. I inhale deeply. He doesn't smell like cologne or beer or even "guy." He just smells clean, like soap and cold water.

When we get on the other side of the door, the flow of people carries me away from him. I turn back towards him and scan the crowd, but all I can see is the back of his head, and Johnny's arm around his shoulder.

CHAPTER·13

My dad's wagon looks out of place among the convertible Cabriolets and soft-topped Jeeps in Richard's driveway. I wish I had the RX-7. It wouldn't make walking into the party alone any less awkward, but at least I'd feel cooler.

Around the back of the house, some boys are poking sticks at a fire, and a bunch of girls I know from school are watching them. Meredith is perched on a tree stump, her knees up to her chest. She's holding a red plastic cup with both hands.

"Whoa, bitch!" she yells, raising her cup towards me. She doesn't sound like herself. She must be drunk. "I did not expect to see you here."

I lean down to hug her. She kisses my cheek.

"I didn't feel like going home."

"Nothing happened with The Hottest Guy Ever?"

"Dennis Burton strikes again."

The girls by the fire are the birth-control-bitches. The ones on the lacrosse team wave to me, and I wave back. The other girls whisper to each other. I'm sure they're trading accusations of my supposed eating disorder.

"What's that?" I motion to a large metal barrel that's surrounded by a bunch of people.

"That's a keg, Chicken! The beer! Have you really never seen one?"

"Richard's mom doesn't care about any of this?" I look around the backyard, half in awe, half in disgust.

"Puh-lease, she's so far gone. Richard said she started drinking when his dad died and hasn't stopped yet. She's likely passed out for the night already."

I cringe. It's a sad thing to say, but Meredith doesn't seem the least bit sad about it.

Richard comes over and kisses Meredith hard on the mouth, like he's marking his territory.

"Hey Alice," Richard says with a cool-guy chin-tip. "Is Nate in town?"

"He comes home tomorrow."

I hadn't expected to see my brother all summer, but with the reemergence of Karl Bell, everything's changed. Nate's coming in to see a game.

"You should bring him over."

"My brother?" I know he and Richard know each other from Aiken, but I didn't think they were friends.

"Sure." I hate that I feel cooler now that Richard's talking to me.

Dylan walks up to us holding two cups.

"Wanna beer, Alice?"

I take a cup, but before I can even try a sip, he kisses me, sticking his tongue in my mouth, and I let him. I guess some things haven't changed since last summer.

The beer tastes like I imagine pee might taste. Meredith looks like she's trying to downplay her astonishment as I take a large swig. On the drive from the stadium, I decided to get fabulously drunk and fool around with Dylan. Because a normal sixteen year old would be hanging out in a backyard with a keg and kissing boys her own age. So far, so good.

I don't know what's more intoxicating, the beer, the fire, or the boys at the party paying attention to me and my new body. The Doors are blaring from a boombox. Everyone got so into them last summer when the movie came out, and then forgot about them again. But now that the VHS is out, I guess they're back "in." The Doors aren't my favorite, but they do add to the air of debauchery in the backyard.

Meredith ushers me to the bathroom. She pulls makeup out of her boho and "fixes" my face. She goes to her car and finds one of her signature tank tops for me. I don't see the point to any of it, as it was clear from the moment I showed up that Dylan is still into me. But I let Meredith fawn over me because dressing me up is how she shows affection.

Dylan follows me around. Every time there's a lull in the conversation I turn my head, and he's there with another drink and a kiss that doesn't feel bad, even if it doesn't feel great.

Things get increasingly blurry.

Dylan takes my hand and leads me from the backyard into his bedroom. His bedside lamp has a red bulb, which I think is supposed to be sexy or dangerous or mature, but instead seems silly. On his bed, his kisses are rough and greedy. Our teeth bump. He kisses me like he's hungry or in a rush. Like I'm not even in the room. His hands start nudging under my clothes. It doesn't feel bad, his hand against my stomach, his mouth on my shoulder, but it doesn't feel as good as I think it's supposed to. Things didn't go this far last summer.

All I can think about is Chris Thompson. I'm doing this, letting this be done to me, got drunk enough to let this be done to me, to get past the devastation I felt when he made it clear I didn't exist if I was Burton's kid, but it isn't working. I imagine him bursting in the door and saving me, but while I'm indulging in this fantasy, I let my guard down. My shirt's off, my bra's unhooked; Dylan's hands are pushing lower. It takes a fair amount of leverage to redirect him above my waist, but he complies … for a while, and then the whole thing starts all over again. I do like the sensation of his fingers firmly grasping my breasts, but only when my eyes are closed, and I'm imagining it's not him. It's unclear whether these moves, this series of pushes and pulls, has worked on other girls, wore them down into submission, or actually turned them on, or if he's just never gotten this far before. Eventually, I allow his hands into my underwear, but I resist when he tries to take off my pants.

"Come on," he coos.

These are the first words he's uttered since we've come inside. I don't say anything. Instead, I grab his crotch, and he shuts up. When he's satisfied, he turns over and goes to sleep. I get up, throw on the first shirt I can find, and wander out back.

The yard has cleared out, and the fire has burned down. I pick up an abandoned cup of beer, but it tastes warm and fuzzy in my mouth. I leave it on a ledge with some other cups. I'm on my way back in through the living room when Meredith slips out one of the other sliding glass doors that make up the entire back of the house. It's a sprawling ranch with wings stretching out in every direction.

"What are you doing out here?" she asks me.

"Nothing. Why?"

"You look pretty out of it. How much did you have to drink?"

"I have no idea." My lips feel raw and puffy. "Does it matter?"

"Where've you been?"

"With Dylan."

"Ooohhh," she teases. "And look, you're wearing his shirt! Did you do him? Are you two together again?"

"Stop it, no," I say. "And we were never together. He barely talks. It's like I'm just a bunch of body parts to him. I jerked him off, and he went to sleep."

"Sheesh, Alice," Meredith feigns disgust. "So crass."

"Shut up."

"You're not yourself."

I detect a note of sincere concern. "I guess I'm drunk."

"Did he pressure you?"

"No." I snort a clumsy laugh. "Are you worried about me?"

"I just don't like seeing you like this – it's not you."

"Listen, Dylan doesn't scare me. And he didn't force me. It was just easier than trying to talk him out of anything."

"I guess that's one way of looking at it." Her face contorts in what might be pity. "Come inside. Let's get some water."

Meredith leads me into the kitchen. She takes real glasses out of a cupboard. She opens the correct door on the first try and moves around the kitchen like it's her own. It's the way we move around each other's kitchens, a familiarity that means a lot to me.

"What's going on?" She hands me a glass, and I gulp down the water.

"I don't know what you mean. It sort of feels like you're judging me. Isn't this what you wanted? You and Richard. Me and Dylan. Wasn't this your plan?"

"I don't know … I thought that's what I wanted … but it doesn't feel right."

"That's what I've been trying to tell you. Listen, it would appear Chris Thompson might have, *maybe*, been interested in me, but then he wasn't. And it just sucks. I thought this would make me feel better."

"Did it?"

"No. But I don't have a better plan. I feel like someone punched me in the stomach and ripped out my heart and is laughing at me. All at the same time."

"What actually happened? Did he say something?"

"No, he just sort of shut down after my dad got there. Like all of a sudden, I didn't exist. Which pretty much proves he had been … interested? But a lot of good that does me now."

"Yeah, that totally sucks."

Dylan's mom wanders into the kitchen but shows no sign of noticing us. She takes something out of the fridge and leaves again. She's wearing a strange flowy, floral robe, and she glides rather than walks, which helps create the impression she's a ghost.

"That was Joan," Meredith says with a sigh. "It's so sad."

"She doesn't care about all of this?" I motion beyond the kitchen.

"She's heavily medicated," Meredith says. "But let's talk about you. I'm worried about *you*. What are we going to do with *you*?"

"I'm touched you care."

She narrows her eyes at me.

"You should just tell him you like him." She sounds authoritative but not altogether convinced she's right.

"Come on. That's not a real option. I can't say, 'Hey, college-guy,' who is by far the most attractive person I've ever met in my life, 'I like you.' Where does that conversation even go?"

"I can't imagine it goes anywhere worse than where you are right now."

"Thanks." I channel Meredith's own champion eye-rolling.

"Hey," she says. "Don't get pissed at me. I know you don't like how much time I'm spending with Richard, but I'm still your best friend. I want what's best for you. And getting drunk and hooking up with someone you don't like isn't what's best for you."

"Wow, it's almost like you care." I put my hands over my heart and pantomime extreme gratitude.

"Shut up!" She flicks me with water from her glass.

"I'm sorry. I'm not pissed at you. It does feel a little like you're moving on. Like now that you're a birth-control-bitch we're not going to be friends senior year. But that's not going to happen, right?"

I don't mention the part where I might not even be back at school with her.

"No, that's not going to happen. We're always going to be friends. Especially senior year. Those birth-control-bitches can't hold a candle to you, Alice. You're so much angrier than they are."

"I'm not angry. I'm just not satisfied being arm candy to a dumb boy."

"Exactly," she says. "You just proved my point."

"And I don't 'not like' Dylan," I continue. "I *could* like him, I guess. I just don't really know him. And he's not Chris Thompson."

"I can't argue with that."

"So now what?" My mouth feels chalky, and I'm exhausted. I want Meredith to tell me what to do.

"I think …" She trails off when Richard enters the kitchen.

"What do you think?" The words come out of his mouth slowly, like he's indulging a small child, and then he kisses her. "Nice shirt," he says to me.

My eyes dart from door to door looking for an escape. "I'm gonna find somewhere to crash."

"Did little man pass out already?"

"Leave her," Meredith says, taking his hand. "Let's go to bed."

They seem like adults as they walk out of the kitchen – the pretty girl and the popular boy – like they've just stepped out of a movie where thirty-year-old actors play the prom king and queen. I don't belong in this movie. I'm the sixteen-year-old who looks twenty-one but feels thirteen. Richard and Meredith's nonchalant intimacy highlights how alone I am.

Meredith turns back to me. "Go in the guest room at the end of the other hall. No one ever goes back there. It's next to Joan's room. We can go to lacrosse together in the morning?"

"Don't worry about me," I say. And I mean it.

"Obviously I'm going to worry about you."

Richard's already leading her down the front hallway. "Love ya, Chickie," she says over her shoulder.

The first door I try reveals two couples already passed out on all available surfaces. The next door is a bathroom and beyond that is clearly Joan's room, though she isn't in it. What part of the house is she currently haunting? Beyond her room is a tiny room with a daybed, a desk and a small television. I let myself in, lock the door behind me, and collapse on the bed. Being upright I hadn't felt very drunk, but lying down is a different story. The room spins. I curl up in a ball and try to make myself disappear.

CHAPTER 14

I sneak out of the house before anyone else is up. The drive home through the quiet streets would be peaceful if my head weren't throbbing. I've never been out on my own this early, and the city looks different – lonely or sad – or maybe that's just me.

I get home just after six, and I need to be at the fields by nine. The Tylenol I found in Joan's medicine cabinet hasn't made a dent in my headache. I put the Wasted Pretty tape in my Walkman and crawl into bed. It's not music meant for falling asleep, but I can't pass up the opportunity to hear Chris Thompson's voice in my head, even if it's only on backup vocals.

I've just fallen asleep when the door creaks open. Meredith and my dad are standing in my doorway. None of the doors in my house latch, let alone lock. It's so annoying.

"Uh, hi ..." I say. "Dad, aren't you supposed to be on air?"

He ignores my question. "I thought you said you were staying at Meredith's."

Meredith's the only person I know who my dad can't rattle, but she's rattled now. She looks at me as if she's trying to communicate something telepathically, but I don't know what it is.

"Yeah, I woke up and didn't feel well, so I came home a couple hours ago. Sorry, did I freak you out?"

"Yes!" Meredith shouts, but I can tell she's relieved. I must not be contradicting whatever story she told my dad.

"What do you mean, you don't feel well?" Ever since I switched to my mom's don't-call-it-a-diet plan, I haven't been sick or missed a day of school.

"I'm probably fine." I rub my eyes. *Just hungover after being drunk for the first time ever.*

I want to get out of bed and show them I can walk upright, but I'm not dressed to be on display. The three of us stare at each other, each one expecting the other to move first.

Finally, I say, "I'm not dressed."

My dad backs out of the room, and Meredith pushes the door closed behind him.

"Holy crap!" she whisper-yells at me. "I looked all over that damn house for you."

"Sorry." I pull on a new pair of underwear and Umbros. I dig two sports bras out of my hamper.

"I saw way too many naked people way too early in the morning," Meredith complains.

"I said I'm sorry. I just woke up and didn't want to be there anymore."

"You don't look so hot."

"I don't feel so hot."

"We'll get some coffee on our way to the fields."

"What does my dad know?"

"Nothing. I covered for you. But you should have left me a note or something. If I'm going to be your cover, you need to let me know what's up."

"I didn't plan on leaving. I'm sorry."

I walk back and forth across my room. I'm looking for something, but I don't know what. Eventually, I sit down on my bed and put my head in my hands.

"Let's go, Chicken," she says. "You'll feel better after we get some caffeine in you."

*   *   *   *   *

I don't feel better. When we get to the parking lot at Fox Chapel, Meredith sings one more verse of TLC's "Ain't 2 Proud 2 Beg" at the top of her lungs before she shuts off her Cabriolet. I lug my lacrosse bag from the car out to the field, happy to be far away from her custom sound system. We sit next to each other while we're stretching. I can feel everyone checking everyone else out and determining who they can clearly beat and who's going to be a challenge. I'm not sure how I'm going to make it through the day, let alone how I'm going to look better than these girls. Getting drunk last night may not have been the smartest move. I can't believe any of this is happening.

When we get up to do warm-ups with one of the coaches, I lose my balance, and Meredith catches me before I hit the ground.

"What is going on?" she hisses.

"I don't know. Maybe the caffeine and the alcohol are a bad mix."

"Pull your shit together."

The rest of the day doesn't go any better. I have no speed. I have no strength. The light of the sun stabs my forehead and pierces right through my brain. We're doing attack drills when I lean over and heave. One of the assistant coaches is standing right behind me.

"What's the problem, Burton?" She's not as tall as I am, but she could definitely take me.

"No problem." I wipe my mouth with my purple terry cloth wristband.

"There is a problem," she says. "You want to tell me what it is?"

"Too much coffee, maybe?" I turn towards the field hoping this will be a short talk.

"You think I don't know what a hangover looks like, Burton? I coach at the college level, Division I. I see this kind of thing all the time. Those girls don't make it."

I turn to face her.

"I'm not hung-over. I don't have a problem. I'm going to get back out there, if that's ok?"

"You know, Burton, I can tell you have skills; you wouldn't be here if you didn't, but everyone here has skills. We look for hard work. We look for coachability. And we look to avoid problems. Are you going to be a problem?"

I've never been anyone's problem in my life.

"No ma'am."

We stare at each other wordlessly. I'm waiting for her to dismiss me. I don't know what she's waiting for.

"Not everyone's going to make the team," she finally says. "You better hustle."

"Yes ma'am." I take my place in the crush of girls waiting for their turn to sprint across the field.

When we break for lunch Meredith leans against her Cabriolet sucking down Powerade. She's sweating, which is a true testament to how hard they pushed us this morning, because no matter how hard she plays, Meredith never breaks a sweat. For my part, I threw up a second time.

Meredith and I take our lunches across the field. On the way, we pass a group of girls, and I can tell Amanda wants us to invite her to eat with us, but we don't. Meredith unpacks her food under the shade of a tree. My mom has allowed me a few hard-boiled eggs in addition to celery and the meal bars, but it's hard not to covet the buffet of carbs and sugar Meredith has laid out.

"How long are you going to wallow?" She bites into a massive sandwich.

"I'm not wallowing." *I'm wallowing.*

"Right."

"What do you mean?"

"So a hot guy thought you were cute, but he's either too principled – gag! – or too scared of Burton to make a move, so what? Find a different guy. You don't like Dylan? No problem, Richard has friends. You're looking at this totally wrong. You look really good. I mean, not today – sorry! – but in general. Try to enjoy it."

"It's not that simple. It's not like I can just like anyone. The way Chris Thompson looked at me was different. It made me feel different. It may have actually changed who I am."

"Gross. You need to lose your virginity. You wouldn't be talking like this if you weren't a virgin."

I shoot her the finger, and she throws a bag of chips at me.

"Just give me a few more hours of wallowing."

"Don't wallow too much, you'll get yourself cut."

"Thanks for the vote of confidence."

*   *   *   *   *

The afternoon session is a beast. I like lacrosse, but I like it better when I'm the best one on the field. My dad has always called my play effortless, but this damn Summer Team is probably the most effort I've ever put into anything. Meredith looks great, and even Amanda looks like she can handle this better than I can. I'm guessing Amanda isn't hungover, but Meredith must've had as much as I did last night.

Every time I think about getting cut – about missing my chance to be seen by the coaches and scouts – I have to force the thought out of my head. What's the worst that will happen to the other girls if they get cut? Nothing. Amanda will have another chance next summer, and Meredith … well, Meredith won't get cut. Unfortunately, the next thought is if my dad can't pay for Frazer, he can't pay for college. I waste a ton of energy trying not to think about it.

The coaches divide us into three teams, and we're playing round-robin fifteen-minute games. One team is always resting but after we cycle through the three games they mix the teams up, and we start all over again. I hate playing against Meredith. She always smiles on the field, but I know the smile is just about psyching out the opponent. She's fierce, and I don't like being her opponent. The first time we face each other, she rushes me hard trying to get to the goal. I plant myself, and we both end up going down. Her smile doesn't waver the whole time. Amanda doesn't look as confident, but as defenders, we don't have to go head to head.

When everyone has played everyone else a bazillion times, they let us rest. We end up throwing our bodies on the ground on the small hill next to the fields. The shade from the high school provides limited relief from the heat. The coaches congregate by a tree and pass a few clipboards back and forth.

"That looks serious." Meredith passes me a water bottle.

"I don't know." I push the bottle away. I don't want to accept her kindness while I'm lying to her. I know it looks serious. I know in my bones they're going to announce cuts, and I'm not going to make it. They weren't supposed to do it until the weekend, but what they put us through this afternoon felt like a final test. They saw all they needed to see.

"Sorry I knocked you over." Meredith pours the water I refused over her head.

"You didn't knock me over. I knocked you over."

Meredith's about to argue the point when the head coach walks towards us and blows her whistle in three short blasts.

"Thanks for all your work today, girls. I think we're going to get out of here a little early." There are sighs of relief, but I hold my breath. "We're gonna split you into two groups before you go. The list I'm going to read is going to come with me. Everyone else is going to stay here on the hill with Coach Shelly."

She reads the list. Amanda and I are on it. Meredith isn't.

I push myself up to stand. "I just got cut."

"Shut up."

"Meet you at the car."

We follow Coach Kim back to the tree where the coaches had been huddled. Everyone seems oblivious to what's about to happen, but the tree's by the parking lot. She's marching us out of here.

"You looked good out there." Amanda tries to stay close to me.

"Not good enough."

"Oh, come on."

I ignore her. I owe her nothing. My future is being destroyed. I'm going to go to public school for senior year. Alone. Without Meredith. Without lacrosse. I can't go to college if my parents can't pay for it. All day I felt woozy from the hangover and the workout, but now I feel nothing. I'm numb.

We sit on the grass by the tree, and Coach Kim says things. I don't hear complete sentences, just strings of words.

Solid effort.

Hard decision.

Cream of the crop.

At some point, she must have stopped talking because girls have started making their way to their cars. I can't move. I'm the last one on the ground, which is fitting, given the day.

"You wanna talk?" Coach Kim squats down next to me. I have to work to resist the urge to tip her over.

"I'm good."

"You're gonna be fine. You're good enough for D1. You just didn't have the focus today."

I don't respond. I silently will her to go away.

CHAPTER 15

The Pirates lose to the Padres again tonight, but no one in the station box seems to care. We all walk across the street to a bar with a bunch of the players. I'm used to the looks we get when we walk in places with my dad, but walking into a sports bar with Karl and half a professional baseball team takes it to a whole new level. First, the place goes silent and then it's taken over by a hushed murmur. My family sits at a high table near the bar. Karl comes and goes, sitting with us for a few minutes and then getting pulled away to be in pictures or to sign autographs. I have to listen to Nate regale my family and people from the station with stories from his life as a Division I athlete. Meanwhile, I haven't come to grips with the fact I've been cut from the Summer Team, and I certainly can't bring myself to say it out loud.

"This is exciting!" My mom has an eager smile on her face.

It's hard to say if she's excited by the game or the bar or just that we're all here together. I don't bring up that she and my dad barely spoke to each other in the box or that we all drove separate cars.

My mom orders plain grilled chicken for the two of us. My dad gets a burger. True to form, Nate chooses plain grilled chicken for himself as if he wants to – but doesn't have to – eat health food. Karl puts our dinners on his tab.

"I'm going to the bathroom," I say to no one in particular.

I pass a set of payphones in the dark hallway leading to the bathroom. For some reason, I want to call Chris Thompson. I want to tell him I got cut. Given his history with my dad, he'd understand. But I don't even have his number.

From inside the bathroom stall, I hear two drunken women by the sink talking about the ballplayers and which ones are hot and which ones might take them back to the hotel. They're discussing their past conquests when I open the stall door. They look at me like I'm intruding on them. They wear acid wash and lace, like the secretaries with big hair at the radio station. It's what the girls at public school look like. I'm never going to fit in. I might never fit in anywhere ever again. I move in between the two women to wash my hands.

As the water falls between my fingers, I really look at my hands. They used to be pudgy, like my dad's. But one morning before school I was tying my shoes, and I looked down and saw my mom's hands, slender fingers with defined knuckles. I didn't recognize them. That's when I knew my mom's shakes and bars, with the dumb butterfly stickers, were working.

"Which one are you with?"

It takes me a minute to realize one of the big-haired women is addressing me.

"Um, I'm in high school."

"Are you one of their kids?"

"No." I shake my hands dry. The room really isn't big enough for three people, and they're blocking my way out.

"Do you know any of them? 'Cause if you do …" Her words trail off as her eyes lose focus.

"I know Karl Bell."

"So you'll introduce us?" the first one says.

"Ummm, I don't know you."

"She's Jodi, and I'm Dawn. Got it? Jodi and Dawn? We gotta do touch-ups." She pulls some lipstick out of her bag. "But when we come out, you're doing this."

"And I've gotta pee," adds Dawn.

"Yeah, she's gotta pee," says Jodi.

"Ok, but he's married."

"I heard she doesn't travel with the team!" Jodi's head wags in a way I've only seen on TV.

They laugh viciously, like wild animals, if wild animals could get drunk.

"I gotta go." I push past them.

My eyes haven't adjusted from the fluorescents of the bathroom to the darkness of the hallway when I run into Karl.

"Having fun, Ally?"

"Sure." I feign the excitement I know I'm supposed to feel.

"Really? You look a little down. I could get you a drink. In a soda cup, of course."

"No thanks."

"So, are you really not dating? You sure you're not just sneaking around and lying about it? You can tell me."

Karl Bell is drunk.

"I'm not dating."

"But you've grown into this beautiful woman." He reaches down for my right hand, the one with the scar from the bike accident.

"Thanks," I say, uncomfortably. "I'm just tall."

I try to wiggle my hand away, but he doesn't let go.

"Do you have fantasies?"

I look away from him. The hallway's dark, and we're alone, but that can't last.

He tightens his grip on my fingers. "You know, like, when you touch yourself?"

I don't say anything.

"You must touch yourself," he says. "And you should know, not everyone is afraid of your dad."

A lump in my throat makes it painful to swallow. His cologne fills the space around my head. I try to get my hand free, but he pulls me closer. He cups my hand around his dick, which I can tell, even through his black jeans, is hard. I'm frozen in place and can feel his breath on my neck when Jodi and Dawn burst out of the bathroom behind me. Karl pushes me away.

"There you are!" Dawn says, pretending we know each other. "Who's your friend?"

At first, I can't find my voice, but Dawn stares at me like she might actually hurt me, so I make the introductions and get back to my parents' table as quickly as I can. I don't look back, but I can feel Karl's eyes on me. Cold sweat runs down my neck into my T-shirt.

"What's your problem?" Nate asks.

I wince at the attention my family is focusing on me. I know I need to respond, but I can't get enough air.

"Alice, what's wrong?" my mom prods. They're all staring at me. I need to say something, anything.

"It's Meredith," I croak. "I called her from the payphone. She and Richard had a fight."

"That's just something you say when you don't have anything better to say, isn't it?" my dad asks.

"What?" He always seems to know everything. Why doesn't he know what just happened?

"Aren't they always fighting? What makes tonight any different than any other night?" This is a line my dad uses on air all the time. It's a reference to a Jewish prayer, but most people don't realize that.

"Oh," I say. "Yeah, they're hard to keep up with."

Karl rounds the corner from the hallway and heads towards us. Jodi, or Dawn, I can't remember who is who, is hanging on him, but he moves smoothly through the crowd of people shaking hands and smiling. Women are hugging him, and guys are giving him high-fives. My body feels hot, and all my airways seem to be constricted like the time I had an allergic reaction to a bee sting on my chest.

"I really need to go." I don't wait for anyone's response.

In the parking lot, I climb into the driver's seat of the wagon and turn it on so I can put the windows down. I can't tell if I'm hot or cold, but the confined space of the car feels too tight, even though it's enormous. My heart's racing. I feel completely exposed even though I'm sitting inside a virtual tank. People filter out of the restaurant laughing and holding hands. I watch for Dawn and Jodi. I watch for Karl. I look at my right hand. The one with the scar. The one that touched him. I want to cut it off.

What was he thinking?

What about Samantha?

And what about what he said?

Was I supposed to be touching myself?

But really, he didn't actually do anything all that bad. They were just words. He was just drunk. I don't want to think about his crotch.

I'm putting the car in gear when my brother appears in my window.

"What's going on? Who did you really call?"

"Meredith."

"That's a lie. She and Richard aren't fighting. I talked to him before I came out."

"Why are you talking to Richard?"

"He's having a party tonight."

"He has a party every night."

"Well, he wants me to come over tonight."

"Of course he does." Because what I really need right now is my brother partying with Meredith's boyfriend.

"What does that mean?"

"Nothing."

"What's wrong with you? Where are you going?" Nate has never taken an interest in me before, and I wish he wouldn't now either. "Mom's really pissed you didn't thank Karl."

"For what?" The idea of speaking to him disgusts me.

"Dinner?"

"Oh, uh … I think he'll get over it. I need to go."

"Fine." Nate steps back from the car. "But I'm not lying for you."

"Then it's good you don't know where I'm going."

CHAPTER 16

Where other cities have squared-off grids, Pittsburgh has triangles. Zigzagging through the confusing streets of downtown I find my way to Oakland. When I drive by Chris Thompson's place, I see a light on in the kitchen. He said I could come by anytime, but I don't know if he meant it. I have plenty of time to second-guess myself as I look for a place to park the Wally Wagon. As much as I don't really want to see anyone, I do want to see Chris Thompson. Because seeing Chris Thompson trumps everything else. I should be thinking about far more important things, but all I can think about is him.

I ring his bell instead of Johnny's this time and flop down on the porch-couch. I'm too tired to be grossed out by it.

When he opens the door and smiles, it puts me at ease, but when he starts walking towards me, I feel trapped. I want him to console me, but I don't want to tell him why I need to be consoled.

"Hey." He sits next to me on the couch. "You ok?"

"Not really."

"You wanna come upstairs for tea? I know how much you like tea."

"Not really."

He takes my hand, my damn right hand that just touched Karl Bell's crotch. I grab it back and shake it like a freak. I don't want Chris Thompson touching my right hand. I don't want a right hand anymore.

"What's going on?"

"Uh, you know … I'm sorry I bothered you. I should go home."

"Princess," he pleads, and I like the sound of his pleading. "Why'd you come here?"

I don't want to tell him, but I don't want to lie to him, either. I want to be myself and have him like me for it. But I can't tell him what happened. I'm not really sure what happened. I take a deep breath and decide I won't tell anyone ever. I'm not even sure there's anything to tell.

"It's actually nothing." I try to laugh it off. "Sorry, I'm overreacting. I'm gonna go home. I'm really sorry."

"Is it more stuff with your dad?"

"Something like that." That's not really a lie, is it?

"I don't think you should drive right now. Can you come upstairs for a bit? I promise I won't make you drink tea."

"Kind of you."

He looks at his watch. "You have a curfew, right?"

It's a punch in the gut, hearing this gorgeous college guy talk about my high-school-girl curfew.

"Yeah. I really need to go. I'm sorry I bothered you."

"Listen, I have off tomorrow. You wanna learn how to drive?"

I should be at practice tomorrow, but I don't have practice anymore. And a day in the country with Chris Thompson seems like the perfect distraction.

"Ok."

"Pick me up in the morning? I'm going to fill that boat with laundry. And here –" he digs through the couch cushions and produces a pen and a receipt. "This is my number. Give me yours."

The receipt he hands me feels heavier than it should. It's like a golden ticket to my own future. Maybe I won't have a Frazer senior year, or a lacrosse scholarship, or go to college, but I can call Chris Thompson anytime I want. I stuff the receipt in the back pocket of Nate's jeans and write my phone number with his pen in my shaky right hand.

Chris Thompson takes it and gives me a cool-guy chin tip nod. "See ya."

* * * * *

My house is empty when I get home. I go right to my room and lie in bed perfectly still, almost frozen, but I can't sleep. Eventually, I hear my parents come in, about 15-minutes apart, and I know my dad is probably heading up to check on me. I pretend to be asleep when he sticks his head in my room. Thoughts are coming in and out of my head, and I can't get my brain to turn off. On one hand, it feels like what happened in the dark hallway at the bar is a big, big deal and, on the other, I feel like maybe I've blown it out of proportion. The sounds of my parents getting ready for bed intensify and peak, and then the house goes quiet.

12:07 a.m.

1:32 a.m.

2:22 a.m.

When my cordless rings, I pick it up before the second ring but don't say anything immediately. I listen to see if my parents stir across the hall. While I assess the situation, my body warms with the thought that Chris Thompson is calling to check on me.

"Hello?" I whisper.

"Were you asleep, Ally, or thinking about what I said?"

It's like having Karl Bell in bed with me.

"I have to go." My voice can't hide my fear.

"There's nowhere to go. Your mom gave me your number. She said you'd want to say thanks for tonight."

"Thanks," I mumble. I want to hang up, but I can't move.

"You're welcome. But it doesn't sound like you mean it. Can you say it while you're touching yourself?"

With great effort, I manage to press the right button to end the call. When it rings again, I scramble to unplug the base from the wall.

CHAPTER 17

I wake up sweating. The dream always starts like a good one. An early summer day: the perfect temperature, a light breeze, clear afternoon light. I straddle my bike at the top of the hill on our street. It's the day of my accident in fifth grade replaying itself; I haven't had this dream in a while.

Nate didn't want to let me play. He said the game was for boys only. They were matched up one-on-one to race down our hill in an elaborate game of chicken. The goal was to beat the other boy to the intersection of the main road, but stop before you crossed it. You got a point for getting there first and an extra point for getting closer to the main road. They didn't want to let me play, but they had an odd number, so Nate matched me up with the smallest boy. We went last. Everyone else was already at the bottom of the hill. I felt invincible, like I was practically flying, but I misjudged how long it would take me to stop and rather than crossing the road, which could have gotten me killed, I bailed off my bike and ended up under a parked car. Everything went black.

When I opened my eyes, the neighborhood kids were crowding around me. They were looking down in horror, checking me for signs of life. On the day of the accident there were no adults, just the boys who had been racing and the girls who had been roller-skating nearby, but in the dream the kids are joined by Burton. And Karl Bell. And Chris Thompson. And Johnny. There are two Nates: the childhood one and the now-one. Both of them look pissed.

*   *   *   *   *

When I pull up to his place, Chris Thompson's sitting on the porch surrounded by laundry baskets. He's wearing light blue Umbros, soccer flats, an Indiana soccer shirt, and a maroon baseball hat turned around backward. It's clear I've spent too much time on my "going to the country" outfit: cut-off jean shorts (cut slightly shorter this morning with a steak knife); my standard boxy white tank top (hovering slightly above the button of my shorts and showing just a bit of my newly flat stomach); and a button-down short sleeve cotton plaid shirt. I'm wearing Birkenstocks, but if I had cowboy boots I would have put them on instead.

"Hey," Chris Thompson says with a cool-guy chin-tip. "You feeling better?"

"I'm fine."

"Oh, I believe you," he teases.

After he's done loading his laundry into the back of the Wally Wagon, he hands me a cassette tape. "Dubbed the new Cure for you."

"Thanks." I look at the blank tape case. "No song list?"

"You can be pretty demanding sometimes, Princess, can't you? Put the tape in."

I laugh, and so does he when he realizes the wagon only has an 8-track player.

"You're kidding?"

I shift into drive and pull out.

"Burton's tapes are under your seat."

Chris Thompson pulls onto his lap what looks like a small suitcase.

"What year is it in here?" He sounds mildly annoyed. "Queen? Steely Dan? Barry Manilow?"

"That one's my mom's."

"Oh, Princess, we gotta get you out of this car. Does the RX-7 have a cassette deck?"

"It does."

He settles on a Beatles tape.

Chris Thompson directs me through the city and over bridges and out past the boundaries of where I've driven before. Occasionally he says, "You're going to want to get in the left lane in a bit," or "Get in the left lane now," but mostly we're quiet. It's weird being alone with him in a car. We made these plans as if spending the day in the country is the most natural thing for us to do, but I'm pretty sure my dad would kill one or both of us if he saw us together.

The cold sweaty feeling I had when I woke up is gone, but I'm still uneasy. I don't know what to do about Karl Bell, I don't know what to do about lacrosse, and I don't know what to do about the fact that even though it probably means nothing, I think Chris Thompson might actually like me.

My right hand is itchy. More than itchy. It's tingling and pulling my focus.

I can't believe I'm able to function right now, at least in the sense that I'm able to put one foot in front of the other and look normal on the outside. Inside I feel tainted. It's actually a physical sensation just under my skin, and not just on my hand. Between Karl's behavior, my father's financial issues, and the way I've been sneaking around, I wonder if everyone's hiding something. Maybe this is what being an adult is all about.

I pay attention to the road and the directions Chris Thompson is giving. Every once in awhile Karl's face enters my consciousness, and I have to physically shake my head to rid my mind of the image; I probably look like I have a tic. While the Beatles sing, Chris Thompson uses his thumb to drum on his thigh. I want to touch his thigh. I think about easing my hand across the front seat, but I look at my hand, my stupid, skinny right hand, and the scar on it, and I feel like damaged goods. Also, I feel like an idiot for hating all men but thinking Chris Thompson might be different.

As we drive farther away from the major roads, the countryside becomes breathtakingly beautiful and quaint. I can't believe we're less than an hour away from where I live. I'm having trouble integrating the beauty I see with the dark thoughts swimming in my head. And I'm alone in a car with Chris Thompson. All in all, I'm surprised I haven't crashed the wagon.

"Turn down that road." Chris Thompson points ahead of us. It's a dirt drive dividing a huge expanse of grassy rolling hills. On one side, not far from the main road, is a white clapboard church with a small parking lot and an even smaller walled in area with headstones. On the other side of the dirt drive, set back even farther from the main road, is a stone farmhouse with a few evergreens out back.

"You're kidding me, right?" I pull onto the gravel drive next to the house.

"What?"

"You live here? The next Kurt Cobain lives in a Little House on the Prairie?"

"My parents live here."

"Do you like it here?"

"It's boring, but it's nice, I guess."

The setting doesn't jibe with how I think of Chris Thompson. I wonder what else I'm missing when I look at him.

Chris Thompson takes his laundry inside, and I head right to the garage. The truck is probably as old as I am, and it's big. I crawl into the passenger seat, and things become real. I've been so preoccupied with everything else going on that I haven't had time to be nervous about Chris Thompson teaching me to drive. My father's attempts failed miserably, ending with us screaming at each other. I'm not sure why it hasn't occurred to me until now that Chris Thompson's attempt could go the same way.

I hate doing things I'm not good at, especially in front of people I'm trying to impress. Like an idiot, I've been looking forward to Chris Thompson teaching me to drive stick, but as it's actually happening, it feels like a horrible idea.

I crack each of my knuckles as he throws some things into the back of the truck. Then he goes back into the house leaving me alone with my increasingly queasy stomach. When he comes out again, he has a large dog who he puts in the bed of the truck.

"That's Buddy," Chris Thompson says, climbing into the driver's seat. "Do you like dogs?"

"I'm not really a dog person."

"Not a dog person? Not a country person? Can't drive stick? Sometimes I wonder what the hell we're doing with each other!"

Chris Thompson says it in that way guys like Chris Thompson can say things. That way that's either flirting or making it clear that the idea he could be flirting with me is nothing more than a joke.

I narrow my eyes at him, adding a pushed-out pout with my lower lip for good measure. He laughs the whole thing off and starts to school me on the stick shift as he backs out of the garage.

"We're not going to talk about reverse yet. Reverse will come later. How much do you know already? Can you drive stick at all?"

"Not really. Burton took me up to the reservoir, but mostly I just stalled out, and we yelled at each other."

"I can imagine." Chris Thompson says this with more bitterness than seems necessary. "He can explain things one way, and if you don't get it, he's done with you."

"He's not that bad." I find myself defending my dad, but I'm not even sure I believe it. "I mean, mostly we get along, but I know he rubs some people the wrong way."

"Most people ..." he mumbles.

We're on the dirt road going deeper into the woods, away from the main road. It occurs to me that no one knows where I am. Not Johnny. Not Meredith. Certainly not Nate or my family. I wonder if I should be concerned about that.

"Ok, let's do this," Chris Thompson says. "You know the basics, right? The truck has five speeds plus reverse. Reverse on the truck is down and to the right, but I bet on the RX-7 it's up and to the left. Mostly you just want to get a feel for what you're driving. You'll start to know when it's time to shift. Do you know why you were stalling? Was it a timing thing or the mechanics? How's your hand-eye coordination?"

My heart rate quickens, and despite the cool breeze coming in from the open windows, there's sweat forming everywhere. I shake my head, shrug my shoulders, and don't know what to say.

"Ok." He stops the truck. "Less talking, more doing." When he hops out of the cab, I remain paralyzed in the passenger seat. He comes around the back, stopping to pet Buddy, and then opens my door. "Hop out or slide over Princess, let's do this."

I push myself over to the driver's seat, avoiding the stick shift that aggressively sticks out of the floor of the vehicle. It doesn't look anything like the shift on the RX-7, and I'm not sure this day is going to help at all. When Chris Thompson gets in, he talks me through the gearshift again. I adjust the mirrors, but only slightly. He's taller than I am, but not by much. Not like Karl Bell. I shake my head, trying to dislodge an image of him in the hall.

"Go for it," Chris Thompson says in the same cheerful tone he has maintained in the face of my paralyzing fear. "Show me what you got."

I turn the key. The truck sputters on in neutral. I sit there for too long. Chris Thompson is about to say something when I remember what to do. I push the clutch in; I move the gearshift into first and press tentatively on the gas. The engine revs. I get spooked and let the clutch out too quickly. The truck bucks, then stalls and Buddy barks so loudly that I yelp in response. I shut the truck off.

"Shit!" I blurt out and put my head on the steering wheel.

Chris Thompson reaches for my hand. It's the same hand Karl touched. It's the same hand with the scar. I pull it away, quickly, with more force than I mean to, and I begin to cry loudly. I'm becoming increasingly embarrassed which makes me cry even more. It's a horrible loop I can't get out of. I'm wringing my hands in my lap like a total freak. Every time I try to calm myself down, I feel Karl's hand on mine again. I rub my hands harder because it feels like if I rub off a whole layer of skin, I could fix my problem.

"Alice," Chris Thompson finally says tentatively. "Are we going to talk about what's going on with you?"

I shake my head. There are tears and snot everywhere, my cheeks, my nose, my chin. I look away and try to wipe my face with the back of my hand, but I just manage to smear the gunk all over my face. I turn back to Chris Thompson and see he has taken off his shirt and is handing it to me like a Kleenex. His naked abs are arresting.

"Put your shirt back on," I manage to say with a laugh. I slide my own button-down off, because I still have on a tank underneath, and use it to wipe my face.

"Seriously, Princess … "

"It's nothing." I manage to croak.

"Why do you keep shaking your hand? You did it last night, too."

He noticed. He's been paying attention, but I don't want his pity.

"I don't want to talk about it."

"Come on," he coaxes, like he thinks I'm just holding out on him, so he'll have to beg me to tell him. "This is our 'thing.' You're the girl who shows up crying and says she doesn't want to tell me all her problems and then she does anyway. Would it help if we went back to the house and you locked yourself in the bathroom?"

My brain cannot process flirting from him right now, not with his shirt off and the certain knowledge that nothing will ever happen.

"Now we have a 'thing?'"

"Yes, we have a 'thing.' That whole not-telling-me-telling-me thing and the whole you-can't-sing-for-shit-but-for-some-reason – probably because you're so damn pretty – I-like-to-listen-to-you-butcher-my-favorite-songs thing. In exchange, you don't ask me what I'm going to do with my life."

My brain shorts out, but I manage to stay in the conversation. "What is next for you? And did you just call me pretty?"

"Come on, you know you're pretty."

"What I know," I say deliberately, "is that I have big boobs. There's a difference."

And that shuts him up for a moment, but then he says, "I'm not going to deny you have … a big … you know, though it's not something I really want to talk about, but do you really think that's all you have going for you?"

"Yes. And I know it's true because a year ago, no one ever looked at me twice, and now …" I trail off and start rubbing my hands again. I don't want to be doing it, but I can't stop. And then I am shaking, because, right now, I can't tell the difference between Karl Bell and Chris Thompson and the interns talking about my rack. They are all paying too much attention to me.

I fling open the door of the truck and throw myself out. I run from the road, but there's nowhere to run to, just an open field for what feels like forever. When it becomes hard to breathe, I sit down on a fallen log and Buddy is practically on top of me. He nuzzles my face, and I'm surprised to find it comforting. Chris Thompson is not far behind. He sits down next to me, our knees barely touching. Buddy looks at Chris Thompson but stays firmly planted at my side.

"Alice, you need to tell me what's going on. And if you're not going to tell me, you need to tell someone. I don't know why I feel so protective of you. Maybe it's because I saw you faint, and I've never seen anyone faint before. Or maybe because I saw you sleeping, curled up on my couch. Or maybe because it's so clear to me that being Burton's kid is really hard, because I remember what it was like when I was on that team, and I wanted his approval so badly and didn't get it so publicly. But whatever it is, I can't do anything to help you if you don't tell me what happened."

I don't look at Chris Thompson, because I can't look at Chris Thompson. It always feels that way, except for the moments when it doesn't. I can, however, focus on our knees touching. And I hate myself for it, because right now I want nothing more than to hate all men because I know I can't trust any of them. But I can't hate Chris Thompson. Not just because I'm incredibly attracted to him, which I am, in a powerful way that scares me, but because he's not like the stories I've heard about CJ Thompson and that means maybe everyone I've always trusted has been wrong about everything. I'm reeling.

I focus on my hands in my lap. I can't help thinking that if they were still pudgy like my dad's, Karl Bell would have left me alone, but if I were still chubby, I'm sure Chris Thompson wouldn't have noticed me either, which is unpleasant, but probably true. Finally, I lift my head and speak more calmly than I think I'm capable of.

"Yes, something happened last night, but I've already decided not to talk about it. I am ok, or I will be, and there's nothing you, or anyone else, needs to do. I'm sorry I freaked out. I would love it if we could just start over. Please. Teach me how to drive stick so I can give the wagon back to my dad and drive a normal car again."

He looks at me for a long time. I know he's trying to decide whether to let me off the hook or press harder. I'm touched by how much he cares, but I hope he doesn't care too much.

"Princess." He takes my hand, my damn right hand. I make a concerted and successful effort not to pull it away.

"I'm good." I'm holding his hand, not just letting mine be held, and I feel a flutter in my gut I wish I weren't feeling. "For real. I promise. Teach me how to drive."

I drop his hand and start back to the truck. Buddy follows at my knee.

"Looks like you made a friend," Chris Thompson says.

"He's sweet."

"Maybe you are a dog person?" he says. "And a country person? And all kinds of things you didn't realize. Maybe you can even drive stick."

I appreciate that his voice doesn't seem as heavy as before.

"Teach me." I mean to sound coy, and for the first time in my life, I think I succeed.

CHAPTER 18

Chris Thompson helps Buddy into the back of the truck and slides in next to me.

"Ok, just put it into neutral and try to start it up. Let me see what you're having trouble with."

"All of it," I say, turning on the ignition.

I put the gearshift into first, push in the gas pedal slowly and let the clutch out: sputter, jerk, stall, deep breath, repeat, repeat, repeat.

"Shit!" I pound my fist on the seat.

"Ok," Chris Thompson says. "So, I can't tell if you know *what* to do but not *how* to do it, or if you don't actually know what you should be doing. Are you a very technical person or a hands-on person?"

"What do you mean?"

"Are you good at following instructions or figuring things out?"

"I'm good at a lot of things," I say matter-of-factly. "Actually, I generally don't do things that don't come easily to me. I'm good at Chemistry *and* Biology. I'm good at Pre-Calc *and* Geometry. Two years ago I built a house with Habitat for Humanity. I'm just not good at this!"

"Ok, um, what did Burton tell you about how the transmission actually works?"

I shake my head. "Nothing?"

"Hmmm, Burton probably doesn't know how a transmission works." The edge in his voice is always there when he talks about my dad. "Ok, you know those toys you played with when you were little where you could move one circle, and it had teeth, and it would move other circles, but all the circles were different sizes and would move at different speeds?"

"Yeah." I nod. "Gears."

"Exactly. Imagine you need to line up those gears while they're moving. Hard, right?"

"Yeah?"

"That's essentially what you're doing when you're shifting ... and the clutch is like your free pass. If you push down on the clutch the teeth won't eat each other up, but you can't hold the clutch in too long, or they won't catch. Also, the clutch will wear out, and you'll have to replace it. But for now just think about the fact that the clutch, when pushed in, protects everything but also keeps the gears from engaging. So you only want to push it when you need to, and you'll want to let it out as soon as you feel the gears engage. Does that make sense?"

"I think so?"

I turn the truck on in neutral, push in the clutch and slide the gearshift into first. As I push the gas pedal down, I feel the clutch engage, and I let it out. We're moving. We pick up speed, and I successfully shift into second. I practically squeal with glee. I'm too focused on driving to look over at Chris Thompson, but the vibe in the cab is good. We drive all around his parents' property while I upshift and downshift. He makes me stop the car and start all over. I don't stall again for the rest of the afternoon. We even practice reverse, but he reminds me, reverse will probably be different on the RX-7. He says eventually I'll be able to drive any stick, even though gearshifts come in different configurations and each clutch is calibrated differently. When I'm really good, I'll be able to control any car.

Back at the house, Chris Thompson moves some laundry around, and then we take the truck out on the main roads around Zelie. There isn't really any traffic, so I'm not nervous. When we come back to the property, we take Buddy for a walk. He runs into some trees, and we follow after him. From a spot on a rock, we watch as he plays in a stream.

When I see a hairy caterpillar crawling on a fallen leaf, I hop down to pick it up. I've always loved caterpillars – especially the hairy ones. I let it crawl through my spindly fingers and move my hands around to keep it from falling back to the ground.

"Keep that away from Buddy," Chris Thompson says.

"Why?"

"He'll eat it." He says this without emotion, but it makes me unbelievably sad to think of the big dog devouring the small hairy caterpillar. "You wouldn't want to deprive the thing of turning into a butterfly."

"I don't know. Maybe some caterpillars don't want to be butterflies. Maybe sometimes they break out of the cocoon and think, 'Oh shit, now I have to fly all the time, and everyone's going to be pointing at me and chasing me.'"

"Maybe. But I doubt they think, 'Oh shit, I wish a big dog had eaten me while I was still a caterpillar.'"

"Hmmm."

"I've told you you're weird before, right?"

I nod with a smile. I don't even mind him calling me weird, not now that he's also called me pretty.

The country is growing on me. The dog is growing on me. It's easy to pretend this is my real life instead of a crazy, bizarre, once-in-a-lifetime experience. To make it even stranger, a couple times it seems like Chris Thompson is about to kiss me; it looks like he wants to, but each time it dawns on me that it could be happening, the look evaporates.

When we get back to the house, Chris Thompson offers me some food, but I reach into my boho bag and pull out a meal bar and some stuff to make a shake.

"Can I try one?" he asks.

"Are you sure?"

"How bad could it be?"

"Pretty bad. But it's filling and good for you."

"I want to try one."

"You're not going to like it," I say.

"You don't know that."

"Are you trying to impress me?" I try the coy thing again, and it sounds ok.

"Maybe."

His smile is broad. I take a deep breath and bite my lip. We seem to be leaning towards each other when the phone rings. It's so loud it takes my breath away.

He picks up the receiver from the army green rotary phone on the kitchen wall.

"Hello? ... Hey, Johnny, what's up? ... For real? Yeah, we, uh, I can get back. I'll leave right now. I'll meet everyone there."

When he hangs up his demeanor has changed.

"Rain check on the smelly shake – we gotta go."

"What's up? What did Johnny want?"

I feel dread in the pit of my stomach. I feel busted even though there's really nothing to bust me for. I mean, no one actually knows where I am, but I haven't lied to anyone either. Not today.

"I'll tell you in the car."

"Seriously, what's going on?" I find myself unable to move.

"Nothing's wrong. It's good. It's more than good. Can I drive though? We need to get back to the city quickly."

I follow him around the house and grab a basket of laundry to throw in the wagon. We say goodbye to Buddy; I'm actually sorry to leave him. Chris Thompson pulls the wagon out onto the main road as if he's driving his motorcycle. I can tell he's frustrated by the lack of pick-up.

"Are you going to tell me what's up?" I'm nervously bouncing my knee and holding onto the door with white knuckles.

"We got a gig at Graffiti tonight. But we're opening, so I need to be there early."

"Aren't the Flights playing Graffiti tonight?" I ask.

"Yeah. We're opening for them. Their local openers cancelled. This is sort of big," he adds.

"I know."

Fifty-Seven Flights is a Pittsburgh band that has been touring nationally for the past few years. It's always a big deal when they make it back home. I haven't seen Chris Thompson excited about anything before and it adds another layer to his cool-guy persona that throws me off a bit.

"That's really great." I only half mean it. I can't get into Graffiti unless they're having an all-ages show, and tonight's show isn't all-ages. I know, because I checked when it was first announced.

"Listen, I'm quitting school," he says.

"Huh?"

"I'm quitting school. I stopped going to my summer classes. It's just not for me."

"What do you mean?"

"I'm too far behind to get credit for this summer and without that my soccer eligibility is shot."

His mood is still upbeat; I can't figure out why we're talking about this or why he isn't more bummed about it. Not finishing college seems like a big thing.

"Are you sure you want to quit?"

"Yeah. School was fine while I was working to get my eligibility back. It got all messed up after Indiana, but the band's more important to me now. Tess is rushing through courses so she can graduate early and we can start touring. Being in school would just be holding the band back."

And then it makes sense to me.

"Like the Flights?" I ask.

"Like the Flights," he says.

We're speeding down the highway, and the scenery is whizzing by. I'm embarrassed by the thought that pops into my head: I could be dating a rock star. Except we aren't dating and he probably, realistically, isn't going to be a rock star, but that's what I'm thinking. A rock star and a college dropout. I don't think I even know anyone who has dropped out of college. The idea of what Meredith would say about me dating a college dropout pops into my head, which is so embarrassing, because I shouldn't care, but I do.

"Does anyone else know?" I'm in completely over my head in this conversation, but I feel the need to keep him talking, like this is some hostage situation I'm trying to negotiate.

"No. I think I just decided."

"Do you want me to talk you out of it? Because, college is sort of a big deal, and I don't think you should just give up."

"I'm not giving up. I was just doing it for soccer, and I don't need it for what I really want to do."

With a jerk of the steering wheel, he cuts off a car, and it honks at us. I gasp.

"What do you want to do?" I ask cautiously. "I mean, besides the band."

"I don't really know, but whatever it is I don't think a college degree is really going to help. I don't see a desk-job in my future. I'll probably do sound engineering or roadie stuff."

"Well, my dad –" I stop myself mid-sentence.

"What? Your dad runs a radio station? He could get me a job? That's what you were going to say, right?"

"It's a habit," I say. "My dad's helped a lot of people out."

"Yeah? Not me." He switches lanes again.

Neither of us says anything for a while.

I turn the idea of Chris Thompson as a roadie over in my head. He's too pretty to be a roadie. They have scraggly beards and missing teeth. And the fact that I'm infatuated with someone who would drop out of college to maybe be a rock star but would probably end up being the manager of a copy shop is threatening the idea I have of myself and what I think is important in life. All I want to do is finish Frazer and get to college. I can't imagine ever giving up on that, even though it's currently all up in the air. But then he weaves through some cars and seems so sure of himself, so in control of the huge car with me in it, and he's so damn pretty it's hard not to swoon inside.

Back at his place, we unload the laundry onto the porch, and then he pulls around the corner to a space that is magically free. Walking back to the house he quizzes me on various stick shift related facts; I pass all his tests.

"Are you going to come out tonight?" he asks.

"I don't think I can get into Graffiti. I don't have an ID." I hate bringing attention to how young I am.

"I don't either. Not a good one."

It's hard to believe he's not 21 yet.

"Do you want to come with me now?" he asks. "I can probably get you in during sound-check."

"I can't do that."

"Why?"

"What would Johnny say?"

Chris Thompson doesn't say anything; he just grimaces in reluctant agreement.

"It's fine," I say. "I'll figure something out."

But even as I say it, I'm freaking out on the inside, and Chris Thompson knows it.

As we pick up the laundry baskets on the front porch, I blurt out, "It was Karl Bell."

"What was Karl Bell?"

"Last night. It's why I freaked out. It's hard to explain, but it's Karl Bell."

As I say it, I feel a powerful rush of both relief and nausea, like a valve in my head has been released, but the pressure is leaving my body too quickly, causing an uncomfortable vacuum.

"Oh, Alice," Chris Thompson says, and I know he's concerned because he doesn't call me Princess. "That's not good."

"No, it isn't." I shake my head and end up twitching.

"Are you ok?"

"I don't really even know how to answer that."

He puts his laundry basket back down, and I do the same. He wraps me into him, and I let myself be held.

"Well, first of all, are you physically ok?"

I nod.

"Do you think you're in danger?"

I shake my head.

"Ok, let's go upstairs. We need to sit down."

"We don't need to do anything. I just wanted you to know because

I was acting so weird. Not so you would do anything. Just so ... I don't know ... so someone else knew. But you can't tell anyone."

"Let's just go upstairs."

"Promise me you're not going to make me do anything or tell anyone."

"Listen," he says sternly. "I don't what's going to happen, but I don't make promises I can't keep."

"What do you mean?! You can't make me do anything. I'm just gonna leave. Pretend I didn't say anything."

I make a move for the steps but it's a flimsy one, and Chris Thompson stops me.

"Princess, come upstairs. You can't leave like this. I'm not going to make you do anything. Just come up and sit down."

I appreciate he's taking me seriously and not trying to minimize the situation. I've already tried that, and it didn't work. But I don't want him to tell me what to do.

Upstairs we throw the laundry in his room and sit on a gross couch in the living room.

"There's more," I say.

"More?"

"Yeah, and it's worse."

"Really?"

Now that I've told him the Karl Bell thing, there doesn't seem to be any reason to hold anything back.

"I got cut from the Summer Team."

He lets out a snort of laughter.

"What?"

"That's not worse."

"Sure it is. It's my future. Karl Bell is a jackass who doesn't even live in town. I can probably arrange to never see him again. But in case you forgot, I'm probably not going back to Frazer in the fall, and without a college scholarship, I won't be able to go to college. I mean, I know you think it's a big waste of time, but I actually want to go to college."

"Hold up. I don't think it's a waste of time for everyone. I just think it's a waste of time for me. But, I also know there're loans and other kinds of scholarships, and I just don't think your biggest concern right now is lacrosse."

"Ugh, I knew I shouldn't have told you."

"Why did you?"

I don't really know, but I'm afraid the real reason is I wanted his sympathy, and I'm pissed at myself for the miscalculation.

"I don't know. I just had to tell someone."

"What about your bitchy friend? Did you tell her?"

"She knows about lacrosse. She was there. She doesn't know what it means though."

"What about Karl Bell, did you tell her about him?"

"No."

"Why not?"

"She wouldn't understand. She thinks he's hot. She'd say go for it. This is such a mess, I'm sorry."

"No, don't apologize to me. Listen, can you do me a favor?"

"I guess."

"I know it sucks, but I still need to go. I need a shower, and I need to get changed, and I need to get to sound check. And I know that's all bullshit because what you're dealing with is more important, but it's just bad timing."

It does suck. I had no intention of telling anyone about what happened with Karl Bell, but once I said it, part of me wanted Chris Thompson to cancel his plans and sit with me while I figured it out.

"Will you just stay here?" he asks. "I'll go do the sound check and the set. I'll leave before the Flights play. Just stay here so we can talk when I get back?"

I don't hate that he's asking me to stay.

"I guess." I can't think of anywhere else to go. "I am pretty tired."

"Take a nap. I'll be gone, like, three hours. Tops. Sleep. And we'll talk when I get back. Ok?"

"Yeah, ok." I get up to get the sheets out of the closet, but he stops me.

"Just take the bed. Don't worry about the couch."

And although everything is about as messed up as it can be, I can't help but be excited to climb into Chris Thompson's bed. I'm asleep before he even gets out of the shower.

CHAPTER 19

I wake up slowly to the sound of Chris Thompson quietly playing The Smiths' "Please, Please, Please, Let Me Get What I Want," on his acoustic guitar. He's sitting in his desk chair with his feet on the bed near mine.

"Hey," he says when I open my eyes.

"Hey," I say. "How was the show?"

He looks at me tenderly, like I'm his. Or maybe that's just what I want his look to say.

"It was good. Those guys are cool. They're touring with this Australian folk-rock band. They were cool, too. And Tess sounded amazing."

"That's great." I played the Wasted Pretty tape for Meredith the other day, and even she was blown away by Tess' voice.

"And your brother isn't as much of an asshole as I remember."

"Ugh. He was there?"

"Yeah, with Johnny."

"Of course." Because if he's not infiltrating Meredith's boyfriend's backyard, he's hanging out with Johnny and Chris Thompson.

"How are you?"

"Hungry."

"I bet."

"I missed dinner." I'm sure there are meal bars in my bag or in the car, but I'm not eager to eat one.

Chris Thompson helps me out of the bed and holds my hand as we walk across the living room into the kitchen. He pretends to bump into me and tries to trip me. I give him a swift hip-check in return.

"You're wearing my clothes," he says.

I had fallen asleep quickly but woke up with a start in the empty apartment not long after.

"Yeah, I took a shower and didn't have anything to change into." He hands me a bowl for cereal. "I'm sorry?"

"No, that's cool." He sounds amused when he says it.

I salivate over the Marshmallow Mateys as I fix myself a bowl.

"Can we talk some more about Karl Bell?" he asks.

"We can. But we don't need to. I mean, I actually feel better. I'm glad I told you. It feels good to know someone else knows. But I don't need you to do anything. I mean … it's not like it's going to happen again. I can avoid him. It's not like he's some lech down at the station I have to see every day. I'm sorry I was such a freak. And I really appreciate you being cool about the whole thing."

He's still as he looks at me.

"You're really ok? 'Cause I'm not really ok. I'm sort of pissed. It was all I could think about during the show. I just don't like the idea of someone getting away with … whatever he got away with. I'm sorry … but … did he touch you?"

"Yeah," I say, more with a nod than my voice. "But it didn't go far. I'd really rather not talk about it anymore. I think I'm ok."

"Ok, how about this? I agree to let this drop for now. If you agree I can ask you about it later, because I don't actually think you're as ok as you think you are."

"Deal."

"And you'll let me know if you start not being ok?"

I nod. I really am moved by his concern, but I want the conversation to be over. I'm both grateful and disturbed by the way he's looking at me, like I'm a wounded cat.

"One more question," Chris Thompson says.

"Ok."

"I'm not getting those pajama bottoms back, am I?"

"No." I smile. "Definitely not."

"Ugh. I love those pants."

"Sucks to be you." My smile broadens.

His eyes sparkle when he smiles back.

While I get up to fix myself another bowl of cereal – actually it should just be called candy with milk, and I can't believe I'm eating it – Chris Thompson moves into the living room and starts playing guitar again. I bring my cereal in and sit across from him. Our feet touch, and he plays "Stretch Out and Wait."

When Tess and Johnny walk in, I'm formally introduced to Tess. She's even more captivating up close.

"He said you sounded awesome!" I gush.

"Thanks, luv." Her British accent is thick and vowel heavy. "Did Chris tell you Fifty-Seven Flights loved him and he fixed some amp or level or monitor problem they were having, and now they want to take him on tour with them? Can you imagine? Chris Thompson, a roadie?!"

He hadn't said anything about that. I look at him with narrowed eyes, and he gives me a sheepish look I interpret as guilt mixed with modesty.

"What are you doing here?" Johnny asks, with a mildly disapproving look. "I've been calling you all day. Your machine didn't pick up."

Shit. I must have forgotten to plug the phone back in this morning.

"I was taking care of some stuff." I want to know if Chris Thompson flinches at this explanation, but I don't look at him. "Why, what's up?"

"I have excellent news for you." Johnny is beaming.

"Do tell." I flop back onto the couch. I'm used to the puff of dust it spits out now.

Johnny puts a six-pack of beer on the steamer trunk, and he and Tess each open one. No one offers one to Chris Thompson or to me. I assume it's because neither of us is 21 yet.

"Well, Make-A-Wish Karl was at the station today – " Johnny always calls him that, even though it wasn't really a Make-A-Wish thing when I met him – "He bought everyone lunch from Hotlicks – you totally missed out."

"I love those ribs!" Tess interrupts.

"So good," I add. Ribs are miraculously on Lois' food plan, but I don't eat them anymore because I don't like people watching me drip sauce down my chin.

"Anyway," Johnny continues. "You know how your dad handed 5K Fest over to me this year, and how we couldn't decide about doing a celebrity-normal person relay race or a male-female relay race?"

"Really dumb ideas," I interrupt, but he keeps talking.

"Well, your dad decided today it's going to be a celebrity/non-celebrity/male/female relay race. And Make-A-Wish Karl agreed to come in for it, you know, provided the Padres aren't in the World Series, which let's be honest, they won't be, so he's our first committed celebrity, *and* he said Samantha's pregnant, so your dad offered you as his non-famous, female partner. Cool, right?"

I know I'm supposed to act happy, but I falter just a bit before I'm able to force words out of my mouth. "Samantha's pregnant?"

"Yeah. I would've thought you would've known, but your dad was surprised, too. But whatever. There's more."

I focus on my breath. I'm sure I'm visibly sweating. I feel simultaneously paralyzed and like every atom in my body is individually trying to jump off the couch and run in different directions.

I steal a glance at Chris Thompson. He's sitting up, very straight.

"More?" I try to sound like I'm not going to cry or puke or flee.

"Yeah, I overheard Burton and Make-A-Wish talking. He's gonna invest in your mom's weird butterfly food company. And he's going to pay your tuition, last year's and next year's. I didn't hear all the details, but Karl seemed really happy to help out. Talk about Make-A-Wish! He's bankrolling your whole family!"

I almost feel sorry for Johnny. He's so genuinely excited to be sharing this news, and he deserves a far more grateful reaction than I'm capable of providing. Instead, I shoot off the couch and into the bathroom. I know I can't latch the door behind me, so I don't even bother closing it. I throw up two bowls of cereal, splash cold water on my face and sit on the side of the tub. I'm not sure I can go back out to the living room, but the longer I stay in the bathroom, the more I'll have to explain.

As best I can, I put myself together.

In the living room, I avoid eye contact with Chris Thompson because I know it will undo me again.

"Sorry," I say with as much of a smile as I can muster.

"It's pretty cool, right?" Johnny says, confusing my terror for excitement.

"Mmhm," I mumble.

"Are you sure you're alright?" Tess has never met me before, but reads the situation far more accurately than Johnny.

"Yeah. There's just been a lot going on lately. And this was … unexpected."

Chris Thompson is now standing. I can't avoid looking at him anymore. We make eye contact. Tears are collecting in the corners of my eyes.

"Can I talk to you?" he asks, as if he shouldn't even have to say the words out loud.

Johnny and Tess give each other confused looks.

I'm following Chris Thompson into his bedroom when the door to the apartment opens, and Nate bursts through.

"The fuck are you doing here?" he says to me. "No one's been able to find you all day."

"Who's been looking for me?"

"Johnny, for one."

"Well, he found me." I pretend I have not just been caught somewhere I definitely shouldn't be. "What are you doing here?"

"Did I forget to mention Nate was down at Eddie's getting food?" Johnny asks. "I told him he could just come up."

"Alice, I need to talk to you." Chris Thompson's tone is stern.

"No," my brother says, "I need to talk to her."

"Nate, give me one minute with her." Chris Thompson seems to know the request is risky.

"The fuck I will." Nate spits his words. "She's sixteen years old. Has everyone in this apartment lost sight of that?"

"Stop," I say to both of them, but mostly to Nate.

"No," Nate says.

"Dude," Chris Thompson says. "Ease up. She's going through some shit."

"Don't call me 'dude,' *guy*." My brother always calls people guy when he's super-pissed.

I shoot Johnny a look. Tears are freely rolling down my face. It's obvious Johnny doesn't want to get involved, but Tess sees my panic and pushes him to get up.

"Stay out of this, Johnny," Chris Thompson says.

"No problem!" He sinks back into the couch, his hands up in surrender.

"Why don't *you* stay out of it?" Nate says to Chris Thompson. "I don't know what's going on here, but how 'bout you just back off?"

"Nothing's going on here!" I yell.

"Something's going on here." There is pure venom in my brother's voice.

"It's not what you think," Chris Thompson says.

"Oh, what do I think, CJ?"

"Stop!" I yell, stepping between them. For once, I am glad for my height. I place one of my hands on each of their chests and nudge them apart. I look at Chris Thompson first.

"Don't say another word. To anyone. About me. I know you think you're helping, but you're not."

Then I turn to my brother. "Let's go." He follows me into Chris Thompson's room and shuts the door.

We stand silently in the dark for a moment. I hear Johnny through the door trying to explain things.

"They can be like this sometimes. There's a lot of yelling in their family," he says. "You know Burton…"

"You're embarrassing me," I say to Nate, wiping the tears from my face with the heel of my hand.

"You're embarrassing yourself, Alice!"

"Keep your voice down," I say through clenched teeth. "How am I embarrassing myself? You don't even know what you're talking about."

"Alice, you're wearing his clothes. Your clothes are in a pile on his floor." He picks up my clothes and throws them at me. "I'm not an idiot."

"Nothing's going on."

"I don't believe you."

"I don't care," I say.

"Do you think Dad would?"

"Are you threatening me?! Because I know you have a fake ID."

"What do you really think he's going to care about more? Me with a fake ID or you fucking CJ?"

"I am not fucking him. And don't call him CJ." I try to keep my voice down even though I'm furious. "I showered and took a nap when he wasn't even here."

"I don't believe you. He left the show early. Johnny was bitching about him not packing his stuff up."

"I don't have to prove anything to you. We're ... friends, or something."

"Really? Friends?" my brother prods. "How well do you know him?"

"I don't know. Like, not real friends. He's Johnny's friend."

It feels horrible to negate the connection I know we shared today, even if it's in both of our best interests.

Judging by the silence on the other side of the door, I know Tess and Johnny and Chris Thompson are listening to everything we're saying. It's beyond humiliating.

"So, he's told you about what happened at Indiana?"

"No." I remember my dad telling Nate that CJ went to Indiana for freshman year and came home before exams, but that was before I knew him as Chris Thompson.

"You should ask him about that," Nate says coolly, like he's won.

"Are you still pissed he broke your leg? Because you healed and got a college scholarship, so no harm, no foul?"

"That wasn't his fault. It was a clean play. Dad was just looking for a reason to get rid of my competition."

"What?! You let that happen? Getting cut from that Summer Soccer League team practically ruined his life."

"I doubt that. Seriously Alice, how well do you know him? It's not dad's fault he bombed at Indiana. If he's telling you that, he's lying."

"No, I just know Dad was hard on him."

"And what, he's using you to get back at him?"

"By not sleeping with me?"

"Gross. And I still don't believe you."

"Whatever. Can we just agree nothing's going on here and be done with this?"

"No. Because that's total bullshit. Why don't you tell me what's really happening?"

Something in his voice makes me want to tell him about Karl Bell. Partially because it will take the heat off Chris Thompson, but also because I'm not sure I'll be able to keep it in much longer. But I know what telling Nate will mean. I can keep Chris Thompson quiet while I figure out exactly how I want to handle it, but I know my brother cannot be controlled. My mom could lose her business. I could lose my senior year. And why? Because some creep did something gross to me? I'm not ready to let someone else make this decision for me.

"There's seriously nothing going on. I went out to Chris Thompson's parents' today to learn how to drive stick. That's the big secret. There's nothing for you to worry about."

"Then why did he say you were 'going through some stuff?'"

"I'd rather not talk about it."

"I don't really give a shit what you'd rather not talk about, Alice. You're not staying here unless things get a whole lot more clear."

"Fine, then let's go."

I shove my clothes into my bag and throw open the door to the living room.

"I gotta go. Apparently, to prove to my brother, I'm not fucking anyone, I need to sleep at home tonight."

"Manners!" Johnny calls after us.

CHAPTER 20

I plug my phone back into the wall before I go to bed. It rings an hour later.

I know it could be Chris Thompson, but it could also be Karl Bell. I turn the ringer down and wait for the machine to pick up. Whoever it is hangs up. A minute later it starts ringing again and, with hopes of it being Chris Thompson, I pick up.

"Hello?" I say tentatively.

"Hey," Chris Thompson says. "It's me."

At the sound of his voice, my body relaxes for the first time all night. "Hey."

"Can you talk?"

I mumble an affirmative.

"That was intense."

"Nate usually is. He gets that from my dad."

"I hate that you're not here right now."

It might be the sweetest thing I've ever heard in my life. It almost makes everything else melt away, even though it solves nothing.

"Me too."

"Do you want to talk about what happened with Nate?" he asks.

"No."

"Do you want to talk about what's going on with Karl?"

"No."

"Do you want to talk about anything?"

For a moment I entertain the notion that we could talk about "us." He could admit to liking me, because I know he does, and we could figure out how to make something work for real. But if that were going to happen, that would have happened in the country today, not after Nate went ape-shit.

"You know, I think maybe I don't want to talk right now. It's not you, it's just everything."

"Can I play you a song?"

"Really?"

"Yeah."

"Ok."

"I have to put the phone down to play, but I'll pick it up again, and if you're asleep, it's ok."

"Ok, but …"

"What?"

"Why are you being so nice to me?" Nate's words are pulsing inside my ears. Is Chris Thompson fucking with me just to piss off my dad?

"Why wouldn't I be nice?" he asks. But it's not really an answer.

Then he starts to play Billy Bragg's "Greetings to the New Brunette." At first, it makes me cry, but then I'm able to calm down and listen to the tune. When he's done, he gently asks if I am still awake.

"I am."

"Listen, I know you don't want to talk. But can you listen? I have some stuff I want to tell you."

"Ok."

"You know I only came to Pitt in the fall, for sophomore year, right? I went to Indiana last year. It was a big deal, full-scholarship, all that. But it was harder than I thought it was going to be, and I didn't fit in.

"In high school, there were two groups on the soccer team. Half of the guys drank a lot, and half of us didn't drink at all, but we all hung out, and it wasn't a big deal. I was one of the ones who didn't drink. I never had a drink before I went to college. So I get to Bloomington for pre-season and everyone's drinking a lot and all the time. They clearly had more practice at it than I did. So I started drinking, and it got out of hand pretty quickly. And the team itself was more competitive than high school, and the freshmen stuck together, but everyone else was sort of shitty.

"So my parents knew things weren't going well; I guess my brother probably told them. So my dad called this guy he knew from college who lived near campus, and I started having Sunday night dinners with his family. They were really good to me. They had a twelve-year-old, Timmy, who was really goofy and he liked to play soccer, so we always kicked around in the yard before dinner. And they had a daughter, Stephanie, who was also a freshman at Indiana but she still lived at home. She was always very quiet at dinner, mostly she helped her mom in the kitchen while her dad was giving me kind, but stern, lectures about focusing on school and soccer and not screwing up. It was weird because, on one hand, it felt really comfortable and familiar because it was like my dad talking to me – we'd had all of those conversations before – but on the other hand, it was weird having them with someone I barely knew."

"Ok ..."

"So I was trying to get my shit together, but it wasn't easy, because drinking was a lot of fun and, as you know, school isn't my thing. And they had the athletes take a light load their first semester, but it didn't matter, because I just wasn't good at it, but I wasn't good at drinking either, because I kept getting into fights with people in my dorm and guys on my team, and I'd hook up with girls I just really shouldn't have hooked up with. And then one night, Steph came to my dorm with a couple of her friends and wanted me to go to a party with them, and I told her I wouldn't, because I didn't think she should be drinking, just like I shouldn't have been drinking, and she said she didn't care, because she was going to go anyway. It turned out she was actually completely wild, and she and her friends knew where to party, so I tagged along mostly to try to keep her safe, at least that's how it started.

"Are you still there?"

I mumble a yes. I'm not sure where this is going, but I don't like hearing about some other wild party-girl.

"So then, I started to fall for her. And she liked me. And we started drinking together. A lot. And it was weird because I'd go to her parents for dinner and there'd be like, no recognition, no nod, no sneaking off to her room, nothing; it was like she barely even knew me at her house. And then she'd show up on campus, and we'd party really hard. I wasn't going to class, and I knew I was screwing up my eligibility, but I just didn't care because it was pretty clear to me whether or not I drank, I wasn't going to pass any of my classes, so I just kept drinking and partying and hanging out with Steph. And I felt like such a screw-up.

"You have to know what it was like for me playing soccer in high school. I'm sure it was the same for Nate. I mean getting kicked off the summer team was rough, but I still had high school. And I was really good, and we were like the 'cool kids' at school. It seems so dumb now, but I went from being really popular to being a screw-up, and I just didn't handle the whole thing well ... and then, well, I'm sure you know where this is going ..."

"Not exactly."

"Well, I didn't go home for Thanksgiving, I spent it with Stephanie's family. It was insane to be in her house, with her family, but not with her. It was amazing to me how she totally didn't even look at me twice at her house. It was always me and Timmy, or me and her dad. We watched sports or talked about sports, and she and her mom would be in the kitchen or serving food or doing dishes, but that day seemed different. At first, I thought it was the holiday, but then I realized it was something more. She was actively avoiding even being in the same room as me, even with other people around. I tried to get her alone but she wouldn't let that happen, so I went back to the dorm after dinner and was just really messed up, so, of course, I started drinking by myself. Then late, really late, someone's knocking on my door and it's Steph, and she tells me she's pregnant. And she's crying, and I'm crying, and I tell her we can make it work and even though I'm scared to death I tell her I love her, even though I'm not sure I did.

"I tell her I can drop out of school – I think I was actually happy to have a reason to drop out – and I'll go with her to tell her parents and maybe we can just make this all right by being together. And I'm holding her, and she's just crying and crying, and I'm starting to sober up, and I realize again, something's off. Like, I know how bad this is, I know how scary it is, and still, she seems to be even worse than I would expect. I try to get her to talk to me, and when she finally does, she tells me she's not sure it's mine, and she's been seeing this other guy the whole time she's been seeing me.

"So that felt like shit.

"And then she tells me she's definitely getting an abortion, which felt like shit even more because I know that's not how she was raised and it wasn't how I was raised. But then she asks me to go with her because she doesn't think the other guy can handle it, and even though she has no way of knowing whose kid it is she would feel better if I came with her to the clinic.

"You still there?"

Between dropping out of school and maybe getting someone pregnant, it occurs to me that Chris Thompson's issues are a lot more serious than Dylan's dumb love of The Doors and his stupid red bulb in the lamp by his bed. But I manage to say yes, even though my head is spinning.

"So I tell her I'll take her, because what else can I say? And she spends the night. The dorm is mostly empty, but quiet, and I can't sleep, so I'm up all night holding her and she sleeps peacefully. I think about maybe trying to convince her in the morning not to have an abortion, even if it isn't mine, because I just really want her to be ok.

"I must have fallen asleep at some point because then there's banging on the door, and I'm all out of it and then the door flies open – because we never locked our doors in the dorm – and it's her dad. He grabs her out of bed and doesn't say a word to me, and they're gone. I'm standing there in my shorts, and I'm looking around like maybe none of it actually happened. Like maybe I was drunker than I thought and imagined it all.

"I know this all sounds really crazy."

He wants me to say something, but I'm just shocked. The feeling of being in over my head is no longer something I feel every once in a while, but it's something I feel all the time. Chris Thompson's life and my life, I don't want them to be so different, but they are. I can't help him, and he can't help me.

I manage to say, "I guess ..."

"So I go back to sleep, because I don't know what else to do. A little while later, someone pounding on the door wakes me up again, and again the door flies open, and this time it's Stephanie's mom. She walks in right as I'm getting out of bed, but she doesn't say a word. She just throws a plane ticket at me and slaps me across the face and leaves. She doesn't even close the door behind her. So I figure it's real. The ticket is for the next morning, and it seems like it would be best to just leave, so I do. I spent that day packing and drinking and deciding when I got home everything was going to be different. It's why I got help and don't drink now."

And then he doesn't say anything. And I know I am supposed to say something, but my whole body is buzzing from being up too late and being completely overwhelmed by this information, and my own situation, and not knowing where to begin or what I'm supposed to be feeling, let alone saying.

Finally, I ask, "Does Nate know about this?"

"Alice, are you kidding me?" He's more than annoyed. "I tell you all that, and that's your first question."

"I'm sorry! I have no idea what I'm supposed to say."

"Yeah, well, that's why I don't tell a lot of people."

"I don't even know why you're telling me."

"I'm telling you because ..." He trails off.

Please say you're telling me because you want to be with me and you know I'll accept you as long as you're honest with me.

"I'm not exactly sure," he says, "Except, I guess, I care that you don't hear the other versions of the story that are out there."

I consider his explanation in silence for a moment. "You only told me because you thought Nate already did."

"Did he?"

"No."

"Oh."

"I don't want to talk anymore right now," I say. "I want to sleep."

"Are you going to be ok?"

"I don't know how to answer that question. I'm not ok, but … I mean, I'm not gonna die."

"That's a pretty low standard for 'ok.'"

"I'm sorry. I don't know what else to say."

I get the sense I'm supposed to make him feel better, but I'm not interested.

"Ok, so listen." His voice is almost sweet, like he understands I'm not going to ease his fears about my well being or anything else. "Get some sleep. But call me tomorrow, ok? Johnny thinks he's our manager now and apparently booked me and Tess at some acoustic day show tomorrow, but I should be home before dinner. Or leave me a message, so I know you're ok."

"Ok."

"Don't make me call you," he teases. "The last thing I need is to get caught on the phone with Nate."

"Alright."

I lie in bed staring out at the black sky and the dull glow of the street light in the alley behind my house. I want to sleep but the voices in my head, which seem to be yelling at each other, won't quiet down. I don't fall asleep until the sky starts to turn from black to grey to lavender.

CHAPTER 21

"Mom wants you up." Nate is standing in my doorway. I wish the damn doors in this house locked.

"What do you mean?" My vision is blurry. I couldn't have slept more than three hours.

"She wants you downstairs. She made a frittata. It's gonna get cold."

"What the hell are you talking about?" I don't really have time to remember anything that happened last night, but when I look down and see I'm still in Chris Thompson's shirt, it all comes back pretty quickly.

"A frittata, Alice. You know, an omelet, with potatoes on the bottom, starts on the stove, finishes in the oven. My favorite breakfast food?"

"You are such a freak," I say. "Can you get out of here?"

"You need to get up. Mom needs help setting up for her thing."

"What thing? What mom? She hasn't made a hot breakfast since you left for college. Frankly, she hasn't been home since you left for college."

"Well, she's home now, and she wants you downstairs." He leaves without closing the door.

I get out of bed slowly. I can smell the food downstairs, the baked eggs, the coffee, something sweet. The house smells the way it used to when Nate still lived here, and I ate real food. Before my mom finally hit on the perfect recipe for weight loss. Suddenly, I'm hungry, and the hunger propels me downstairs. I don't even care I'm wearing Chris Thompson's pajamas. Still, in a haze of sleep, I take the bottom two steps in one motion and see Karl Bell sitting at the kitchen table. For a split second, I think I'm hallucinating. I hope I'm hallucinating. And then he smiles at me; it's a smile I couldn't dream up in my own head.

"Good morning, Princess!" *Princess?!*

I freeze long enough to see my mom, looking like Suzie Homemaker, turn around from the stove and smile at me, beaming with pride. I'm supposed to be happy she has brought Karl to the house. I make it to the half-bath just in time to hit the toilet with bile. Maybe the rumors the birth-control-bitches started are right about me. Everything makes me puke.

Propped against the door, I'm shivering. My fingers feel like they're dissolving. I shake them to try to get more blood into them. I feel unmoored, like I might float away, but the reality is, I'm trapped in my own house. When I let myself out of the bathroom, I concentrate on putting one foot in front of the other. The smells of coffee and eggs, which moments ago filled the house with warmth I had desperately missed, are now mixed with the smell of Karl Bell's cologne.

"Late night, huh?" He and Nate are eating while my mom opens and closes cabinet doors, looking busy. She's pulling out all sorts of products with the butterfly stickers on them to show Karl Bell, her new investor.

"I'm not hung-over," I say, too defensively. "I just don't feel right."

"I think you missed curfew last night," my mom says, without looking at me.

"She was with me," Nate assures her, as if being with my brother means nothing could possibly go wrong. I'm not sure why he's covering for me. He probably likes having something to hold over me and wants to wait until Burton's around to use it.

I feel Karl's eyes on me. I cross my arms to cover my chest.

"Where's Dad?" If he were here, he'd certainly ground me for missing curfew, but at least I wouldn't feel so exposed.

"Carpet store opening, I think," my mom says. "He's going to meet us at the fair."

"What fair?"

"Family trip to the church carnival!" Nate says with thick sarcasm.

"We're Jewish," I say, but I finally understand what's happening.

St. Raphael's Church Fair is a family tradition. Both my parents grew up in this neighborhood, so they've been going to the fair since they were kids. What started out as a way for the church families to sell Italian pastries to their neighbors now involves carnival rides, cotton candy, and caricature drawings. We go each year as a family, though Nate has found a way to miss the past couple outings.

"I'm setting up a booth, and Karl and Dad are going to put in celebrity appearances!" My mom is overly cheerful.

"Gotta see what I've got myself into with The Butterfly Food." Karl's making sure we all know he's bankrolling her, but he's looking at me when he says it. He wants me to understand what's at stake if I talk.

"What time do you have practice?" my mom asks.

Shit.

I quickly calculate the risk of coming clean. I look back and forth between my mom at the counter and Nate and Karl at the table. I'm going to have to tell them sometime, and strangely Karl creates a buffer. She won't yell at me in front of him. Her Suzie Homemaker image is too important to her brand.

"Uh, I'm done with practice. I didn't make the tournament team."

My mom turns around from the counter. "You got cut?"

All eyes are on me.

"It's no big deal," I lie. "I didn't like the coaches anyway."

"Your dad will make some calls." My mom's cheerful tone cracks just a bit. "But don't tell him until after the fair. I need him focused on the product, not riled up about the team."

Shit.

If my dad calls the coach she's going to tell him I was hungover, distracted, and that I deserved to be cut. He'll defend me, but she'll be right.

I want to get out of the room so badly, but my feet feel like they're stuck to the floor and planted all the way through the foundation of the house. Nate stuffs his face. Karl smiles that smile again.

"Eat something and then go get ready," my mom says. "Try a muffin."

Try a muffin is code for: *Don't eat anything else; that other food is just for the men.*

The muffins must be sugar-free, full of carob, and sweetened only with fruit juices and honey. As quickly as I can, I step just close enough to the table to grab a muffin with an outstretched arm. Karl runs a finger down the scar on my right hand as I snatch a blueberry-orange rind-spiced monstrosity. No one seems to notice his touch.

* * * * *

In the church parking lot, I'm unloading boxes of meal bars stamped with the butterfly logo when I turn and find Johnny, Tess and Chris Thompson standing with Nate and Karl Bell. Everyone but Johnny looks awkwardly uncomfortable. One of Johnny's gifts is being at ease anywhere. I try to make eye contact with Chris Thompson but he avoids my gaze. This is worse than being a prisoner in my own bathroom.

I make the only move I can.

"Hi Tess! What are you doing here?"

She takes a drag on her cigarette. "Johnny thought it would be cute for us to do an acoustic set … here … at a fair … in a church parking lot … I'm pretty sure it's just a ruse to get us in front of your dad." She flares her nostrils, rolls her eyes, and laughs with a guttural cough.

Of course. Now that Johnny's managing the band he's going to try to get them on the radio.

"Do you always smoke this early in the morning?" I ask.

She smiles with a provocatively raised eyebrow. "A morning cigarette is how I maintain my 'raspy perfection.'"

She's quoting from a City Paper review of the band.

"So … last night …" She talks quietly and moves me away from my mom's tent. "You ok? Nate came down on you pretty hard. And Chris was completely freaked when you left. It was our first gig at Graffiti, and with the Flights, and no one wanted to party. We all just sat there staring at each other."

"Sorry. I guess I'm ok. There's just a lot going on."

"It's cool about Karl taking care of the tuition, right? I mean, I'm sorry, maybe you didn't want me to know about that – "

"No, it's ok. I don't mind you knowing. I assume Johnny tells you everything."

"He does, like, everything. Like, he talks *sooooo* much. But it's growing on me. He's growing on me."

She almost giggles which doesn't fit how I think of her. Her attitude and style and brusque British-ness make her seem so old, but she's probably only a year or two ahead of me. And it hits me how moving to a new country and being in college makes a world of difference I'd never even considered before. Maybe I should give up lacrosse and go to college in Canada.

"Seriously, your brother seemed really pissed. He didn't believe you that nothing's going on, did he?"

"I don't know what he believes." I sneak a glance at the guys. "I didn't sleep much last night. Like I said, lots going on."

"But *nothing's* going on, right?"

"With me and Chris Thompson? God no!"

"Yeah, I just wanted to make sure. I mean, I saw the way you two were looking at each other last night. You seem really connected. But you know nothing's going to happen, right?"

I know she's right, but it stings to hear her say it, matter-of-factly, as if it's completely obvious to everyone. Like I'm crazy to hold out hope.

"I know, I know, I'm still in high school. I'm such a baby, blah blah blah."

"Oh, luv, it's not about that. Puh-lease." She moves me further away from my mom's tent. "It's not that he's not interested. He's talked to me about you, and you don't look at someone like that unless you want to shag them."

I feel a strange mix of embarrassment and glee.

"Then what is it?"

I'm not sure I want to know the answer.

"Well ... I don't know if it's my place to say ... you know about Indiana, right?"

"I do, as of last night ... or very early this morning, yeah."

"Here's the deal, Alice. He clearly likes you. But he's not going to allow himself to be with you because he's not going to allow himself to be happy. Like, ever. He still blames himself for everything at Indiana. And I don't think he wants to hurt you, but I'm a little worried this isn't going to end well."

"You think?" My sarcasm is thick.

"I'm sorry, luv."

"I like him so much. It doesn't even make sense."

"You'll get through this. Just don't expect too much from him. He's always going to keep you at arm's length."

"Then what's the point?"

"Um ... I'd like to have another girl around. Hanging out with the band is such a sausage fest."

I'm actually flattered, but I respond with sarcasm anyway. "Oh well, that makes perfect sense. Feeling like I'm going to throw up all the time is totally worth it if it makes you happy."

"Don't be a shitehawk," she says with a laugh. I assume that's a British-ism that means smart-ass, or something like it. "Maybe he'll surprise all of us. Just promise me you won't shag him."

I blanch at her crassness. "Can we stop talking about this now?"

"So ..." she says with a devilish smile, "Tell me about Hot Karl Bell!"

I roll my eyes. She may think he's cute, but I'm pretty sure if I told her what was going on, she'd kick his ass herself.

"What?" She throws up her hands. "We need to break through. Having a celebrity at a show could help. I mean, not this show – at a damn church fair, I'm going to kill Johnny for waking me up for this – but at a different show. Getting a good review here and there in the City Paper isn't going to cut it. We need airplay. We need to break through soon, or I'm going to lose Chris Thompson. The only reason he's still even playing with us is that he hasn't graduated yet. If we're not ready to tour nationally before he gets his degree, or gives up on his degree, he's going to flee Pittsburgh, and I'm going to be without a pretty-boy frontman."

"You don't need a pretty-boy frontman," I say. "You're the pretty frontman."

She laughs, but I feel horrible. Chris Thompson has already given up on his degree, and I'm probably the only person who knows. It simultaneously makes me feel special and gross. It's like everybody's lying to everybody about everything, including me.

"That's nice of you to say, but we're sort of nothing without Chris Thompson. You haven't heard us yet, have you?"

"He gave me a tape. You're great."

"No one's gonna sign a band fronted by a half-Black English girl. I need him up there next to me. He's appealing and approachable. I'm off-putting."

"You're not off-putting. You're fierce. I've read the reviews."

"You don't understand," Tess says. "It's America. Pearl Jam. Nirvana. Soundgarden."

"Hole just toured with Smashing Pumpkins! L7? PJ Harvey Trio?"

"No, we're nothing without Chris Thompson."

I know the feeling. The thought of Pittsburgh without Chris Thompson, my senior year without Chris Thompson, me without Chris Thompson, is depressing. I barely know him, and I need him as much as the band does, but he won't even look at me.

I wonder if I'm supposed to tell her he dropped out. Is that why he told me? Does he want me to expose him? Or am I supposed to keep his secret like he's keeping mine? While I'm wallowing in this sad confusion, my dad appears.

"Hi Dad. How was the carpet store?"

"It was a bagel place. Better food than a carpet store," he says with a self-satisfied smile. "Who's your friend?"

I introduce my dad to Tess. She does her best to seem put out. Like she doesn't need my dad or wants him to think she doesn't need him.

"How do you two know each other?"

"Through Johnny." I'm happy to have something non-incriminating to say, but Tess is not happy with my answer.

"I play in a band, Wasted Pretty, you've heard of us, right?" Her tone is pure aggression. "You work at a radio station, don't you?"

Thankfully, my dad is amused and not offended.

"Yes," he says with a nod. "I work at a radio station. I'm Johnny's boss. I think he's played your tape for me."

"You should play it. It would mean a lot if you liked it."

"But I don't." My dad's tone lacks any sort of apology.

I look around for an escape route, see the guys talking to Karl Bell, and stay frozen.

"Well," she scoffs, "That's ok. You're not exactly our target market."

"And you're not mine."

My dad is used to people kissing his ass, not challenging his authority. I'm not even sure why Tess is doing it. It's kind of a disaster.

"Who's that kid?" My dad motions to where the guys are standing.

"That's Johnny's friend, Chris," I say cautiously.

"He looks familiar. You were talking to him in the box, weren't you?"

"Probably."

Oh no, here it comes. Today actually can get worse.

"What did you say his name was? Did he play soccer with Nate?"

"Chris Thompson?"

"Are you kidding me? That's the kid I kicked off the soccer team when he broke Nate's leg. Chris Thompson? CJ Thompson?"

Tess looks at me as if I need to respond, but I can't.

"He's in my band," she says.

"Let's take a walk," I say to Tess.

We make one loop around the church parking lot and end up sitting on the stage. She gets out her guitar, and I lie on the hot black surface while she tunes. My eyes are closed, but I can hear the sounds of the fair, so familiar and comforting, as she plays a few songs.

My dad finds us and picks up with Tess right where he left off. "You know there are no health benefits to smoking and a whole host of risks."

"I did know that," Tess says, barely making eye contact with him. "I guess I just like to live dangerously."

Burton's trying to get a rise out of her, but they appear to be well matched, so he turns his attention to me. "Your mom wants you over by the tent."

"I'm the real-life after-photo," I tell Tess with a forced smile.

"You make a great butterfly, luv."

Burton follows me through the crowds of people that have begun to fill the parking lot. Kids are running around and chasing each other, just like my brother and I used to. As we approach my mom's booth, I catch Chris Thompson's eye, and my chest feels warm and full. For a moment we are the only two people on the planet, but my insides turn to ice when I realize he isn't looking at me, but through me. By the time we get to the tent, he's walked away.

I remember what he said about Stephanie and how she never let on there was anything going on between them when they were at her house. I know how that feels now, how confusing and jarring it is. When he walks right by me without even a nod, I feel abandoned in a sea of people. I want to shout, "You sang me to sleep!"

At my mom's product table, people are fawning over Karl and asking him detailed questions about ingredients. He completely makes up his answers – mixing up the ratio of protein to natural carbs – and no one seems to mind. My mom grabs at me to show a customer how fit I am.

"We need to get you new clothes!" she exclaims, as if I haven't been asking her to take me shopping for a month.

She pulls at my t-shirt hem and ties it into a cheesy knot at my waist. I swat her away, but mostly I play my part as spokesmodel telling heavyset women with jiggling arms how full I always feel and how the weight just melted away. Which is true – it's not like I was even really trying. I didn't think I needed to lose weight – I was just following my mom's don't-call-it-a-diet plan to help her test out her formula. I say this over and over again for hours. The whole time I'm walking weird circles around the booth trying to keep as much distance, and at least one of my parents, between me and Karl Bell. It doesn't always work, and when I let my mind wander to why Chris Thompson won't even look at me, I get caught next to Karl who is schmoozing with an older woman and talking knowingly about my body. When she buys a box of meal bars, he runs his fingers along the small of my back, which my mom has exposed by tying my t-shirt up.

"We make a good team, Ally," he says.

I look at my parents to respond to this clearly inappropriate interaction, but neither of them is paying attention to us.

When Chris Thompson and Tess play their set, I ask my mom if I can go over to the stage, but she says she needs me at the table, so I stay. It doesn't seem worth the fight. When they're done, Tess and Johnny come to say goodbye, but Chris Thompson doesn't. My brother's leaving, too, to go back up to State College. I'm left alone with my parents and Karl Bell, which seems both horrible and fitting.

CHAPTER 22

After the fair, I ask my dad if we can take the RX-7 out because I want to prove to him I'm good enough to drive it now. He makes me take him to Friendly's for a Fribble and a late lunch, even though I've just watched him consume his weight in cotton candy and kettle corn, no small feat.

The parking lot at the restaurant is full, and the lobby is packed. As usual, my dad walks right up to the hostess, and we're seated within moments. A few years earlier, when things like this started happening, I'd been embarrassed. Not anymore. Now when I'm out without my dad, I get annoyed if I have to wait.

He orders a cheeseburger, fries, a Diet Coke and a strawberry Fribble. I miss the days when I could do the same. But if I ate that now, I'm sure my body would revolt. I order a grilled chicken sandwich with no bun. The waitress looks at me like she has never taken that order before.

"You're not bad with the car," my dad says. "Who did you say taught you?"

"This guy on Meredith's street." I balance the need for details against the potential of getting caught in a lie. I'm surprised how easily it comes to me. "He just graduated. He taught us both."

"You probably just needed more practice."

I realize he doesn't care who taught me or that I'm lying. He's just pissed he couldn't figure out how to teach me himself.

"Totally," I say.

"So, what's new on the Summer Team?"

Shit.

Just like this morning with Karl Bell, the restaurant provides a bit of a buffer, but Dennis Burton is not above making a scene.

"Alice?"

"It's not a big deal, but I'm actually not on the team."

He slams his glass down, and I brace for the yelling.

"You got cut?" he snarls.

"A lot of us did."

"When did this happen?"

"Thursday night. It was a long shot to begin with, you know that."

"No, it wasn't. You deserve to be on that team." His voice is too loud, and people are looking, but he's used to that and doesn't care.

"Dad, there were a lot of good players out there. It's not a big deal. The coach said I was Division I material."

"Not if you don't get seen by coaches. Talent only gets you so far."

"I still have senior year." *As long as Karl Bell makes good on his promise.*

"Did Amanda make the team?"

"No, but Meredith did."

"Anyone with Meredith's last name gets whatever they want." I don't like it when he says mean stuff about Meredith, even if it's stuff I say myself.

"Come on, Dad, you know it's not her fault. We play different positions."

"Did something happen?"

Yeah, I got drunk and puked on the field, and I'm distracted all the time because this one hot guy might sorta be into me, and this other old guy won't leave me alone, and you didn't pay my tuition and ... "No. Nothing happened. It just didn't work out."

"I'll figure out who to call on Monday."

"No." It comes out of my mouth before I realize how defensive it makes me sound. "Please don't. Can we let it go?"

It's totally my fault I didn't make the team, and while I'm glad he's not taking his anger out on me, I don't want him yelling at some coach and finding out the truth.

He takes a long last sip of his Fribble and then, without even looking to see where our waitress is, he puts his arm up in the air and snaps his fingers, like a total asshole.

The waitress practically trips over herself on the way to our table just so he can order a second Fribble. I'm mortified.

"Screw the Summer Team," he says when she's gone. "We'll figure out a way to get you to Penn State."

I know this isn't faith in me – it's faith in his ability to manipulate any situation to his benefit – but I'm grateful it seems to be an end to the conversation. I just wish the whole restaurant wasn't looking at us in the wake of his obnoxious dining behavior.

"So, if we're not going to talk about lacrosse, what do you want to talk about? Are you seeing anyone?"

I scrunch up my face. "You've found the only thing I want to talk about less than lacrosse. Good one, Dad, you should interview people for a living!"

He chuckles. "Tell me more about Johnny's girlfriend. How well do you know her?"

"How do you know they're dating?"

"Johnny can't keep his mouth shut about anything."

My least favorite thing about Johnny.

"We've talked once or twice. She's nice."

"And CJ's in her band?"

Hearing my dad say "CJ" sends an uneasy feeling down my spine. My fingers get tingly again.

"Yeah." I pick up my cup and sip some water just to put something, anything, physically between my dad and me.

"He's been hanging out with Johnny more lately," he says. "I knew they grew up together, but I didn't realize they were still friends."

I have to tread lightly. I can't talk about Chris Thompson without smiling in a way that could give everything away, not that there's really all that much to hide. Just me on a dirty couch, a dusty road, and an empty bed.

"He was always such a dick," my dad continues. "When he broke Nate's leg, I wanted to kill him. I was right to get him off that team. He was pulling them all down." He says it as if it's a distant memory he's just recovered, and he's proud of himself.

I avert my eyes because I know they're filled with rage. If I tell him that Nate said it was a clean tackle, it will open up a whole line of questioning I can't handle.

"Have you heard them play?" he asks.

"Just today at the fair. And I have their tape. Johnny gave it to me." What's one more lie at this point?

"Are they any good?"

"They are."

Our food is placed in front of us. My plate looks as unappetizing as his looks appealing.

"What do they sound like?" my dad asks. "Sell them to me."

"You heard their tape. You told Tess you didn't like them."

"I say a lot of things."

"They do some covers of The Smiths and The Cure. They're hard to categorize. I think they're moving away from the British stuff into grunge, but really it's all just rock 'n' roll, right?" I hear myself parroting Chris Thompson's words from the night we first talked. "And Tess writes all the original stuff. And she's got a great voice – "

"So, I've heard," my father interrupts. "'Raspy perfection.'"

"I knew you read the City Paper. You say you don't, but I know you do."

"So, would you book them?"

I look at him perplexed. He seems to be asking a serious question, but I find it hard to take him seriously because it's just so absurd.

He reads my mind.

"I'm really asking. Johnny's been too afraid to ask me. He knows I know he's screwing her. He knows if I do him the favor of booking them I'd never let him forget it. And if they stink, it'd be his ass. Why aren't you eating?"

I've cut a piece of chicken, and it's been on my fork for too long. I shove it in my mouth.

"Who says I'm not eating?" I say while chewing.

"Where were you yesterday? Why couldn't anyone get in touch with you?"

I try to remind myself that getting the third degree from my father is preferable to being back at the fair with my mom and Karl Bell, but it's a struggle.

"Like who?"

"I think Nate was looking for you."

"He found me. As did Johnny."

"Were you with Meredith?"

"Yesterday? No, I was at the library."

"The library?" my dad scoffs.

"Where would you go if you needed to read *Moll Flanders* in June?"

"I don't know anything about *Moll Flanders*," he says, "but I think I'd probably stay home if I needed to read a book."

"Moll Flanders is a prostitute," I tell him. "And I end up watching too much MTV if I stay home, so the library's better for me."

"Which one?" he asks.

"Which library?"

"Yes, Alice, which library. Where were you yesterday?"

"Oh, Meredith's library," I joke. I always call the Pitt library that because when we were kids, she told me it was named after her, which it basically was. "And I wandered around Oakland a bit."

He doesn't say anything for a moment while he really looks at me. I force myself to eat more chicken. He eats more of his burger. He doesn't let go of my gaze once, not to pick up the burger, not to put it in his mouth, not while he chews and uses his napkin to blot his face. When he's finished chewing he just stares at me with one corner of his mouth tipped up in half a smile that says, I've got you, or, if I don't have you, I want you to at least think I do, which may be enough to scare you into an admission of guilt. I stare back, knowing I can't actually admit to anything if I don't say anything.

When I was younger, I thought he could read my mind. He had an uncanny ability to know what I was going to say before I said it. And it wasn't just me. He was a master at deflating big, exciting news because he always seemed to know it first. But it's just now occurring to me that his stare is increasingly becoming a bluff. There was a time he probably did know every thought in my head – we're so similar in so many ways – but that's becoming a thing of the past.

We sit in silence. He continues to eat his burger; I continue to force small bites of bland chicken breast into my mouth.

"Is there a problem?" I finally ask, unable to stay silent any longer.

"I hope not." His face softens, and then it's taken over by something that appears to be pride, like I have passed some sort of test. "So should we book them?"

"Yeah." I try to conceal the high I feel.

"We could move some stuff around at the end of the Flagstaff season, or we could just book them for the 5K Fest pre-party. They'd have to wait until fall, but it would be a more important crowd."

"Are you sure?" I let myself smile. "It's up to me?"

He nods as he takes the last of the cheeseburger off of his plate.

"Let me think about it," I say. "I'll get back to you."

"Have your people call my people." He laughs at his own joke. "Or just leave a note on my desk. But I'm not done with the lacrosse thing."

He's done though. I can tell by the tone of his voice he's not going to push the issue.

We spend the rest of the day running errands. When we finally get home it's seven o'clock, and my mom has left to cater a dinner party in the suburbs – probably for the parents of one of the rich kids at Frazer. My dad and I hang around in the kitchen digging through the fridge for anything she might have left that could be construed as dinner. We find half a roasted chicken and stand at the counter picking it apart. My mom's chicken is much better than the crap from Friendly's. I actually sort of hate that everything she makes is so good.

I know my father is in large part responsible for most of the problems I'm currently facing, but while we tear into the roasted chicken, I remember what it was like to think he was the most perfect man in the world.

CHAPTER 23

After our stand-over-the-counter-dinner I shower and put on one of Nate's V-neck undershirts and a clean pair of purple Umbros that I roll at the waist. Each time I walk by my phone, I remember that I was supposed to call Chris Thompson today, but I don't want to talk about what he wants to talk about. Also, I'm a little pissed about how he ignored me at the fair. And I want to tell him in person my dad is going to let me book Wasted Pretty for one of the live events. I want to see his face when I say it, and I want to be alone when I tell him, in case he wants to express his gratitude by kissing me. I decide to drive over to his place to tell him in person. I tell my dad I'm headed to Meredith's, and I'm taking *my* car. I practically skip out to the RX-7 with Chris Thompson's cassettes in my bag.

When I get to his place, he's on the porch-couch eating a sandwich.

"Nice car," he says, a slight edge in his voice.

"Thanks …?"

"You said you'd call."

"I came over instead. What, have you been sitting by the phone all day waiting?"

He holds up his cordless phone in response.

"Wow. That's … touching … and weird."

"I was worried about you."

"You don't have to be." I don't want him to think of me that way.

"I didn't like seeing you with them today. And I didn't like that I didn't like it."

"Well, I didn't like watching you walk right past me."

"What was I supposed to do, stop and hang out with you and your dad and your brother and Karl Bell? How do you think that would have gone down?"

"I don't know, but you could have, I don't know … looked at me?"

"No, I couldn't have. You get that, right?"

There's a long pause. I was so dumb to think I could show up here with good news and have him just fall all over me.

"Listen, Karl's leaving town." I try to diffuse the situation, try to get the conversation back on my terms. "I think they fly out in the morning, so while I appreciate your concern, you don't have to worry about him for a few months. Actually, you really don't have to worry about him at all. I'm fine about all of that. But you know, my dad? He's not going anywhere. I get you don't like him and, to be fair, he doesn't like you, but he's my dad. You can't be bothered that I'm with him. I was with him all day today, and it was kinda nice, actually."

"Alice, your dad is basically pimping you out to Karl Bell. I wanted to punch him in the face. I wanted to punch both of them!"

"I highly doubt my father knows Karl Bell made me touch his dick, so if anyone's pimping me out, it's me!" A quality of rage I'm not familiar with has overtaken my voice. I sound like Nate when he's really mad. "Fuck you!" I spit.

Chris Thompson leaps up from the couch.

"Fuck me?" he snarls in a guttural whisper. "Fuck you, you spoiled brat."

I don't know how I get angrier, but a spike of vehemence materializes and instantly produces hot tears. *Brat* is too much. It's a window into how he sees me, and it destroys me.

"I'm outta here." I turn towards the steps.

"Wait!" Chris Thompson grabs my right wrist, and I jerk my arm away.

He puts his hands up to show he won't try to touch me again. We end up standing several feet apart with our hands up like we're being robbed by each other. Tears are rolling down my face; my breathing is heavy and loud.

"I'm sorry," he says in his standard, almost inaudible voice. He runs his hand through his bangs and looks down at the ground.

"It doesn't matter." I wipe my face.

"Alice, I like you." He's still looking at the ground.

"You like me?" I don't know how it's possible, but I get even angrier. "What does that even mean? You want to be with me? You want to save me? Take me to the prom? Fuck me?"

"Alice, come on, it's more complicated than that."

"Exactly," I shout. "Let's just agree this is a little too complicated. You just called me a whore and a brat and quite frankly, I'm not sure which one I'm more pissed about. Let's just agree we don't even know each other."

I storm off the porch. If he tries to stop me, I don't notice.

CHAPTER 24

Pulling up Richard's driveway in the RX-7 feels infinitely cooler than arriving in the Wally Wagon. Parking my car, which is probably half the size of the wagon, should be easier, but I'm so upset I struggle and stall out a few times. I give up trying to parallel in the line of cars and pull onto a patch of grass.

I know I look good. After I left Chris Thompson's, I went to Meredith's. With the spare key from under the birdbath, I let myself in the back door. I punched my alarm code into the beeping panel by the pantry – each family member has their own, and Meredith convinced her mom to make me one this summer. Even though no one was home, upstairs, I locked Meredith's bedroom door behind me. Of all the things I love about her house, being able to lock the bedroom door might be my favorite. Raiding her closet is my second favorite. I pull together a suitably sexy-yet-classic combination of frayed jean shorts and a white oxford shirt, half unbuttoned without a tank top underneath.

Walking into Richard and Dylan's backyard is like going back in time to Wednesday night, but I feel like a different person.

"Can I get a beer?" I ask Meredith when I find her.

"You clean up nice – are those my clothes?"

"Is it a problem if they are?"

"No."

"Beer, please?"

"Bitchy much?"

"How's Summer Team going?"

"Oh, that. Don't be mad."

"Beer, please," I repeat.

"Behind the shed."

"Thanks." I head off to the back of the yard near the woods.

Some guys who graduated with Richard find me a clean cup and fill it.

I down the beer quickly and ask the guys for a refill. After chugging half of my second beer, I wander through the crowd, executing a plan that hatched, fully formed, in my head on the drive over. I find Dylan draped across Tracie, a blonde who has just finished her freshman year at Frazer. She and I are wearing virtually the same outfit. I take it as a sign I nailed preppy-suburban-cool-girl style perfectly.

"Hi Alice," Tracie says brightly. Our school is small, and the social order is fairly defined. Even a cool girl in 9th grade is below an 11th grader whose only claim to social status is being Meredith May's best friend. "How's your summer?"

"Interesting." I dismiss her. "Hey Dylan."

"Alice," he says with his version of a cool-guy head nod. He's happy to see me, but he's trying to cover it.

"Dylan, can I talk to you for a minute?" I ask.

"Sure!" He hides his excitement poorly.

"See ya, Alice!" Tracie says with a wave. "Dylan and I are just friends!" she adds nervously as we walk away. Apparently, she doesn't think I'm cool; she's just afraid of me, or afraid of Meredith, which is basically the same thing.

"What's up, Alice?" Dylan asks.

He's too skinny. He can't possibly weigh more than I do; I hate him for that.

"Listen, I want to do a shot, do you have anything hard?"

"Sure!" He's unable to maintain his tenuous grasp on a cool-guy demeanor.

I follow him to Joan's stash of liquor, and we each do a shot of room temperature Jagermeister. It's disgusting.

"Hey." I wrap my hair around my hand then flip it to the side. "Can we go to your room?"

"Yeah!" He's clumsy when he pulls me close to him. "If you want to, but where's this coming from?"

"Do you care?" I feel the alcohol all over my body, especially behind my knees.

"No, I don't care."

He leads me down the hallway and gives me a sloppy kiss on the mouth before we even get to his room. Once inside he pushes his hand down the front of my shirt and grabs one of my boobs before I manage to shut the door. His eagerness feels like an empty space I have no desire to fill, but right now I'm not motivated by desire.

I push him away just long enough to see his eyes in the dim, red light of the bedside lamp.

"You have a condom?"

"Really Alice, are you sure?" His eyes are wide and hungry.

And because I can't change the fact I'm sixteen, and I can't change whose kid I am, and I can't change who's writing the checks, I change the only thing I can.

"I'm sure."

When we're done, which is pretty soon after we start – we do the whole thing standing up and not completely undressed – I ask Dylan to find me a cigarette. While he's out looking to bum one off of someone in the backyard, I find my way to the guest room. I spend the rest of the night in there with the door locked, smelling like sex and watching reruns of "Saved By The Bell."

CHAPTER 25

Flagstaff is full tonight. I'm alone at the table because three weeks into the summer, Meredith is already bored and pretty busy with lacrosse. She vastly prefers drinking in Richard's backyard to handing out bumper stickers with me. Lucky for her, she doesn't need an internship to list on her college applications. The movie "Annie" is about to play. Meredith and I loved this movie when we were kids. We convinced her dad to buy out a whole theatre so we could watch the movie the way Annie does with Grace and Daddy Warbucks.

The walkie-talkie crackles.

"Wonderland, Wonderland, come in Wonderland. This is Johnny-Five do you copy?"

"Why are you such a dork?"

"Sorry, what was that? Don't copy."

"Affirmative. This is Wonderland. Can you hear my eye roll? Over."

"Where are you? Over."

"At the table where I'm supposed to be every Flagstaff for the rest of time. Why? Over."

"I can't see you. Over."

I look up to the table at the top of the hill and see Johnny peering through his binoculars.

"I'm at the table, dork. I got my haircut, but it's still me. Over."

"Whoa. Tess said it was short, but whoa ..."

"Why are you and Tess talking about my hair? Over."

"I'm coming down. Over."

Johnny went away with his parents, and I've been avoiding him since he got back last week. Tess and I hung out a lot while he was away. It seems I was the perfect size to fill her empty Johnny time and she filled my empty Meredith time. She kept trying to get to me to come out to a Wasted Pretty show, but I thought it was best to stay out of Chris Thompson's way for a while.

"Who's up top?" I ask when Johnny takes the empty seat next to me.

"One of the interns; I still don't know all their names. Was I that useless my first summer?"

"No, you were much more useless. My dad would have fired you if it weren't for my constantly fixing your mistakes."

"Cute Wonderland."

"So what's up?" I ask, even though I know what's coming.

"Well, I can't believe I'm even saying this to you, because I sort of don't want to know, but is everything ok with you and Chris Thompson?"

I give him my best mock-innocent-confused-librarian face.

"Tess said she kept inviting you out and you never showed. And you've been MIA since I've been back in town. And he's been moping, more than usual. And you let me book them for 5K Fest and take all the credit. And I swear to god, I don't want to know too much, but I'm actually kind of worried … about both of you. I still don't know what was going on that night after Graffiti."

"I told you, he took me out to Zelie to teach me how to drive stick, and then I crashed out while you guys were at the show. What's the big deal?"

"I don't know. What *is* the big deal?"

"Seriously?"

"Listen, I'll never admit to this conversation, and I don't want to know what I don't want to know, so just tell me everything's ok, and I don't have to worry. Like … he didn't … do anything to you … right?"

"What?!"

"Tess is worried. We can't get anything out of him. He's back to being his sullen, bitchy self, which he wasn't when you were around. And Tess said girls do weird things to their hair when bad things happen."

My hand shoots up to my head. "You think my hair looks weird?"

The day after I fucked Dylan I cut off all my hair, 13 inches. It's a short, curly pixie cut now. I didn't even know my hair had any curl in it.

"I actually think it looks nice, if you want to know," he says, quite sheepishly. "To be honest, it's hard for me to see you as anything other than a pudgy thirteen-year-old, but now … well, it's pretty clear you're not that anymore."

I'm touched by how far out of his comfort zone he's going to look out for me.

"Listen," I say. "I'd be lying if I said everything was ok, because it's not. And I don't feel like lying to you. But Chris Thompson hasn't done anything wrong. And there's absolutely nothing you can do to make anything better. So, thanks. I really appreciate your concern. Even though I think it's weird you and your girlfriend were talking about my hair."

"I think you're weird, Wonderland!" He puts his arm around my neck in a half-chokehold, half-hug, and our heads smash into each other. I push him away, but not too hard.

"No offense," he says, "but I liked you better when your biggest concern was which fast food restaurant had the best strawberry milkshake."

"That was never a concern. It was always Burger King."

"Um, get out! It's totally McDonald's."

"You're crazy. That shit might as well be Pepto Bismol."

Johnny starts rummaging through the station crate under the table and doesn't lift his head when he starts talking. "In all seriousness, you'd tell me if there was anything I could do. If you were, I don't know, in trouble?"

"Yeah." It's not exactly a lie.

"Will you come out tomorrow night?" he asks. "Wasted Pretty's headlining at The Decade. I'll put you on the list. Teach you how to work the soundboard."

"Really? I thought you didn't want me anywhere near Chris Thompson?"

"I don't. But something tells me I need to keep my eye on you this summer."

"As long as you're not doing covert surveillance for Burton."

"Why? Do you have something to hide?"

"Stop. Your dad may be a cop, but you're a horrible detective."

"Will you come? If they're playing 5K Fest, I'm going to need someone to cover the soundboard. I'll be too busy doing everything else."

"Well, if you really need my help …"

I act like I'm put out by his request, which is hilarious, because he's begging me to go to my first Wasted Pretty show. It seems my plan to be conspicuously absent is working.

CHAPTER 26

I'm wearing Meredith's denim overall shorts and a tie-dye T-shirt I took out of Nate's closet and cut into a half-shirt. The outfit is put together specifically to get Chris Thompson's attention but has the added benefit of making me feel invincible as I walk down Forbes Avenue in the dark. Summer air wraps around my exposed waist.

When I round the corner onto Atwood, I see Dom, the Bouncer at The Decade, who's twice the width of most people. I'm so nervous; I stop before he can see me and duck into a doorway. Leaning up against the brick wall, I run my hand through my cropped hair. I'm still not used to my mane being gone, and for a moment I panic and consider going home. Most of the people who have seen my haircut like it, but Chris Thompson isn't most people. As I approach the club I can tell Dom doesn't recognize me.

"Hey Dom, it's Alice!"

"Alice Burton?! I saw your name on the list, but I never would've recognized you."

Dom was an intern at the station Johnny's first summer. I'm not surprised he doesn't recognize me.

"It's me," I say with an awkward twirl. "Been a while, huh?"

"Your dad still crazy?"

"As ever."

"I won't tell him I saw you here, if you don't tell him I let you in."

"Thanks, Dom!"

"Johnny says you're working the board tonight. Going into the family business?"

"Something like that!"

He opens the door for me, and I'm so giddy I kiss him on the cheek as I slip into the club.

I get myself a club soda at the bar and weave my way through the crowd to join Johnny at the table where he's working the small mixing board. The bar is packed. I had no idea Wasted Pretty had gotten so popular this summer. Maybe the show at Graffiti really was a big deal. Maybe I'm here to flirt with a burgeoning rock star. Maybe this is a bad idea.

"You're here." Johnny beams at me, and I nod.

"Things good?" I ask.

He nods – speaking in The Decade is nearly impossible.

"Wanna learn how to mix sound?" Johnny yell-whispers in my ear.

No, I want to stare at the beautiful person playing lead guitar, but if it will make you happy, I'll learn to mix sound. "Sure."

Johnny wordlessly points to knobs and levers and mimes what he wants me to do with each. I'm nervous about taking the controls, but he offers an encouraging smile. He tells me to listen with my eyes closed to get a sense of the balance. Their music, which I've been playing non-stop in my Walkman when I run – and on my stereo in my room, and in the tape deck of the RX-7 – is so much more powerful live. And I feel like I'm a part of it. For some reason, it feels right to be in the bar surrounded by cigarette smoke and sweat and energy that radiates out from the band and right back to them from everyone who loves them, including me. It's far better than being in a backyard with a bunch of high school kids who only care about their social status and getting wasted. I open my eyes. From where I sit, I have an unobstructed view of Chris Thompson, and I stare unapologetically.

It's a moment before I realize who else is in the room. Girls. Pretty girls. Lots of pretty girls. Tess may have been right. She may need Chris Thompson more than I realized. The girls look at him with a particular longing I feel in my gut. I can't compete with them. It's sobering, and I'm not even drunk. For his part, Chris Thompson looks at his shoes, black Chuck Taylors, or maybe at his hands. I can't tell, but he's not looking at the girls and their exposed, tan stomachs. They're all old enough to be here, and they hold their opaque plastic cups of beer like proof of their belonging. It reminds me of the birth-control-bitches and their Evian. I had thought staying away a while would make him realize he wanted me, but it hadn't occurred to me I wasn't the only girl vying for his attention.

The band comes offstage shortly after midnight. There are a bunch of them, and I want to tell them how great they are, but I just hang next to Johnny and smile. Chris Thompson is still on stage messing with some equipment. Tess pantomimes disgust for her sweaty body and then gives me two exaggerated air kisses, one on each cheek. She makes a big deal about how "fit" I look and how glad she is I came out. The band makes their way to the bar, and I hang back, so I'm alone when Chris Thompson steps off the stage. He hugs me, and I let him. His arm threads through the back of my overalls so I can feel his forearm up against the bare skin of my lower back. His head is nuzzled into my neck. It's exactly the reaction I was hoping for, but I have no idea what comes next.

"Let's get out of here," he says into my ear.

"Don't you have to –"

"I packed up my guitar. They'll bring it back. Come on!"

He's deliberate about taking my left hand instead of my right. He leads me through the crowd to the exit. I have just enough time to grab my boho bag.

"Johnny's gonna call you a diva," I tell him.

"He'll deal."

We burst through the door and run right into Dom. We're giggling like schoolgirls who have been caught breaking all the rules, which, to be fair, I sort of am.

"Alice." He looks at the two of us suspiciously.

"'Night Dom!" I call as Chris Thompson leads me down the street towards his place.

I trip over my feet trying to keep up with him. Halfway down the block he finally slows his pace, and I'm able to walk next to him without the fear of falling over. Then he slows down even more until he stops. Our fingers are intertwined. He's looking at me the way I've always wanted him to look at me. The ability to control my breath leaves my body. I want time to stop moving. I can tell this is the moment that will separate "before" from everything that will come "after." I drop my bag. And then Chris Thompson kisses me. His left hand holds the side of my face with his fingers just touching my ear, and his right hand holds my ribcage firmly, his thumb just grazing my breast, the thin cotton of my t-shirt barely separates our skin.

There's nothing hungry or greedy about his kiss. He isn't taking anything from me, though I would happily let him. He pulls me closer. If his arm weren't wrapped around my back, I'm not sure I'd be able to stay upright. My knees are literally, embarrassingly, weak. It's the same feeling I had after the shot I did with Dylan, but I'm sober. When Chris Thompson finally pulls back, I can't look at him. I immediately bury my face in his chest. Despite the sweat of an entire set, he still smells clean, and I breathe him in deeply.

"We're ok?" he asks.

We.

"Yes."

"And all of this is ok?" he asks, with my face in his hands.

"Yes." I'm breathless.

"So, don't disappear again," he says quietly in my ear.

"I won't, but don't call me a prostitute again."

I was actually more upset about being called a brat, but I don't want to remind him.

"I didn't call you a prostitute."

"You sort of did."

"Well, I didn't mean to. I just meant your dad was letting someone incredibly dangerous get too close to you."

I narrow my eyes a bit. "Listen, I appreciate your concern – "

"No you don't."

"You're right, I don't."

"But Princess, what if you're in over your head? Those lottery tickets? Your dad's an addict. Like me. Except he's not dealing with it."

"Also not your problem."

It's my fault Chris Thompson knows more than he should about my father, but I'm not going to let that ruin this.

I pick up my bag, but he takes it from me, and we continue walking towards his place. He's careful to stay on my left side. His right hand rests on my lower back, inside my overalls and just above my underwear, skin against skin. I amaze myself by putting one foot in front of the other.

"I've been worried about you," he says. "I don't like to worry."

"I'm sorry."

"Like, really worried. Tess told me about your hair and said sometimes when bad things happen to girls they do drastic things to their hair. So she was asking Johnny what could have happened. And obviously I'm thinking of Karl Bell, but I'm not gonna tell them. And they're obviously thinking it's me, since Tess keeps trying to get you to come out and you won't. So Tess says girls try to make themselves look ugly in an attempt to distance themselves from whatever happened, but they end up looking hotter, which is clearly what happened here –"

I blush. "I wasn't trying to look ugly. I just wanted something different."

"Well, you look amazing. I don't want to let you out of my sight. Ever."

He uses his hand on the small of my back to guide me closer to him, and I try to relax into the pressure, but I'm feeling things too intensely. I have to focus consciously on walking. I'm more than grateful when we finally make it upstairs to his place, and he pushes me playfully, onto the bed. Then he lies down on top of me. The weight of his body pressing into me, which should be suffocating, actually makes it easier to breathe. Everything he does feels amazing. I've really only ever hooked up with Dylan, and I spent most of my time with him trying to get him to stop doing what he was doing. Being with Chris Thompson is different.

Everything he does, I want him to do. And then he does things I don't even know I want him to do. At first, I'm paralyzed – worried I'm going to make a mistake that will show my inexperience, and then thinking about my lack of experience makes me freeze up even more. It isn't until he's kissing me behind my ear that I'm able to take a deep breath and ease into the moment. I let out a sigh that stands in for a question I don't know how to ask, and he lets out a groan in response. It's an answer I don't know I'm looking for.

Eventually, Chris Thompson stops kissing me, but his weight is still on top of me. He props himself up, his elbows on either side of my head, and he traces my eyebrows with his thumbs. Our noses are inches apart, and I panic, slightly, sensing he's about to say something I'm not ready to hear.

"You're very pretty." He kisses my cheeks and then my collarbones and then the part of my chest that is exposed above my shirt. "Very, very pretty."

I had thought hearing Chris Thompson say those words would give me a sense of peace I'd been longing for, but in the silence that follows his declaration, I'm overcome by the realization that being pretty, if I am pretty, is never going to be enough. There's already a sense of loss in the air around us.

"Everyone's going to be home soon," he says, as if he's reading my mind.

"Right. Everyone."

"They'll probably have pizza," he says, smiling his wide, face-altering grin.

"Oh yay!" I say with mock enthusiasm. "Pizza. Woo-hoo!"

"Come on." He pulls me up off the bed and leads me into the living room where I sink into a couch. He leans down and kisses me gently on the lips before going into the kitchen to get us two cups of water. With his acoustic guitar, he sits opposite me on the couch, our legs stretched out between us. Our feet rub against each other.

"Requests?" he asks.

"Whatever you want."

I can't imagine ever making any demands of him. I suspect I'd be grateful for whatever he wants to do ... play, sing, say, touch ... but even in the moment, even in the bliss of the new way he's looking at me, I can't ignore what's at stake. What's happening between us is no longer part of a potential future thing I want. Now it's something I can lose.

We hear "everyone" on the steps at the same time. Chris Thompson stops playing for a moment and says, "You can stay tonight, right?" and I nod. Then he goes back to playing.

Johnny bursts through the door as if on cue. He finds us on the couch the same way he did the night after the Graffiti show, except everything is different, and no one can tell but us.

PART 2

CHAPTER 27

By the middle of July what seemed impossible in June has become positively routine. I spend every Saturday night at Chris' place while my parents think I'm at Meredith's. After a while, I don't even have to lie about it anymore because it's just assumed. Chris and I haven't had sex. This is something we do not discuss.

"Why aren't they leaving?" Tess has her head on my shoulder, and she's complaining about the rest of the band.

Johnny and Tess always hang out at Chris' until everyone else is gone so no one but them sees me alone with Chris. This is also never discussed, but it's obvious to me.

"Isn't it time for you all to go home?" she says loudly, but to no one in particular. She opens another beer. "Maybe if I drink all the beer they'll leave."

She offers me a swig, but I shake my head, like always. While everyone else scarfs pizza and beer, I eat celery and drink water. I don't want anything to dull my senses, and because Chris doesn't drink, it doesn't seem right for me to.

Tess keeps drinking and playfully shouting at the guys in the band to leave, but they just laugh at her. "It's like they want me to get as little sleep as possible!"

Chris generally keeps his distance from me when everyone is around, but I love to catch him looking at me from across the room. Right now he's standing by the kitchen talking to Johnny, but I see him eyeing me over Johnny's shoulder.

"You're not going to hurt him are you?" Tess slurs.

"Tess, how drunk are you?"

"I just mean, look at him looking at you. He's smitten."

I love that she saw it, too. It means it's not all in my head.

"I'm not going to hurt him," I reassure her, but I can barely contain my own laugh at the absurdity of it.

"You think I'm kidding, but I'm not. He doesn't let people in. He didn't before Indiana, and he certainly doesn't now. But he let you in."

"I won't hurt him. Promise." The idea is absurd.

"But don't fall in love with him, either. You promised you wouldn't."

I didn't actually promise that. She warned me not to, but that's not the same as a promise. I don't know what love is supposed to feel like, but I do feel something charged and new when I'm alone with Chris. And not just in his bed. Sometimes we sit at the kitchen table, and he drinks tea, and I read magazines, or he writes songs, and I listen. Everything else in my life is falling apart, but here, in this grimy apartment, where I'm not supposed to be, I feel most at home. Maybe that's love?

"Let me get you some water," I tell Tess.

I walk by Johnny and Chris in the doorway, but by the time I'm back with a cup for me and a cup for Tess, the room has rearranged itself. Tess is forcing Johnny to dance with her, and Chris has taken my seat in the corner of the couch. I sit on the floor in front of him, his knee touching my shoulder, casually, as if I were anyone else in the room. As if we won't be in bed together, almost naked, as soon as all these people are gone.

I'm dealt into the next game of cards. Tess continues to yell at people to go home. She must want to get Johnny alone as much as I want to be alone with Chris.

*　*　*　*　*

The Pittsburgh summer melts into August and gets sticky. Chris' apartment doesn't have air conditioning. It's a good excuse to lounge around in very little clothing revealing various parts of my body. Today, I've banished him to the living room, and I'm in bed reading *Moll Flanders*. The box fan ruffles the pages. I have to finish my summer reading, and he's too distracting. Even with him in the other room, fooling around on his guitar, he still steals my attention.

"Pat Benatar!" I yell. "'We Belong.'"

"Shoot!" Chris yells back. "How do you know all these songs?"

All summer he's been trying to learn songs I can't name in three bars.

"It's like you don't know me at all!" I call back. "If you're trying to stump me, you should probably stay away from 1980s-power-ballads-with-female-lead-singers as a general rule. They're sort of my thing!"

"They're not your thing! What does Pat Benatar have in common with Billy Bragg and The Smiths?"

Now he's standing in the doorway.

"MTV?" I say with a coy shrug. "I think you underestimate the amount of time I spent at Meredith's watching MTV before I started hanging out here. I have an encyclopedic knowledge of '120 Minutes' and 1980s power ballads. I'm complicated."

"Oh, I know you're complicated."

He starts to walk towards me, but I hold my hand up.

"You're not allowed in here until I read at least two more chapters."

He works through a couple different smiles trying to get me to let him into his own room, but I shake my head.

Chris goes back to puttering. He does that. He wanders from room to room, sometimes playing guitar, sometimes reading a magazine, and sometimes, when I let him, curling around me and kissing me while I try to concentrate on whatever it is I'm trying to concentrate on. I often lose the battle, happily, which is how I've ended up so far behind in my summer reading.

The phone rings, and I hear Chris pick it up in the kitchen. Moments later he's in the doorway again.

"Permission to enter, Princess?"

I make a big deal of pretending to consider the request and then give him the smallest of nods.

He plops down on the bed next to me, still holding the cordless. He doesn't say anything for a moment, but he traces the length of my left side with his fingers. Little pulses of electricity radiate from his touch. It's been more than two months, and we still haven't had sex. Hooking up with Chris is remarkably chaste, all things considered, and it's unnerving. With Dylan, I was always trying to hold him off, except for that one time, but with Chris I'm constantly trying to make myself available.

I'm wearing one of Chris' shirts and my underwear and nothing else. It's pretty much all I ever wear around the apartment unless other people are here. There were a couple of close calls early on, when Johnny used to let himself in unannounced, but he has taken to knocking. It seems his desire for plausible deniability is of greater concern to him than my virtue. Now it's me who walks in unannounced. I use the trick Chris taught me at the beginning of the summer on the front door and the key above the doorjamb of his apartment.

"You're away next weekend, right?" he finally says. His tone matches the thick, heavy sky I can see out the window. We've been bumming around the apartment waiting for the rain to let up.

"Yeah. Meredith and I are taking the varsity girls up to a cabin at Hidden Valley. I'm sure she has some horrible hazing rituals planned. I'm just looking forward to swimming one last time before school starts."

"Ohhhhh, Princess in a bathing suit," he coos.

"Please." I pretend to be annoyed. "You've seen me in less than a bathing suit."

Chris has not seen me naked; I have not seen him naked. The whole thing is starting to concern me.

"Aren't you going to Ohio?" I ask.

"No. That was Tess on the phone. She says hi. The mini-tour got canceled. Apparently, the headliners are having trouble with their van. Tess thought she could convince the bars to let us headline, but they weren't going for it. So now we have no shows booked, I have no shifts to work, and no you."

"I can see if I can get out of Hidden Valley," I say too eagerly.

"You could stay all weekend. Neither of us would have anywhere to be ..."

I lean down to kiss him. The fact I can do that whenever I want, as long as we're alone, is intoxicating.

"Give me the phone." I dial Meredith's number. "Hey, it's me. What are you doing?"

"MTV," she grunts. "You?"

"I'm at Chris' working on *Moll Flanders*. Gag."

"Oh, poor you." Richard dumped her when he left for Bucknell. She claims not to care, and there's no way to tell with her. "Please tell me you've had sex with him by now."

"Stop." I cup the phone closer to my face and hope he hasn't heard her. "Have you written the paper yet?"

"Of course. My dad's secretary typed it last week. You haven't finished yours?"

"No, I need to finish the book first."

"What the hell have you been doing all summer? Not screwing Chris Thompson ..."

Sometimes it seems Meredith is more pissed Chris won't sleep with me than I am. Which is saying a lot, because I'm pretty pissed.

"I'll get it done," I say. "Listen, would it be a disaster if I didn't come up to Hidden Valley?"

I make a face at Chris intending to convey how risky the question is. He makes the face back at me, gritting his teeth in an uncomfortable but hopeful smile.

"So ... I'm gonna pretend you didn't just ask that," Meredith says.

"Seriously, Meredith," I plead. She's acting like she hasn't put Richard ahead of me every chance she's had for the last year. Not that Chris is my boyfriend.

"Seriously, Alice, we're the captains. We're taking the girls up there together. You can't leave me with those losers. And I have something really big planned for your birthday."

"No, you don't." Meredith hates birthdays.

"Well, I could have."

"Please ..."

"Why?" She softens only slightly. "What's going on?"

"Um ..." I stammer.

I was so excited by the possibility of a weekend with Chris, I didn't think this through. I weigh whether or not there's any way I can sell it to her without looking like a bitch.

"Um, Chris was supposed to be out of town and now he's not, so I was just thinking I could hang here."

"Whatever," she says. "I don't give a crap."

Anyone else would think she was pissed, but I can tell it's all bluster.

"Thank you, Meredith!" The sing-song-y way I say it is meant to sound grateful, but it comes out sounding facetious instead. "You're the best. But you can't tell anyone where I am. You know that, right?"

"Of course I know that, Chicken. I'll give you the stomach flu or something."

"Really Meredith, you're the best."

"Let me talk to him," she barks.

"Chris? You wanna talk to Chris?"

"Yes, I'm sure he's right there kissing your toes or something."

"Stop." I hold the phone to him. "She wants to talk to you."

I raise my eyebrows, and he raises his back at me.

"Hello?"

I lean in to hear her end of the conversation, but I can't make anything out. I hope that means he didn't overhear anything either.

"You're mine all weekend," Chris says when he's done on the phone.

"What was that about?"

"She wanted to make sure I knew your birthday is Friday. Why didn't you tell me?"

"It's not a big deal."

"If you say so."

He throws my book on the floor and wraps himself around my

body. He kisses my bare thighs, and I let myself be kissed. I run my hands through the corn silk of his hair. I sigh, he groans, and just when I feel like I can't handle not screwing anymore, he pulls back, looks out the window and says, "It stopped raining."

I compose myself, which always takes me a moment after he inexplicably puts the brakes on, and say, "Looks like it."

"Go for a run?"

I let out a deep sigh. "Sure."

I get dressed, pull one of his baseball caps down low on my forehead, and we head out on the streets of Oakland, disguised in plain sight. It's late for us. Most of the time we wake up early on Sunday mornings, eat bananas silently in the kitchen and take to the quiet streets before the college students are stirring. We run through the trash and occasional vomit left over from other people's wild nights – evidence of what people were doing while we were in bed rubbing our nearly naked bodies against each other. The streets and the filth give way to Schenley Park, and I pretend we're back in the country because that day at his parents' still holds a magical appeal for me.

I'm always amazed by how little attention we command in the park. I'm used to being noticed as Dennis Burton's daughter everywhere I go, but when Chris and I are running no one ever looks at us. Other runners nod politely as runners do, but I'm careful to keep my head down, and I never once feel the spark of recognition I'm used to at events or even in the restaurants my dad and I frequent. We run silently, no chatting, no headphones. We're simultaneously together and alone.

CHAPTER 28

I'm asleep on Meredith's plush comforter when a ball of her socks hits me in the face. I wake up to the light streaming in her window illuminating a halo around her head. The comforter is soft, and lovely things surround me: upholstered chairs; tables that have no purpose except to display expensive trinkets; framed, expensive art. Everything with a clear place. I love being at Chris' place, but Meredith's is much, much nicer.

She's proofing my *Moll Flanders* paper, which I wrote in one, long, horrible all-nighter last night.

"It's good."

"Really? Or are you just saying that?"

"No, it's fine. It's clearly not your best work, but that book sucked, and it's only summer reading. It's fine."

It worries me that spending time with Chris has distracted me so much from what little school work I should've been doing over the summer. It doesn't bode well for senior year. It's just like getting drunk for the first time ruined my chances on the Summer Team, even though in the end, Meredith said the tournament was dumb, and the refs ruined all the games. But it's like these little things I'm doing don't seem to matter, until all of a sudden they do.

"I need to head up to Hidden Valley," she says. "Are you ready?"

I parked the RX-7 in front of her house, and she's dropping me off at Chris'. This way our parents will think we're at the cabin together.

"Thanks for doing this," I say as I get into her car.

"Consider it your birthday gift. I'm not getting you anything else."

"I would not expect you to. This is the best birthday gift you could give me."

"Wonderful. Not spending time with me is the best gift I could give my best friend."

"You know what I mean!"

"You don't think he's getting you anything, do you? I hope you didn't get your hopes up. Guys suck at birthdays. I'm sure Chris Thompson sucks at birthdays."

"We didn't really talk about it."

"Maybe he'll actually fuck you tonight."

The thought has crossed my mind. "Why does it matter so much to you whether we're having sex or not?"

"It doesn't matter so much to me," she says. I think she may finally be tired of this conversation. "I think it's weird, and it doesn't make any sense, and I know it bothers you, but I really don't care."

I exhale.

"Don't get pissy at me," she says. "You know it bothers you."

It bothers me. We don't say anything for the rest of the ride. When she pulls up to Chris' place, I lean over, hug her shoulders and give her a kiss on the cheek. At first, she lets me but doesn't reciprocate, but when I pull away, she grabs me and says, "Love ya, Chickie, happy birthday. Try to get some action tonight, ok?"

"Ok." I smile.

I let myself into the front door and take the narrow, steep steps as quickly as I can. Chris is in the kitchen, sitting at the table, drinking a cup of tea.

"Happy Birthday, Princess."

"Thanks."

"I didn't get you anything," he adds.

"It's ok." I know I shouldn't be disappointed, but I am, just a little.

"I thought about making you a mixtape, but that's so cheesy. But now I feel bad." He looks at me sheepishly. "Should I have made you a mixtape?

"It's really ok. Being here is enough." I want to believe it, but a mixtape would have been nice. And the place looks like shit, as always. It does feel a little bit like maybe I should have gone to Hidden Valley with Meredith. Like maybe my expectations for this weekend, for everything with Chris, are just too high.

"Come here." He takes my hand and pulls me onto his lap. He's bigger than I am, but not by much, and sitting on his lap makes me feel self-conscious. I straddle him, and he kisses me. Then he buries his face in my chest.

"You're disappointed." He looks up at me through his long bangs. "I should have made a mixtape."

"I'm fine." I smile, trying to shake us both out of this mood. I kiss him on the mouth, and he responds. He lifts me off his lap, leads me into the bedroom and takes off my shirt.

"But your tea …" I tease.

"Screw my tea!"

Kissing is my favorite part. I know where everything goes when we're kissing. I'm not nervous about where to put my hands because I can put them anywhere. I like it best when he's on top of me, his hands shoved under my ass, my hands wrapped under his arms and clutching his shoulders, one of his thighs mashed between my legs.

"At least I made plans for us tonight." He says when he rolls off me.

"Plans?" We don't do anything. We go to his shows, the only place we can plausibly be seen in the same room and not have it arouse anyone's suspicion, and we hang out at the apartment with Tess and Johnny and the rest of the band. "You make us reservations at a fancy restaurant? Are we gonna wear disguises?"

"No." He pushes his bangs out of the way, and they fall right back in place. "Do you want to go to a fancy restaurant?"

"No." *Yes.*

"There's a band playing at the Banana. We can sneak in the back after they start and watch from the wings. No one'll see you."

"Are you sure? Everyone knows me there now." I try not to let on how much I like how that sounds. Being known at the Electric Banana is pretty cool, but it's a problem tonight when I'm supposed to be out of town.

Coming and going from clubs with the band all summer gave me something to do while Meredith was busy with the Summer Team and Richard. Meredith said Dylan asked about me a few times, but I haven't been back to his house since before I cut my hair. Eventually, I'll run into him somewhere, and that's going to suck, but I've been too busy to worry about his feelings.

Some people at the clubs still know me as Burton's kid, but others know me as Wasted Pretty's sound person. Once Johnny figured out I could work pretty much any bar's sound system, he used it as an excuse to focus on other things. He claimed he was networking for the band, acting as their manager, but to me, it just looked like he was drinking a lot. I never get carded when I come in with the band, and I never drink, so it's really all pretty tame even though I have to lie about everything.

"You don't want to go?"

"I *want* to go. It just makes me nervous. I'm supposed to be up at Hidden Valley."

"Having pillow fights and freezing each other's bras?" He hits me with a pillow.

"You gonna freeze my bra tonight?" I hit him with a pillow.

We start to wrestle, and before I know it I'm beyond turned on, and he's pulling away.

"I'm gonna shower," he says. He always does this. When things get too intense, he finds an excuse to leave the room. I wish I could talk to him about it, but I can't find the words. I pick up a copy of *Rolling Stone* off the floor and flip through it.

When he's done in the shower, he comes into his room with a towel wrapped around his waist. His abs undo me, just like they did that day in the country. I could stare at his abs all night. That would be an acceptable birthday present. I wait just a little bit before I get up to give him privacy while he gets dressed. He wears jeans and a flannel when he comes out of his room.

"I had an idea for tonight. A better one, I promise. But you have to get dressed."

I pout. I'm still in my underwear, and I try to position myself seductively.

"Put your clothes on, Princess. Jeans. We're taking the bike."

* * * * *

We don't take the bike out much. I think it worries him to be responsible for my safety in that way. It worries me. Not because I don't trust him, but because if something bad happened, it would be way too hard to explain.

I'm always nervous before we get on the bike, but once I wrap myself around Chris and we pull out onto the street, adrenaline and swooniness take over. Sometimes I let myself believe this is my real life and not just something I'm doing to avoid my real life.

We ride out past the city in the direction of his parents'. It isn't getting dark yet, but the sun will start going down soon and the light will turn purple, and the breeze will pick up. I wonder if we're going to see Buddy and sit by the creek and make out. That would be an ok birthday present. I knew he wanted to kiss me when we were there before. I wish he had. I wouldn't have been with Dylan if Chris and I had gotten together before that fight. A lot of things might be different.

Chris pulls off the highway before Zelie. We're on a road that seems familiar but I can't place it. It's the outer suburbs. There are car dealerships and places you can buy a swimming pool. I have no idea what we're doing here. It's not picturesque or romantic, though I suppose it is out of the way. Chris pulls the bike into a lot under a pink and green sign. The Venus Diner. Of course.

We take off our helmets in the parking lot, but I don't get off the bike.

"Come on, Princess." He takes my hand and kneels down like he's a footman at Cinderella's coach.

"What are we doing here?"

"Well, I may not have made you a mixtape, but I remember Johnny saying something about strawberry milkshakes, and I thought you might want to try the best one ever made."

"That's so sweet. But I can't."

"It's your birthday. I won't tell your mom you had a milkshake if you don't."

"That's very funny. But it's not that. I'd be happy to share a strawberry milkshake with you for my birthday. But I still can't go in there."

"Why not?"

I don't want to say it. I don't want it to be true. I don't want my father to ruin this night like he always ruins everything.

"They know me in there. They know Burton. I can't go in there with you."

Chris' face falls. "Are you sure?" He looks like I feel.

"I am. Gus works the day shift, and Nick works at night. There's no possible way I could go in there and not be recognized. Unless I left my helmet on."

Chris bows his head and rests it on my chest. I'm still perched on the bike watching cars whiz by on Route 8. His hair is matted down from his helmet, and I run my fingers through it.

It wasn't my outsized expectations that ruined tonight. It was my dad.

"I'm sorry. This was a dumb idea." He brushes his bangs aside so I can see his whole face.

"No, it wasn't. It was a great idea."

I put my hand on his face and kiss his lips for longer than I should in a public parking lot.

"You can get something to go, if you want?" I suggest. "I'll sit out here with my helmet on."

"Nah. Let's head back. You hungry?"

"Sort of."

He reaches into a compartment of the bike and hands me one of my mom's bars. "I thought you might want one of these if I couldn't get you to drink a shake. They're selling them at Eddie's now. I picked up a bunch to have at my place for you."

He bought a Butterfly Bar for me. It's the best present I could imagine.

CHAPTER 29

Meredith plops cookie dough haphazardly onto greased cookie sheets I've lined up on Chris' kitchen table.

"Make the scoops smaller," I say. "They all have to be the same size if they're going to bake at the same rate."

"Why are we baking cookies?"

"For the prom committee bake sale – you know this."

"It's October – why is the prom committee having a bake sale?"

"Meredith, please. The more money we raise, the cheaper the tickets will be."

She looks at me as if I've spoken a foreign language she doesn't understand and then moves on.

"When's Chris coming home?"

"When his shift's over. Why?"

"I want to be gone before he gets here."

"Why don't you like him?"

"Why do you like him?"

Meredith hasn't found a new boyfriend, and she's taking it out on me.

"I can't explain it, really, except to say," and I hesitate because I know how cheesy it sounds, "that when he looks at me, I feel like I was put on earth to be looked at by him. And sometimes I feel like that's the only reason I was put on earth."

"Oh, shut the fuck up, you cheeseball!" She lobs a balled up paper towel at me.

"Stop it." It's not that my feelings are hurt, it's more that I agree with her and it's embarrassing.

"Are you screwing him yet?"

"Are you on something?"

Meredith has been experimenting with diet pills – not to lose weight, just because she thinks they're fun – but who knows, sometimes she's just an in-your-face bitch for the hell of it.

"You've been with him since June, and you haven't screwed yet? Don't you stay here, like every night?"

"We're not 'together.' At least we haven't said it like that. But I stay here on Saturdays," I say nonchalantly, as if the sounds of the words aren't intoxicating. "But you know my parents think I'm at your house." I feel the need to remind Meredith she's my cover story every chance I get.

"I don't care about your lies," she barks. "You're telling me you've slept in Chris Thompson's bed every Saturday night for the last four months and you haven't had sex with him?"

"You really think if I were having sex with him I wouldn't tell you?" I hop up on the counter and take a drink of water.

"Well, if you're really not screwing him, then there's something seriously wrong here."

"There's nothing seriously wrong here."

There's something seriously wrong here, but it isn't what Meredith thinks. Little things have been off since my senior year started. Even though I try to dismiss them, I can't deny the truth; I can only ignore it in spurts.

Part of the problem is Chris isn't taking classes anymore. As far as I can tell, no one presses the issue, but Tess sees him as a flight risk, and it really freaks her out. Whenever they open for national touring acts, which they do more often now, she gets really nervous and twitchy if he talks to their sound guys or roadies for too long. I suppose I should be nervous, too, but I prefer to ignore the inevitable. Sometimes I think the only thing keeping him in Pittsburgh is Wasted Pretty's name on the 5K Fest fliers hanging all over town. They're purple and yellow (Johnny's choice) and have a black and white picture of the band in the corner. Even though Tess is the lead singer, Chris is prominently featured in the photo. The rest of the band has their arms slung over each other's shoulders, flanking him. I'm sure to people who don't know him, or to fans of the band, he looks like the all-American, alternative-rock god. To me, he looks uncomfortable.

There are other things that aren't exactly right. I've started to see the moodiness Johnny always complains about. Not all the time, but enough that it worries me. I see it more as a reflection on me than anything else. In the beginning, I could make Chris happy just by being in the room, but more and more he's been retreating into himself.

I'm lost in my head, and Meredith can tell. Her response is to raise her voice and tell the most scandalous story she can think of.

"You know I almost got caught doing whip-its at school yesterday?" She launches into a detailed account of doing shit with the birth-control-bitches in the history room. It's completely uninteresting, but she clearly finds herself fascinating. She doesn't notice when Chris slips into the apartment, but I'm attuned to his sound on the steps and anticipate his arrival in the kitchen. He leans against the frame of the door and smiles at me while Meredith, completely oblivious, rambles on about her nefarious ways.

I can't help but smile back even though I'm pretending to listen to Meredith. It's funny that my dad would be thrilled to have me practically living at her house, but the idea that I'm spending time with Chris Thompson, with CJ Thompson (who doesn't drink and won't have sex with me) would certainly horrify him. The other thought I have, as I watch Chris watch me with his sly half-grin (even after all this time, I'm still seeing new smiles), is that I will never get tired of him looking at me, even though I'm simultaneously aware it won't last forever.

"What are you smiling at?" Meredith snaps.

I giggle in response. She whips her head around and sees Chris in the doorframe. "Oh! Hi, honey, you're home!" she teases.

Chris shakes his head and makes his way across the kitchen. He leans up against the counter next to me with his elbow resting on my knee. This is as close as he will come to me with anyone else around, and it drives me crazy. I'm always surprised how intensely I feel his touch, even the casual ones, especially the casual ones.

"What's going on here, Princess?"

"We're baking cookies for the prom fundraiser bake sale." I put on my best Suzie Homemaker-Lois Burton voice.

"And why are you doing that here?"

"You think I'd give my mother the pleasure of letting her watch me bake? Anyway, I wanted to use real sugar."

"You're the only person in the world who would sneak out of your house to bake something you'll never eat, you realize that, right?"

"I didn't sneak out of my house. Just because my parents don't know where I am doesn't mean I snuck out."

"Is that an electric mixer?" he asks.

"Oh, the mixer? Yeah, I snuck the mixer out of the house," I say with a laugh.

"I didn't think I had what you would need to bake cookies."

"You don't," Meredith says. "It's as if no one even lives here."

It's true: his apartment looks sparser than normal, and not just in the kitchen. Meredith always makes a big deal about how much she's "slumming" when she comes here, and while it's always been true, it has seemed truer the last few weeks. Seeing the apartment through Meredith's eyes, it's easy to see its flaws.

"How was work?" I ask, still with the Suzie Homemaker voice, as if I'm a married 1950s housewife.

He gives me a look that says, you know how I much I hate work, but he doesn't answer me.

"Sorry."

He takes a drink from my cup of water.

"Do you want to go for a run later?" he asks.

"No, I don't have my stuff."

"Ok, then I'm gonna shower. I have to leave for the show around 7. You're coming out tonight, right?"

I nod.

"Why does he call you Princess?" Meredith asks, when he's gone.

"It's a joke … about where we go to school … because he thinks that means I'm rich."

"But you're not." Kind of her to point that out. If she only knew the truth, maybe she'd be nicer. But probably not.

"I know. He knows that, too. It's just sort of … funny."

"Your whole face changes when he says it."

I shrug, as if to say, I have no idea what you're talking about, except that's a lie. I know there's no way I can feel what I feel when he looks at me and have it not register on my face.

"You look like a dork."

"Shut up."

"You're like an old married couple."

I take it as a compliment even though she doesn't mean it that way.

"Complete with the lack of sex!" she adds too loudly.

She rolls her eyes as she takes a lump of raw cookie dough out of the mixing bowl and shoves it in her mouth.

"I'm out," she says and heads for the door. "See ya, Chicken!"

*   *   *   *   *

When the cookies are done and packed in Tupperware that I snuck out of my basement, I crawl into bed with Chris. He's freshly showered with only shorts on. Almost immediately, he moves down my body with his mouth. Gripping my ass, he uses his thumbs to push the edge of my underwear over my hip. For a moment I think this will be the day he will actually take it off, but instead, he kisses the point of my right hipbone. I raise my hips to push into his face. I hook my own thumbs into the back of my black satin low-rise bikini briefs, purchased at Victoria's Secret the same day I cut all my hair off. I push them down, but Chris stops me with a firm hand.

I look down the length of my body at him.

"No." He shakes his head as he has several times before. "Don't."

"No?"

"No."

Another shake of his head and then he kisses my hip again. Instinctively I raise my hips, my thumbs still hooked around the cool material.

"Leave them on."

And then, to my great dismay, I hear Meredith's voice in my head. *There's something seriously wrong here.*

And then I hear my own voice in my head, *There is something seriously wrong here.*

And then I think about how he snapped at me last week at The Bloomfield Bridge Tavern when he wanted to leave right after the set, and I wanted to stay and hang out with Tess.

And though I've been almost naked for the better part of the last hour, all of a sudden I feel completely exposed. I wrestle my body away from him and curl up in a ball.

He moves his body back up the bed, so his bare chest is against my back. His arms reach around to hold my own forearms firmly against my chest. His breath moves across the sweat on the back of my neck like quick bursts of secrets being exposed.

"Are you … ok?" he asks quietly.

I stare out the window at the greyish sky and press my lips together hard.

"Mmm-hmm," I manage to murmur.

He presses his face close to mine, his cheek on top of my cheek. I focus on the housetops in the distance.

"Alice," he says quietly, plaintively.

The sound of my own name being whispered into my ear by a mostly naked Chris Thompson is unlike anything I've ever heard. It rattles things in my brain. It makes the hard corners of logic turn to mush. I respond by pushing my ass into him.

He tries to turn me over to face him, but I resist.

"Princess, don't be mad." He uses his thumb to trace the features of my face.

I let out a little laugh. I'm not mad. I'm not sure I know how to be mad at him.

"What's funny?"

I shake my head silently, more at myself than at him.

He tries again to turn me toward him, and this time I let him. He threads his legs through mine and holds my face close to his with both hands.

"What's funny?" he asks again.

I can't answer. I can't tell him this whole thing is funny. My body is funny, and his body is funny, and being mostly naked is funny, and not having sex is funny, and the fact that I lost my virginity with a stupid high school boy explicitly so Chris would find me fuckable is funny, but he doesn't find me fuckable, and that's funny, too. But none of it is really funny, even though all of it makes me laugh. I can't answer him, so I kiss him. And he responds, because he likes when I initiate things, as long as what I initiate isn't sex. And he keeps responding until I again turn my back to him and stretch out the whole length of the bed signaling I need a breather if things aren't going to go any further. I wait for him to grab me. There's a rhythm to how these things go. It has become familiar. But he doesn't grab me.

"We need to talk about next week." His lips are close to my ear again.

"You want to talk about that now?" I pull the sheet up over my exposed body.

"Princess, I've been trying to talk to you about Karl Bell for months." He places his hand on my hip and tries to pull me into him. I push his hand away. "And you keep telling me there's nothing to talk about because he's not around. But he's coming back."

5K Fest is next week, and I'm still scheduled to be Karl's relay partner. Despite my best efforts, I haven't figured out how to get out of the role of the female-non-famous person in our male-female/famous-not-famous duo in the dumb publicity stunt Johnny created and my father approved. People from all over the city have signed up to run with newscasters and weathermen and pro-athletes. And I'll be running with Karl Bell.

"Do you ever think about Stephanie?" I ask.

"Why are you doing this?" The words are muffled because he's turned away from me.

"What? You want to talk about something I don't want to talk about. Let's talk about something you don't want to talk about."

"I've told you everything there is to say. There's nothing to talk about."

"But you could have a kid."

"Or I couldn't. It could be some other guy's. Or she could have gotten the abortion. Or given it up for adoption –"

"It could still be yours if she gave it up for adoption."

"No. It couldn't. You're just changing the subject because you don't want to talk about Karl. It's not going to work."

He's right. And it's mean of me. Because I don't want to talk about his ex or his possible kid any more than he does.

"Fine. I don't like it when you treat me like I'm damaged." We're still turned away from each other, but I'm sure he can hear the catch in my throat.

"I don't think you're damaged." He reaches around to wipe my tears even though he can't see them.

"But you won't …" I falter. "You won't fuck me." I finally say it. The words fall out of my mouth with no power. Pathetic.

"Hey." He tries to flip me over. I resist again, but when he succeeds – he's so strong, which is something I love about being with him – I bury my face in his chest, my lips pushed into his taut pec.

He kisses the top of my head and pets my short curls. "You think it's because of what Karl Bell did?"

I mumble an affirmation into his chest even though Karl Bell is only part of it.

"Alice, there are a million reasons we haven't had sex, and Karl Bell has nothing to do with any of them."

I half-believe him. Stephanie. Indiana. My father. My age. The kid he may or may not have. The abortion she may or may not have gotten.

With his fingers on my chin, Chris lifts my face to his and kisses me. I'm surprised by his patience. At this point, even I'm annoyed with me and my inability to just be happy with whatever this is between us.

"You think I'm fragile." I whimper.

"I think you're amazing … and fragile … I like that … especially because it's something only I get to see. Like your skin, right here." He rubs his hand along the inner crease of my hip.

I giggle because it tickles.

"Oh thank god," he says. "I hate it when you cry."

"I'm not done being mortified yet."

"That's fine. Because I'm not done being worried yet."

He flips me around again pulling my back close to his chest and holding me tightly.

"What are we going to do?" he asks.

"This." I push my ass into him.

"About Karl Bell?"

"God, can you stop saying his name?" I extricate myself from his grasp and throw on the first shirt I find, which turns out to be his. "*We* are not going to do anything about him." I sit on the bed with my back against the wall and pull my knees up to my chest. "I've been very clear you don't get a vote in how I deal with this."

"You also told me you would deal with it. And you haven't."

I mumble in reply.

"I'm not doing this to piss you off, Princess. This is me being worried about you."

I get out of bed, pull on a pair of shorts and go to the kitchen. I open a Tupperware full of cookies and eat one. It's good. Too good. I eat another. I consider a third as my hands start to shake from the sugar, but I walk away and plant myself on a couch.

We don't talk much before we leave for the show, but when I go into his room to get ready, he's sitting up in bed playing Billy Bragg's "Greetings to the New Brunette," which I take as a peace offering. Also, while I'm looking through my bag for some clothes to put on, he throws me one of his flannels. It's my favorite.

I wrap it around my hips and tie the sleeves together tight, like they're his arms wrapped around me. "You never let me wear this one!"

"You can have it." He gets up and kisses me, a firm hand on the base of my skull.

CHAPTER 30

My alarm jolts me awake on the morning of the 5K Fest Pre-party. I stayed up too late on the phone with Chris last night. He was trying to convince me to fake being sick, so I would miss 5K Fest altogether, or at least the pre-party, but I don't want to miss his show, and Johnny needs me to mix sound. I assured him I'd be fine in a crowd. I can avoid being caught alone with Karl Bell. Still, we stayed on the phone way too late while he tried to convince me to at least tell Johnny what's going on.

"If I tell Johnny, he'll tell my dad. Not an option."

"I don't understand why you think Johnny'll tell your dad and I won't."

"Because Johnny talks to my dad every day and you don't talk to my dad at all."

"You think Johnny cares more about you than I do, don't you?"

"I didn't say that. I would never say that."

"But you think it, right? It was Johnny you came to see that night. It was Johnny who came up with the plan to get the letter back on Burton's desk."

"Of course I came to find Johnny. I didn't even know you then. If you're looking for some way to prove you care about me, I'd be happy to suggest ways that don't involve my dad or Karl Bell."

"What is it between you two?"

"Me and Johnny? You're kidding, right? He's known me since I was

13. He tells me all the time what a baby I am. You can't be jealous of Johnny. Are you jealous of Johnny?"

It went on like that for a while. Chris is rarely worked up about anything, but last night he was a mess. While we spoke, I looked at the 5K Fest flier I had hung by my bed. It's reckless to have a picture of Chris in my room, but his image is so tiny, down in the bottom corner, that I doubt anyone noticed it. Nate would have, but he hasn't been home. While we bickered, I put my thumb over Chris' face, erasing him from the band and my world. When I moved my thumb, he was still there.

The alarm is jarring, but the rest of the house is quiet. My mom must have left for Penn State's homecoming weekend already.

I find my dad in the kitchen.

"What are you doing home?" I ask.

"There are guest DJs this morning because of 5K Fest."

I hand him the note I prepared last night. "Can you sign this?"

Please excuse Alice Burton from last period for a family obligation, it reads. *Signed, Dennis Burton.*

"Family obligation?" He's already scrawling his trademark, illegible insignia on the piece of paper.

"What would you call it?"

"What would you have done if I had already left?"

I shrug, but he doesn't wait for an answer.

"And why do you have to leave school early? The party doesn't start until seven. Does it take you that long to get ready these days?"

"Dad, I'm mixing the show tonight." I can't imagine he doesn't already know this. "I'm the 'sound-guy.' And Meredith and I are helping Johnny load in for the party."

"Do you really need to miss last period? What are you missing?"

"Actually a Calc test, but I'm going to take it during lunch, so really, I'm not missing anything."

"You have a Calculus test today?" My dad seems more upset about it than I am, which is saying a lot. "Did you study? You were on the phone late last night."

I shudder to think what he may have overheard.

"Yeah, I studied. Before you got home. It'll be fine. I need to get ready – can I have the note?"

I kiss him goodbye and run upstairs to shower. He's gone when I get out.

*   *   *   *   *

After lunch I meet Meredith by the sign-out book, her backpack is slung over one shoulder, and her leg is bouncing furiously.

"Sorry, I had to check-in with the bursar." I lean down to sign out.

"Prom committee?"

"Yeah," I say, keeping my head down.

It's not true. I stopped by to confirm my account is up-to-date. I feel like this is important information to have if I'm going to be spending the next 24-hours in close proximity to Karl Bell.

"So, we outta here?" It's pretty clear she's on something, which adds to my anxiety about the night.

"Yeah. Meet you at the station?"

We drive separately but go upstairs together. The summer interns who have come back to help with the weekend are already in the conference room. Clay has the clipboard we sign in on.

Johnny assigns everyone tasks. I'm the "sound-guy" and Meredith is my runner. She's angling for something more exciting, but I told Johnny I needed her with me. I finally decided that was my plan for Karl Bell – keep Meredith with me and hope for the best.

Meredith and I hold doors and offer mostly unhelpful suggestions while the interns do the heavy lifting. My dad intercepts me outside his office.

"Calculus?"

"Fine."

"What's Meredith on?" His tone doesn't even change; it's the same monotone he used to ask about Calculus. I hate how it seems he's not paying attention but is all-knowing at the same time. I try not to show he has rattled me.

"I don't know what you mean. I think she's just excited. We all are."

I keep walking. I'm going down the stairs when I run into Johnny coming up.

"You ok?" he asks me.

"Yeah, why?"

"I don't know. Chris said you might want to talk to me about something and you seem really off."

"I don't know what you're talking about." I put my head down and take the stairs two at a time.

Meredith is in the crush of people by the van.

"Johnny was looking for you," she says.

"He found me."

CHAPTER · 31 ·

I'm upstairs in the balcony surrounded by interns eating pizza when Wasted Pretty starts to load in. I sip the shake I made in the bathroom and watch the band carry in their gear. Chris looks up and gives me a cool-guy chin-tip. Tess waves, and I wave back.

"I didn't have you pegged as a groupie," Clay says.

"I'm not a groupie. I do sound for the band."

"Yeah ..." he teases. "I think you're a groupie."

"Shut up!" I sound ten years old, but Clay doesn't really bother me. It's actually nice to see him. He's the only intern I can barely stand.

I turn to Meredith, "We need to get ready."

Meredith bought us matching clingy dresses and told me to bring black pantyhose and heels. The dresses are impossibly short but have long sleeves like the dresses from Robert Palmer's videos. They're crushed black velvet; I can't image how much they cost. We put them on in the bathroom backstage. Meredith is applying my makeup in the green room when Tess comes in and plops down on a couch.

"Wow," she says to me. "You look fit."

I'm not sure how to respond. The dresses are shorter and clingier than I thought they'd be.

"Thanks!" Meredith says over her shoulder, taking credit for everything.

"Hey, we're ready," Chris says to Tess. In the mirror we're using for makeup I can see the reflection of his head poking through the door.

"Have you seen Alice? She's not in the sound booth."

Tess points in our direction.

"Oh … I … Um …" he stutters.

As everyone watches, he fixes me with a gaze he normally reserves for when we're alone. Then, after a brief moment of awkward silence, Meredith exclaims, "Hot, right?! You can thank me, I bought the dresses."

He ignores Meredith. "Uhhhmmm, can I talk to you?"

I look around the room and shrug.

He nods towards the door to the alley, and we step outside to the back loading dock. Tess makes a joke about how anyone could "just talk" to someone who looks as good as I do.

"Hi." He's standing closer than he should, but still not close enough to get us in trouble.

"Hi."

"Do you really think that's a good idea?" He motions to my dress.

"Wow," I say, deadpan. "Thanks."

"You know what I mean. Do you have a plan?"

"My plan is that Meredith is going to be strapped to me like body armor. That's all I got. But thanks," I continue sarcastically, "glad you like the dress."

"Princess, there's no question you look good. I mean really good." He shakes his head like it's unsafe for him to look at me. "But you look good in my Umbros and a T-shirt, too. You don't need to try to be something you're not."

"I'm not *trying* to be anything. Meredith thought it would be funny if we wore the same dress. She bought them; I didn't even see it until twenty minutes ago. But I'm glad you're so convinced I can't pull this off."

"I didn't say that." His eyes look at me from behind his bangs, asking for mercy I have no intention of giving to him. "You know I'm worried about you. I don't know why you're making this so hard."

"Oh. I'm sorry this is so hard *for you*. You think tonight's going to be easy for me? But I'm not going to wear a paper bag to make you feel better about it. I'm going inside."

I step past him, and for a moment the heavy door and the loading dock wall form a triangle that blocks us from view. We're standing so close our chests are touching. Chris runs his hand down the length of my torso. His fingers come to rest on my left hip. I push my body into his, and he lets out a sigh that tells me everything is ok.

"Can you stay over tonight?" His lips brush my ear, and a shiver goes down my neck.

"No, I don't think so. I have to be up early for Fest."

"Are you sure?"

Apparently, the dress is magical.

"Will you screw me if I stay over?"

Or maybe the dress has just given me the confidence Meredith got with her trust fund.

"Alice," he says sternly, gripping my upper arms and creating space between us.

"What? That's not a fair question?"

He looks around to see if anyone is in the parking lot, but no one can see us in this industrial cocoon.

"It's not that I don't want to. You know that, right?"

"I don't know that. I don't know anything because you won't tell me anything. You know I'm not a virgin, right?"

"Alice, stop, I don't want to talk to about this here."

"Ok." I take an awkward step past him, but he holds on to my arm.

"Wait," he says. "I don't know that."

"Well, I'm not. And if that's what this has been about, you should have just asked me."

"Who was it?" I can't read his face, but he seems displeased, which isn't exactly what I was going for. I realize too late how it must have sounded to him.

"It's no one you know. I only told you because I thought maybe that's why you wouldn't …" I said it to make things better, to make me sound like less of a child, but now I realize he probably thinks I'm a slut. I can't win, and I'm making stupid mistakes. "Is that why you won't sleep with me? You don't want to be responsible for defiling me?"

"Let's talk about this later. Let's not make tonight any harder than it needs to be."

"Fine." I pretend to be pissed, but I'm actually relieved he's not angrier.

After looking around again, he kisses me on the cheek, and I don't know what to make of that. He never kisses my cheek.

I dart back into the building and take the long way around to the front of the room. When I get out there, Chris is already standing on the lip of the stage next to Tess, his hair hanging in front of his face as he tunes his guitar. I'm looking at him over my shoulder, thinking about how strong his fingers are, when I walk into someone.

"What the hell are you wearing?" my father's voice booms. The caterers and florists who are setting up turn and look at us. I resist looking at Chris on the stage, but I assume he's humored by me getting busted by my dad.

"Meredith bought it for me," I say, as quietly as I can.

"Nice try, Alice," my dad says more loudly than is necessary. "I didn't ask where you got it. I want to know why you think you can wear it."

Finally, something Chris and my dad agree on.

"Because right now my only other option is a school uniform? And that doesn't seem quite appropriate for a cocktail event." I deliver this line with calculated sass.

"And you think that's appropriate?"

I'm sure everyone in the room, including everyone in Wasted Pretty, can hear all of this, and I'm mortified. Beyond that, I'm seriously concerned he's going to make me put my school uniform back on when, out of nowhere, Johnny appears, oblivious to what's going on.

"Burton, we need you out front. Make-A-Wish Karl and some other celebs are here."

And with that, he whisks my dad away to the front bar, and I make a beeline for the booth.

The sound check goes well. Tony, Graffiti's sound guy, adjusts the levels on a board that's far more complicated than the ones I've been working in bars all summer. I stand next to him giving input on how the band would want to sound (more vocals, less bass). I'm relieved I won't be alone on the board, but I'm concerned about the night. The run-ins with Chris and my father lead me to believe I've underestimated the issues at hand and overestimated my ability to keep them from exploding. Focusing on the music helps. Tess sounds awesome, which is important because it's a big night for her. The band will get more exposure tonight than they got playing in small clubs the entire last year. The people at this show are the kind of people who can get them a record deal or a national tour as an opening band. She's hopeful everything is going to break open tonight, and you can hear it in her voice. Everyone is amped up, everyone except Chris, who is his typical low-key self. He just plays his guitar, silky blond hair in his face, shoulders hunched a little forward.

"You have to try this!" Meredith says, when she bursts through the door of the sound booth with a flute of champagne.

"You're pretty wasted, huh?"

"Or am I *wasted pretty*?!" She does the winking thing I hate.

"Meredith, you're going to get us kicked out of here. My dad made it very clear we were not to drink."

"Blah blah blah," Meredith says. "He's not going to tell, are you?" she asks Tony.

"Wait, how old are you?" Tony asks. "Wait, who's your dad?"

"Oh, never-mind," she says to Tony. "This is the good stuff," she says to me. She's bouncing off the walls of the small room.

"No, really," Tony insists.

I look at Meredith in her black dress and dramatic makeup. And I know how I look, more from Chris' reaction than from the mirror. Tony must think he hit the jackpot stuck in the tiny sound booth with the two of us.

"I'm Dennis Burton's kid. I'm seventeen."

"Holy shit," Tony says.

"By the way," Meredith says, head cocked to one side, her long brown hair falling into her cleavage. "Your dad has no sense of humor. He was complaining to Johnny about our dresses."

"Wonderful." I take a swig from Meredith's glass. "Oh, that is good."

"I'm gonna get more." She's halfway out the door when she turns back around. "Karl Bell's here, and he's wearing a tux. I'd totally do him. Actually, I think I am going to do him. Big night tonight!"

She slams the door behind her. My dad is gonna bust her, and it's going to be a disaster. But I don't have time to fix that because Tess is motioning for me to come out of the booth.

Her tiny torso is wrapped in black: black leggings, a short black skirt, a clingy, gauzy black top layered over a black tank. A huge black leather belt with a square silver buckle rests on her hips.

"I need your brutal honesty." She sits on the edge of the stage and talks quietly in my ear.

"Of course."

The doors that separate the room with the stage from the front bar are still closed, but a bunch of people are milling around setting things up for the party.

"We're going to try a new song. We've never played it out. We don't need it for the set tonight, but I think it could make a really big impact. If we play it now, do you swear to tell me if it's horrible?"

"Yeah, sure." I love being taken into her confidence.

"Ok, will you listen from the bleachers? Not the booth. I need you to hear it in the room."

"Of course."

I walk across the dance floor to the back of the room. The heels and dress make sitting on the bleachers awkward, but as soon as Tess starts singing it's hard to focus on anything but her voice. She's singing a cappella, mournfully, while the guys are all looking down at their feet. It's devastating, equal parts beautiful and sad. Even the people setting up turn towards the stage and freeze in place. I can't see anyone's face, but I picture them all with their mouths agape, stunned by the power and intensity of her voice. And then, on the chorus, the band comes in playing extremely disjointed noise. It's raw and angry and aggressive. They go silent as abruptly as they started. The band looks at the floor; Tess looks straight ahead, straight at me. *We're doomed to be together, we're doomed to break apart, I'm doomed to run to you to give you all of my heart, give it back and let me go, give it back and let me go, give it back and let me goooooo!"*

Tears stream down my face. I don't even care mascara is likely streaking black tracks on my cheeks. I'm broken, unhinged. Very physical sobbing replaces the silent tears as Tess and the band trade back and forth, noise and melody, anger and mourning.

It's only because I feel so alone in the back of the room that I'm grateful when a heavy hand rests on my shoulder. I turn expecting to see my father, but it's Karl Bell. Shards of ice and glass puncture my insides as my back stiffens. I know my attire prevents me from moving quickly, but my body wants to flee.

The song comes to an end, and Tess and the guys are all looking at the floor. The people in the room clap and let out exaggerated sighs of awe. The band lifts their heads almost in unison, and I lock eyes with Chris. It's only the sight of him lunging off the stage towards me that reminds me how to move my own body. I push off the seat and clomp down the bleachers, nearly falling as I take the last step. I meet Chris halfway across the dance floor and put my hand on his chest to stop him from moving any closer to Karl who's still somewhere behind me. I don't let myself stop or look Chris in the eye; I just keep walking towards the stage.

"That was unreal," I manage to say to Tess.

"Oh, luv, don't cry. Your face." She wipes my cheeks with the willowy tips of her fingers.

"You don't look at her," I hear Chris say. I can't bring myself to turn around. Tess locks eyes with me, and it reminds me of the day of my bike accident: how the first mom who showed up didn't want me to look at my own body, so she tried to keep me focused on her instead. Tess doesn't want me to turn around as Chris and Karl's argument escalates. I don't want to turn around either. I want to pretend it isn't happening. I take off for the green room.

CHAPTER 32

Meredith pounds on the door to the backstage bathroom and yells my name. I crack it open, but I don't put my face out.

"Is anyone else out there?" I ask.

"It's just me. What the hell happened? Tess said you lost your shit. And Hot Karl and Chris Thompson were yelling at each other?!"

She pushes into the bathroom even though there's not room for both of us.

"I don't even want to know." I gasp for air.

"Why were they swearing at each other? Do they even know each other?"

I shake my head.

"This isn't happening," I croak and start crying again. Dammit. "I have to get back out there."

"You're in no shape," Meredith says. "I'm not even sure I can fix your face."

She roots through her make-up bag.

"It's just the song …" It's not totally a lie. "It's so beautiful and sad."

She doesn't believe me, but she doesn't press. I want to tell her the truth, the truth about Karl Bell, and Dylan, and Stephanie, and how Chris has become moody and distant, but I can't find the words.

We hear the band filtering into the green room. The sound check is over, and I've failed miserably as the 'sound guy.'

"Are you done yet?" I ask her.

"Almost."

I worry if I look at Chris, or even Tess, I will lose it and ruin my makeup again, so when Meredith's finished, I resolve to make it to the front bar without stopping to talk to anyone. I take a deep breath to steady myself before we open the bathroom door. Chris is standing on the other side.

"Your plan sucks," he says.

"My plan only sucks if I say it sucks." I blow past him pulling Meredith behind me.

My plan sucks.

We check with Johnny. He wants to open the doors to the main room.

"Go for it," I say. "Sound check's done."

"Did it go ok?"

"Sure. Have you heard the new song?"

"Not with the full band," he says. "But Tess knocks it out of the park when she sings it to me in bed."

I smirk at him, and Meredith laughs too loudly. He sends her to open the house doors.

"I think your friend Meredith might be a problem," he tells me.

*   *   *   *   *

I'm hanging close to Johnny when Meredith stumbles up to me. She looks almost official with a clipboard, but also drunk.

"Who gave you a clipboard?"

"I'm on photo detail now," she reports, slightly slurring her words. "The photographer needs you with Hot Karl Bell."

"Me?"

I look to Johnny for confirmation.

"Your dad put you two on the shot list." He puts his hands up, disavowing any responsibility for the ordeal. "He wants to use it next to a picture of you two at the race tomorrow. But he's pretty pissed your dress might give the wrong impression."

"Why is he complaining to you about my dress?"

"Why does he complain to me about anything?" Johnny huffs with exaggerated exasperation. "Because he thinks I was put on this earth to fix things that annoy him."

"Weren't you? Weren't we all?"

"It sure seems that way."

"Do you think my dress looks bad?"

"I'd rather not talk about your dress."

"He's blushing," Meredith points out.

"I'm not blushing," Johnny says. "Men don't blush."

"You're blushing," Tess says, sneaking up next to him and folding herself under his arm. "Why are you blushing?" She's using a convincing southern accent, which is a hilarious departure from her typical Eliza Doolittle cockney.

"This conversation is over. Go get your picture taken."

Meredith and I stride across the room in our matching dresses to where Karl is surrounded by fans. Meredith, with her official clipboard, butts in and clears an area for me, but she can't make enough room for the photographer to get a good angle. I can't make enough room to breathe. Karl's cologne engulfs me.

"Let's go into the other room," Meredith suggests. "In front of the stage!"

The photographer, a petite blond woman in black jeans and a tight black V-neck shirt agrees. "You've got a great eye for this," she says to Meredith.

"Let's put her up on the stage," Meredith says. "With a guitar, just like the Robert Palmer videos."

"I don't think that's a good idea," I tell them. But no one listens.

"I like the guitar idea!" the photographer says to Meredith. "But let's keep them on the dance floor. Go ask him for his guitar."

"Chris Thompson," Meredith yells. "Give me your guitar."

"What are you talking about?"

"I'm producing a photo shoot," Meredith says. Her certainty commands respect. "We need your guitar to complete the look."

The photographer is positioning Karl Bell and me on the dance floor while Meredith and Chris are negotiating.

"I don't think this is a good idea," I say again to anyone who will listen.

"Of course it is," Meredith calls over her shoulder. "I don't have bad ideas."

She hops up on stage, not a small feat in the dress and heels, but of course, she makes it look easy. She physically removes Chris' guitar from him. When she hops back down, he follows her. She hands me the guitar, and the photographer asks me to give her my best "I don't give a shit face" while Karl Bell stands behind me. He's right up against me, close enough to say things in my ear no one else can hear over the music. Tony's playing an '80s mix over the PA. It's Dexy's Midnight Runners.

There are a few people in the room, but it isn't as crowded as the front bar. It feels claustrophobic to me. Karl Bell rests his hand on my hip, the same hip Chris held on the loading dock. Chris is standing just beyond the photographer, and I focus on his sparkly eyes. There's rage in them, for sure, but also something protective – like he's ready to pounce the moment something truly goes south. As long as I concentrate on his eyes I can pretend what's happening isn't really happening, just like when that mom found me sticking out from under the car the day I crashed my bike.

The whole thing is absurd. For a moment I leave my body and see how this looks to everyone else in the room. Is it normal for a professional athlete and a 17-year-old to be acting out a risqué music video from 1985? I'm sure it makes for a great picture that will get the station and the photographer a lot of press, but someone has to stop this.

The photographer asks for a different pose and Meredith takes the guitar from me. I lose my balance and have to lean into Karl Bell to keep from falling over. Chris' chest puffs up like this might be his limit. I use my upper arms to try to block my chest from being grazed by Karl Bell. He's holding me close, and I'm resisting, the whole time trying to play it off for the room like it's no big deal. Karl Bell is strong, and when he's holding on to me, I have to use my whole body weight to try to create space between my ass and his crotch.

"Almost done!" the photographer shouts over the music. "This is great stuff!"

I'm furious that I'm going to end up with a professionally documented account of Karl Bell and me, but I have no pictures of me and Chris. The room starts to spin, and I worry oxygen isn't getting to my brain. I try to fill my lungs with air. Karl Bell misreads my attempt to not pass out as acquiescence and hisses, "Yes" in my ear. I try harder to create space between our bodies.

What happens next is a blur. I see my father enter the room and the look on his face is a mix of confusion and fury. Karl Bell must have seen him first because he lets go of me before I can react. Without a counterbalance, the weight I've been using to avoid contact with his body pitches me forward. I fall onto the dance floor, and when I look up, there are multiple faces looking down at me: Karl Bell, Chris, my dad, Johnny, Meredith, the photographer. I put my hand over my eyes in an attempt to avoid their concerned looks. Two hands reach down to help me up. I take my dad's.

"What is going on?" he asks me and everyone else.

"Nothing," I say, when I regain my breath and my balance. "We're just finishing up the pictures you wanted."

"What's wrong with you?"

And as I say, "Nothing," Chris says, "Tell him."

Everyone turns to look at Chris, and while no one is looking at me, I shoot him a look that I hope says *shut up*.

"I said, I'm fine."

"Are you drunk?" my father bellows.

The photographer and Meredith back away leaving me surrounded by a circle of men who each thinks he's protecting me from the other one.

"I'm not drunk. I just lost my balance."

My father looks at Johnny for confirmation.

"I haven't seen her drink. I think it's those ridiculous shoes."

Johnny laughs and then my dad laughs and then Karl Bell laughs. Chris and I don't laugh, but it seems like the weirdness has evaporated. Thanks to Johnny's gift for dispelling tension, I can breathe again. He shepherds my dad and Karl Bell towards the bar. I start to wonder if it's all in my head. Maybe Karl wasn't grabbing me during the photo shoot. Maybe he was just doing what the photographer wanted him to do. Or maybe everything about my life is so strange, so hyper-real and super-charged, I can't tell what "normal" is anymore.

CHAPTER 33

Towards the end of the first set, Johnny squeezes into the sound booth with a large plate of hors d'oeuvres.

"Oh, thank god." I take a bacon wrapped scallop (strangely, two foods allowable on Lois Burton's newly-trademarked Butterfly Food Plan™). I pass the plate to Tony.

"Nice job on the board. They sound great," Johnny says.

"Thanks, but Tony's doing most of it. Things going ok out front?"

"Yeah, everything seems to be going really well. Thank god."

"Cool." I smile at him.

"So, are you drunk?"

"No! Are you crazy? Have you ever seen me drink? Ever? Do you really think I'd pick tonight to start? What the hell?"

"What did Chris mean when he said 'Tell him.'"

"How am I supposed to know?" I snap defensively. "But I'm not drunk."

"I saw your face. You know exactly what Chris meant."

I narrow my eyes at Johnny.

"Drama just follows you, doesn't it, kid?" Tony says to me.

"You can say that again." Johnny huffs as he leaves the booth.

*   *   *   *   *

Between sets, I find Meredith at the front bar.

"That was amazing," she says. "I didn't realize they had gotten so good."

"Yeah, they do sound great."

"You don't look like you're having any fun."

"Because I'm not wasted?"

"Slow down, Chicken. I'm not the enemy."

"Where's your clipboard, and what are you drinking?"

"Straight vodka," she says with a wink. "And we're done, we got all the shots we needed so now the photographer's just getting candids. I've been released to mingle."

"Can you please make sure to stay far away from my dad?"

"No problem." She winks again.

"And stop winking. It's weird."

I storm off and end up alone in the balcony of the main room. We closed it off for the party but I know there's leftover pizza up there, and I'm craving it in spite of myself. My mom has taught me all about stress eating, but sometimes avoiding stress is impossible. I kick off my stupid heels. I'm shoving a piece of pizza in my mouth when I sense someone behind me.

"So, are you fucking him?" Karl Bell asks.

I don't turn around, and I don't say anything.

"The blond one with the guitar. That's your type?"

I keep chewing my pizza because it feels like I'll choke if I don't.

"What do you think your dad would say if he knew about that? And why would you pick him when you could have me?"

I finally swallow. I try to speak. "Leave me alone." It comes out as a shaky whisper.

Karl leans forward and puts his large forearm around my upper chest, holding my shoulder with one hand, my left breast with the other. His cheek is right up against mine.

"I think you want me. I think you just don't know what to do with your feelings. It's ok. I can –"

"Get off me." My voice comes out a little louder than the last time, but still wobbly.

I try to peel his hands off my body, but he clamps his forearm tighter across my chest.

"Come on, Ally," he coos. "I know you wore this dress for me."

"She wore the dress for me!"

The voice comes out of the dark near the stairs. It's low and guttural, like a roar, but it's unmistakably a drunken Meredith. "Get your hands off her. Don't look at her. I will cut you!"

Meredith lurches towards us with a small, plastic knife from the pizza box. Karl Bell stands up and tries to step away from her, but she's in his space and attempts to shove him with little success.

"Crazy bitch!" He flicks her away. She stumbles but keeps herself upright, because she is Meredith and she's awesome, and she doesn't take shit from anyone.

"That's right," she shouts back. "I'm a crazy bitch, and you're fucking with my best friend. That's a baaad combination."

"You don't know what you're talking about," he hisses.

"I know exactly what I'm talking about. I heard everything you said. And you should know, for what it's worth, there is nothing going on between Alice and 'the blond one with the guitar' because he fucking respects her! And if you try to say there is something going on, I will tell everyone you're a fucking disgusting pedophile, and they will believe me. Do you know who I am?!"

"Crazy cunt," he says under his breath. He's on his way to the stairs when he stops and looks down on me. "You know what a big mistake this is, right?"

"Don't talk to her!" Meredith screeches. I trust no one can hear her over the music Tony's playing. "If you so much as brush her finger when you pass the baton at the race tomorrow, I will cut you! Do you understand?"

She lunges at him, but he steps out of the way and disappears down the stairs.

I collapse into Meredith, and she holds me while I sob for the second time tonight. At some point, she starts crying, too. I'm so tired of crying. I sit on the steps, my head in my hands, my elbows on my knees, my dress way too short.

I don't know why I thought I could handle this myself. I've never handled anything in my life by myself. Meredith has always had my back at school. My dad's bizarre local celebrity has made everything from going out to dinner to skipping lines at the amusement park normal. Even with Wasted Pretty all summer, I got into clubs I shouldn't have been in, all because of the people I'm associated with, not because I actually can handle a damn thing.

"How long has this been going on?" Meredith asks me.

"A while."

"Is this why you cut your hair?"

"No. Or maybe. I don't know."

"Why didn't you tell me?"

"You wouldn't have understood. You thought he was hot."

"Well now I know he's gross. You gotta trust me. I'd do anything for you."

"I wanted to do this on my own."

"You'll be on your own next year. This year, I still get to have your back. No secrets."

"Well, there's more," I say.

"What?"

"Karl Bell is paying for me to go to Frazer."

"I thought you were on scholarship."

"I am. But we still have to pay something. And my parents stopped paying. Or, my dad did. I doubt my mom knows what's going on."

"If you needed money, why didn't you ask me? My dad would have paid for you." She says it like it's the simplest thing in the world. But I would never have asked her for money. It's hard enough for me when she pays for us to go to the movies.

"I didn't know what was going on until it already happened. This year's paid for. I made sure. I just don't know what's going to happen with college."

"You'll get a lacrosse scholarship. You don't have to worry about that."

"I hope so."

"Why'd your dad stop paying?"

The lump in my throat makes it hard to answer. "I think he has a gambling problem."

"Oh jeez, Chicken. Why didn't you tell me?"

"I didn't tell anyone. It's embarrassing. I mean, Chris knows, but he found out when I did."

"So that's what's going on with you two?"

"What do you mean?"

"You bonded over your secrets and a mutual distrust of your father."

"I guess." *Is that all it is?* "Really putting Mrs. Charpentier's Psych class to good use, huh?"

"Anything else I need to know? Do you have a secret life as a spy or anything like that?"

I decide to leave the information I lost my virginity to Dylan for another day. Or maybe I'll just keep pretending it never happened. If Meredith doesn't know about it, he clearly hasn't mentioned it to anyone yet. "No, nothing else."

Meredith rubs my back for a while and then says, "Let's get out of here."

"Not an option. Johnny would kill me, and how would I explain it to my dad?"

"They'll live."

"No, we have to stay, but I'm not putting on more make-up. Let's go down to the booth. Tony won't care that we look like shit."

"Speak for yourself," Meredith says. "I'm pretty sure I can pull off this look."

Mascara streaks form long triangles under her eyes.

"You can't," I say with a laugh.

We squeeze into the booth with Tony just as the band takes the stage for their second set.

"Oh, jeez, what now?" Tony asks.

"What?" I say, as if we didn't look like we have just been crying our eyes out. "Can I take the board?"

"Apparently you can do whatever you want. You're Dennis Burton's kid."

"Thanks," I say. "I've never heard that one before."

Meredith perches on the office chair in the corner, and Tony stands over my shoulder making helpful suggestions as I run the board for the second set. Wasted Pretty sounds amazing, and there's little I need to do to make them sound better. Tess' voice is clear, and everyone in the room is really into it.

Midway through the set, I feel my whole body relax with a sense of extreme exhaustion, but also peace. I will see Karl Bell at the race tomorrow; that's unavoidable, but Meredith will be with me. I'm convinced Karl is sufficiently afraid of Meredith – as we all are and as we evidently should be – so I don't expect him to do anything more than say something disgusting. I guess we all need a crazy-bitch who's a little bit drunk and a little bit hopped up on diet pills in our corner; it's just better when her energy is being used for good rather than evil.

CHAPTER 34

Wasted Pretty does The Cure's "Pictures of You" as an encore and then ends the night with the new song. I'm again brought to tears. Meredith pushes Tony out of the way so she can hug me. In the middle of all the shit that has just gone down, that's been going on for months, with Meredith holding on to me, I feel better than I have in a long time.

When they're done, the band goes backstage, and Tony puts his 80s mix back on the PA.

"You're not bad," he says to me. "Is this what you want to do?"

"I grew up in a radio station," I say. "It's what I know how to do."

"Don't listen to her," Meredith butts into the conversation. "She's going to cure cancer, and world hunger, and poverty, and ... what else is there to cure?"

I snort a laugh. I didn't know she knew poverty existed, but clearly, she is paying more attention to stuff than I had realized.

"Hey," Johnny says, sticking his head in the booth and forcing us to cram together to make room for him. "Are you sticking around for cleanup?"

"I don't think so," I answer. "Is that ok?"

"Yeah, I figured you'd want to go because of the race tomorrow. But you're totally doing cleanup tomorrow."

"That's fine. I figured."

"Are you ok?" He asks the question like he might not want to know the answer. "You sorta look like shit. Seriously, are you drunk?"

"No!" I yell. "I just shouldn't wear make-up. Or heels. Or dresses. I'm fine. But I can't really leave the booth. I mean, I can't be seen like this."

"Neither can you," he says to Meredith.

"Thanks, Johnny." She bats her eyelashes at him and then winks. It looks like she's having a seizure.

When he comes even further into the booth, it takes me a moment to realize it's because Chris is pushing him in.

"Hey," he says to us.

"Good set," Johnny says.

"Thanks, man."

"Alright, I'm out." Johnny squeezes past Chris to get out of the booth.

"I'm gonna help Johnny." Meredith doesn't sound convincing, but she follows after him anyway.

And then it's just me and Chris and Tony in the booth.

"Hey, man," Tony says. "Nice set. And congrats. I heard about the Flights."

"Oh yeah," Chris says. "Cool. Listen, can I talk to Alice about some stuff?"

"Yeah, sure." Tony finally gets the message to leave, but he looks slightly more intrigued than I'd like him to be.

As soon as the door to the booth shuts behind him, Chris pulls me close. There's nothing sexual about it; it's pure concern. It feels odd for a moment, like he's holding onto me but maintaining a distance at the same time, and then I realize it's exactly what I need. I don't want to be a sexual being right now. I want to be taken care of. I want to be the caterpillar he's protecting from a hungry dog. I don't want to be a butterfly.

"You're crying again." He holds my face in his hands. "What happened?"

"Nothing. It's just the song. That new one."

"Princess," he protests. "It's not the song. Did he touch you?"

"No. That's over."

He steps back so that he can look at me.

"Did you tell Burton?"

"God no!"

"Then what happened?"

"Actually, Meredith handled it, if you can believe that."

"Oh, I can believe that," he says. "That girl is a tad on the intense side."

"She is, but she's also on my side."

"So you're really ok?"

"I'm ok," I say. "I know you were worried. I know it must have been hard to see … what you saw tonight. And I know my plan sucked. And I know you've been bugging me for weeks to figure it out. But it's ok now. I'm ok."

He kisses my forehead. The lights are up on the dance floor, which makes it hard to see into the booth, but I still pull away, nervous about who might walk in.

"What was Tony saying about the Flights?"

"You mean to tell me you spent all night in the booth with Tony and you didn't notice that nothing he says makes any sense? I thought you were supposed to be the smart one."

"Ha," I laugh. But he hasn't answered my question.

"So, really, you're ok?"

"Yeah, I really am. I know it doesn't look like it," I motion to my mascara streaks, "and I know it's probably hard to believe, but Meredith was on fire. I was up in the balcony just hiding out and … he found me, and he … said some stuff … and she was lurking in the background and she pounced. It was really pretty amazing."

"I'm sorry I couldn't do more. I tried."

"Don't apologize. I know you would have done more if I'd let you. I thought I could handle it alone. I really wanted to."

I lean into Chris, and he holds me. I can feel his heat through the fabric of this dress I've come to hate. I know we shouldn't be touching, not where anyone can find us. But it feels too good, being enveloped by him. The whole night I've felt like a pinball ricocheting between equally uncomfortable situations. Alone in the cramped booth, being held by Chris is a small reward, but one I know could be taken away at any moment.

Chris lifts my chin to kiss me. I pull back, my hand on his chest, my head cocked to the side.

"Not here," I say.

"Who's going to see?"

"Chris, my dad is here somewhere, as are a lot of people who'd love to bust me just to earn points with him."

"You should have been nicer to the interns."

"Yeah – too late for that."

"I'm not worried." He leans over to lock the door to the booth.

"Well, I am."

He pulls me in to kiss me, and I let him. It feels too good and too familiar. Hiding out in a corner of a bar, stealing a kiss, that was my whole summer. It's my every Saturday night. Normally we're just hiding from the rest of the band, not my father, but being alone in the booth with Chris feels like a gift. It goes on like this for a while, building to a crescendo that feels amazing. At one point he bites my lip and doesn't let go. I lean into the pain and let out a moan. The sound of my own intensity shakes me, and I pull away.

"You're clingy tonight," I say.

"Clingy?"

"Clingy? Hands-y? Grabby?" I try to keep the mood light: "It's the dress, isn't it?

"What are you talking about?"

I can tell by the look on his face we're not on the same page.

He tries to kiss me again, but I hold him off.

"Sorry, you just don't normally ... you know ... in public?" I try to explain without making things awkward. "I like it," I add trying to sound coy, "It's just not like you."

He fixes his gaze on me, and I squirm. I rarely know what's going through his head, and right now I'm completely perplexed. After all this time, he still seems unknowable. I want to be home in his bed. More than that, I want to be out of this dress.

I lean up against the counter opposite Chris. Neither of us says anything. I'm getting increasingly annoyed I can't just bask in the glory of vanquishing Karl Bell, when someone tries to open the door.

I raise my eyebrows at Chris. He leans over and unlocks the door. My dad bursts through.

"Oh shit," I say.

"'Oh shit' is right," my dad growls. "Get out of here – go find your friend and get home. That fucking dress."

I look at Chris – he seems unmoved – and I'm momentarily grateful we weren't caught in a truly compromising position. That gratitude quickly dissipates once my father lays into him.

"You think you're going to get away with this?"

"Dad – there's nothing going on," I jump in. "I don't even know how the door got locked."

"Alice, I'm not talking to you," he snaps. "Get out of here. I'll deal with you at home."

"I'm not going anywhere." I'm equally embarrassed and afraid. "I was just dubbing a tape of the set for Chris. He's just waiting for the cassette."

"Alice, stop talking!" my dad yells. "You won't make this any better by lying."

Chris remains silent. I'm frozen in place.

"What do you have to say for yourself, CJ?"

Chris doesn't move, doesn't say a word. He and my father stare at each other. The room seems desperately small. I consider my options. I have no desire to tell my father about Karl Bell, especially now that Meredith has handled the situation. Still, if I'm looking for a way to get us all out of the room alive, it's my best bet. Johnny's warning from months ago echoes in my head: It's one thing for something to have happened; it's another thing for people to know it has happened. While I'm still trying to figure out my next move, Chris speaks.

"Go ahead, Alice. I'll catch up with you later."

He smiles at me like we're alone, like he's in complete control and has nothing to hide. It frightens me how poorly he's reading the situation.

"I'm not done dubbing," I say. I turn towards the tape deck and start pressing buttons. I know my dad won't hurt me, but I'm worried for Chris. I don't know if he realizes just how bad my dad's temper is.

"I'll get it from you later."

"Don't talk to her," my father says. "Don't look at her. Do you know how old she is?"

"Stop!" I say. "Just stop!"

"I know how old Alice is." Chris still doesn't seem rattled.

"Dad," I butt in. "Chris and I are friends. You know he's in the band. There's nothing going on."

"Whether or not something's already happened, I see the way he's been looking at you. And I know all about him."

And then a switch flips in me. "You don't know anything!"

"Shut up, Alice. Don't you ever yell at me!" My dad's words are directed at me, but he's still looking at Chris.

"Stop staring at him!" I yell.

"You can't protect him. You're in over your head, little girl!"

"Oh, I know I'm in over my head! I've been in over my head for months. But you don't know what you're talking about! Have you seen the way Karl Bell looks at me?"

"Leave Karl out of this."

"You really haven't seen it?!" I scream.

"You're not making sense." My dad's yelling but at least he's looking at me and not Chris.

"I'm talking about Karl Bell putting his hands all over me and thinking he could get away with it because you need his money."

The more I sweat, the more the dress clings to me, and the more I want it off. My father stares me down and then looks at Chris who remains stone-faced.

"He knows everything," I tell my dad. "He's known all summer. And he hasn't said a word to anyone because I haven't let him. You should be thanking him for keeping me sane. Not threatening him! Not making assumptions about him. Not making assumptions about me."

I wish I were telling the truth. The technicality that we haven't had sex wouldn't save us if my dad knew the true extent of our relationship, even if I can't define it.

My dad looks back and forth between Chris and me. He leaves the booth as abruptly as he entered it. Chris and I are momentarily still, staring at each other, then I lunge towards him. Even though he seemed unfazed, I can feel his heart racing as I press myself against his chest.

"Are you ok?" he asks.

"God, I wish you would stop asking me that! Of course, I'm not ok! How could you just stand there? I thought I was going to have a heart attack! I think I still might!"

I focus on my breath and put my hand over my chest in an attempt to physically slow the pounding.

"You're going to be ok." Chris puts his hand on top of mine.

I want to believe him, but wanting something doesn't make it true.

"He's going to kill him," I say.

"Or not."

"What do you mean?"

"Are you worried he's going to confront him? Or are you worried he might not do anything?"

"Seriously, what are you saying? I mean, I don't want him to really kill him, but I don't think he's going to do nothing …"

"Ok." Chris runs his hand through my short hair, but I push him away.

"What are you talking about?"

"I don't want to fight with you," he says. "Not again, not tonight."

"Tell me what you mean."

"Alice, all summer you avoided telling him. I think maybe it's because you knew he'd let you down."

"You're wrong. I didn't want to tell him because I didn't want to tell anybody. And I certainly don't think he's going to 'do nothing.'"

"Ok."

He's not agreeing with me. He just wants to stop talking about it, and I'm happy to drop the subject. So much for the "Karl Bell thing" being behind me.

"I'm exhausted. I think I'm gonna take off," I say.

"Are you sure you don't want to stay over?"

"Not tonight. I assume you won't be at the race?"

"I wasn't planning on it," Chris says. "Do you need me there?"

"Nah. I suspect it's going to be a shit show, but it's nothing you need to witness."

"Are you sure?"

Instead of saying *I don't want you anywhere near my dad,* I say, "I'm sure. Just get me back to the green room, so I don't have to talk to anyone else?"

"I'll block for you any night, Princess." He kisses me again before leading me out of the booth, across the dance floor, and backstage.

"Hey," I say to Meredith. "You ready to take off?"

"Sure. You ok?"

"Don't ask me that. You ok to drive?"

"Yeah, Johnny cut me off ages ago."

"I should probably tell my dad."

"Your dad just left." Tess says, coming in from the loading dock. "With Karl Bell."

"What?!"

"They literally just pulled out. They were having some crazy intense conversation on the loading dock and then they took off. Hot Karl Bell was driving your car."

"You can stop calling him that!" Meredith yells.

I wave her off. When it sinks in, I go hot with anger.

"MY CAR?!" I run out to the loading dock to see the empty space where my car should be. The Wally Wagon is right next to the empty space.

"Fucker," I spit.

Chris has followed me out, and he puts his arm around me.

"What a dick," I say.

"Which one?"

"Watch it. Where would they go?"

"Who knows? But do you believe me now? Your dad's an addict. He's addicted to money. And what you told him is asking him to put something ahead of his addiction. He doesn't know how to do that. I go to meetings, and I can barely make the right decisions most of the time."

"Meetings?"

"AA. You know I don't drink."

How is it possible there's still stuff I don't know about him? But I can't go there right now.

"What are you saying? That he's not going to confront Karl Bell because Karl's lending him money?!"

"I guess that's what I'm saying."

"You don't know my dad!" I'm defensive and angry, and I don't want to have to defend my dad to Chris.

"I know him well enough. And I know addiction more than most. You don't have to believe me. It's all going to play out however it plays out. I just don't want you to get too upset if it doesn't go the way you want it to."

"I need to go. Can you tell Meredith to come out here?"

"Hey," he responds. "Kiss me?"

"No," I pout.

"No one's here to see."

"It's not that."

"What? You're pissed at me?"

"I guess."

Even as I say it, it feels false. I can't really ever be pissed at Chris Thompson.

"After the night you've had, you're pissed at me?"

"I just need some time."

"How much time? How pissed are you?"

"You know, pissed for tonight."

"Just kiss me." He knows I'm not really pissed.

"No."

CHAPTER 35

It's after three in the morning when a phone rings, but it doesn't sound like mine. Meredith kicks me awake.

"Alice, the phones have been going crazy. I think you should answer it."

"What are you talking about?"

"Your parents' phone was ringing, and then it stopped, and then your phone was ringing. But now it's both of them."

I climb over Meredith to find the receiver. I didn't even have time to worry about who it might be.

"Hello?"

"Alice, is that you?" It's a familiar voice, but I can't place it. "Where's your mother?"

"Who is this?"

"It's Doug from the station. Johnny gave me your number. No one's answering your parents' line. Is your mom home?"

"Do you know what time it is? Why do you need my mom?"

"Alice, is she there?" He's clearly annoyed with me, but no more annoyed than I am with him.

"No, she's at Penn State with Nate. Why do you need my mom?"

"Alice, are you alone?"

"Jeez Doug, what's going on?"

Meredith keeps kicking me and grunting about how she needs to sleep. I'm kicking her back when it hits me: my dad killed Karl Bell.

"Alice, are you alone?" he repeats.

"No. Why?"

"Alice, there's been a … an accident?"

"An accident?"

"Alice, can you come to the hospital?"

"The hospital? What's going on, Doug? Why do I have to come to the hospital? Where's my dad? I want to talk to my dad!"

"Alice, can you come to Montefiore? Do you know where it is? Do you want me to send Johnny for you?"

Strange thoughts are crystallizing: a hospital is not a morgue. Somehow, this is comforting.

"No, that'll take too long. I can drive. Where should I go?"

I scribble down the words he's saying and then follow the directions he's given me. I can barely read my own chicken scratch. When I pull up to the emergency entrance, Johnny is waiting in the vestibule.

"What's going on?"

"Let's go talk to Doug."

He puts his arm around me to lead me into the emergency room, but I stop him.

"Tell me what's going on."

"I don't know what's going on Alice. We need to talk to Doug."

It isn't until I know Johnny is lying to me, that everything starts to feel real. Things inside me collapse onto themselves. I'm weak and unsteady. He walks me through several hallways until we find Doug sitting in a mostly empty waiting room with orange plastic couches. The room smells like someone has made something fishy in the microwave.

"Alice." Doug gets up to hug me, but I push him away. I only want to be near Johnny.

"What's going on, Doug?"

"Can you get in touch with your mom?"

"No, I told you. I don't know where she's staying. I'm sure my dad does. Where's my dad?"

"Can you call Nate?" Johnny asks.

"No one ever answers the phone in his house! You know that!"
I'm yelling at him, but Johnny is basically holding me upright.

"Alice," Doug says calmly. "I think your dad is going to be ok, but he's in bad shape right now. Let's get the doctor."

Doug walks us over to the nurse's station, and they page the doctor. A man in scrubs with short grey hair walks over to us and starts saying words.

Contusion.

Abrasion.

Fracture.

Hematoma.

Swelling.

Coma.

I stare wide-eyed, leaning on Johnny, blinking and squinting and nodding because I sense that's what I'm supposed to do. The doctor reaches out to shake my hand, and Johnny has to nudge me to extend mine. When the doctor leaves we walk back to the waiting room outside of what I now understand to be the ICU.

"What did he say?" I ask Johnny.

"Who, the doctor?"

I nod. I can't let go of his hand. He looks at Doug for an answer.

"The good thing is the damage is localized," Doug says cautiously. "No organ damage. No bleeding, except for a very small spot on his brain. They're monitoring him for swelling, and seizure, and they have him in what's called a 'medically induced coma' until things calm down a bit."

"A coma?! My dad's in a coma?"

"He's not actually in a coma – it's medically induced. They don't think there's brain damage, but they won't know for sure until they bring him out of the coma, and they won't try that for a day or two."

It sounds bad, but I can't quite wrap my head around how bad. "What happened?"

"There was an argument. A fight ..." Doug trails off.

I look at Johnny. For the first time since I've known him, he looks uncomfortable.

"And?!" I snap when neither of them continues.

"And Karl and your dad got into it." Doug is mopping sweat off his forehead, but I'm freezing.

"With each other?!"

Doug and Johnny nod slowly.

"Karl did this to him? Where is he?"

A thought presents itself fully formed in my head: Karl Bell is dead.

"He's gone," Doug says.

I immediately think of Samantha, and the baby she's going to have any day. And if it's my dad's fault he's dead, then it's really my fault, too. When I realize I've stopped breathing I gasp audibly for air.

"Oh, no, he's not dead," Johnny jumps in.

"No, not dead, sorry Alice." Doug realizes his mistake. "He's … gone. He left. He took your car …"

"He what?!"

They hush me. *Now I want him dead.*

"He's gone? And he took my car?! He's going to get away with this? Johnny! He did this on purpose! This is my fault!"

"Let's not talk about blame right now," Doug says. "Let's wait and talk to your dad in a few days. We don't need to talk about blame. From what the police said no one at the bar recognized them. I'm not sure how they ended up in that part of town. It was late. They were probably looking to get away from … everyone. We're lucky we can keep this quiet for now. It won't be news just yet."

Doug babbles on and on about blame and fault and the media. He's lost without my dad. Sweat gathers at my clavicle even though I'm shivering. Just like that night in June, I look to Johnny to make things better when there's no real way he can.

"I think everything's going to be ok." He sounds less certain than I would like.

"Really?! Ok? This is not ok. And this is my fault. You don't understand."

"Listen, when Tess and I got home from Graffiti, Chris told us what's been happening. And then when Doug called, I knew you were going to blame yourself, but for all we know this has nothing to do with you."

"Does Chris know what happened?"

"No, when Doug called I came right here. Tess didn't even wake up."

"I want to see my dad."

"Alice," Doug interrupts us. "I know I don't know you well, but I have watched you grow up. And I know you are strong and being a teenager you probably think you can handle anything, but I don't think it will help you to see your dad like this. I think what will help you is getting in touch with your mom."

"Johnny, tell him to stop talking to me like I'm ten years old. It's 4 o'clock in the morning. I'm not calling hotels all over State College to wake my mom up and tell her my dad's in a coma –"

"A 'medically induced coma,'" Doug corrects me. "It's different."

"Oh, shut up Doug! I want to see my dad!"

I break free from Johnny and run out of the waiting room. I get turned around in the hallway, and I'm not sure which way to go to get back to the ICU. Johnny catches up to me and wraps his arm around my shoulders.

"I'll take you in. But you need to stay quiet. He might be able to hear you, and they don't want anything stressing him out."

"Fine," I hiss, and then I add, "Thank you."

Outside the ICU, I stop him. "Have you seen him?"

"Yeah, when I got here. They let me in, because they think I'm his son."

"And?"

"I don't think you should see him right now. I'm only taking you in because I know it would be a pain in the ass to talk you out of it."

"He looks bad?"

"His face does, yeah. But they say a lot of it is superficial damage. He's pretty banged up and swollen. The blood on the brain is concerning, but ... I think we just have to assume the best right now."

"I want to go in alone."

"Nope." Johnny steps between me and the door.

"Why not?"

"Because I said so. What does your dad always tell the interns? When he's not around, I'm in charge. And I say no."

"Stop it, Johnny." I try to move him out of my way. "I don't have to listen to you."

"No, you don't have to. But what will it prove if you go in there alone? You want to pass out and hit your head? You want to throw up on something?"

"You'd rather I throw up on you?"

"Honestly, yeah. Or, more importantly, Burton would want you to throw up on me. I know you're not thirteen, but he wouldn't want me to let you go in there alone."

The ICU isn't small, but there are machines everywhere, so there's not a lot of room to walk. I stay close to Johnny, and he leads me to the last bay on the ward. A nurse acknowledges him as he moves a curtain aside for me. My father is totally unrecognizable. His head is bandaged, and what I can see of his face is purple. I hold onto Johnny. We stand silently at the foot of the bed. I can't figure out how to get closer to my dad; there are too many lines attached to too many machines making too many beeping noises. I take a few tentative steps but end up staying next to Johnny and resting my hand on my father's foot.

A nurse enters the bay and glides easily around the room like she could do it with her eyes closed. Her hips don't knock into anything as she checks the machines, presses some buttons, and flips some switches. She moves quickly but not frantically. She becomes still only when she stands next to me.

"Are you his daughter?"

I nod in response.

"It's good you're here. You can talk to him. We don't have proof, but some people believe he can hear you."

"Do I have to?"

"No. Only if you want to. Some people think it helps, but like I said, there's no proof. I'll leave you two with him, but let me know if you need anything."

"Like what?" I can't imagine what I could need from an ICU nurse.

"Like some water?"

"Oh," I say. Of course, like water. I'm such a bitch. "No thanks."

After she disappears around the curtain, I look to Johnny.

"Should I say something?"

"If you want."

"What would I say?"

"Alice, this is so far outside my wheelhouse. I'm literally here to make sure you don't pass out. I add no value in this situation."

"Sorry. And thanks. You're doing a really good job."

I watch my dad's chest rise and fall under the blankets with a rhythmic hiss from the machine. It's calming. Everything in this room is working as it should be: the beeps and the wooshes; the lines carrying fluid, and the blinking lights. I know people generally don't like hospitals, but they don't scare me. It was thanks to a hospital that I have virtually no complications from my bike accident, aside from the scar on my right hand and my family's entanglement with stupid Karl Bell. If he just hadn't wandered into my room, none of this would be happening. If I just hadn't wrecked my bike. If I just hadn't lost all that weight and shot up to be the tallest girl in my class. But that's all in the past now. This is a reset. Karl's gone. My dad's going to be ok. He has to be.

"Wonderland? Are you ok?"

"Me?" I forgot Johnny was there for a minute and I'm startled, but also resolved. "I'm fine. I'm actually fine. You wanna know something really weird?"

"What?"

"I think everything is going to be ok. That's weird, right?"

"I don't think that's weird." Johnny smiles for the first time since I arrived at the hospital. "Why don't you tell him that?"

I make my way through the maze of machines so I'm standing by his head. I put my hand on his shoulder.

"Burton," I say, and Johnny lets out a little laugh. I shoot him a look.

"Fine," I say. "Dad. I think everything's going to be ok. I'm not really sure why, but I just do."

I can't think of anything else to say, so I tell him I love him and we leave.

Back in the waiting room I sit on one of the plastic couches while Doug and Johnny try to talk without me hearing them. But I hear them. They're talking about Fest, which I have completely forgotten about. It is 4:30 in the morning. I leap up to join the conversation.

"Johnny, what are you going to do?"

"We're figuring it out. Don't worry."

"You should go home and get some sleep," I say. "We have to be there at seven for set-up!"

"Don't worry about Fest," Doug says. "You don't have to be there."

"Yes I do! Johnny needs me!"

"Alice," Johnny says carefully. "Your dad needs you. I can manage."

He's right, and I'm embarrassed. I'm probably misjudging the severity of what's going on around me.

"Ok," I say. "But you need to go home and sleep."

"I don't think I should leave you."

"I'm fine, really."

"I can stay," Doug says.

Johnny and I look at each other. Doug is not the person I want to rest my head on.

"No thanks. It's nice of you Doug. But I'll be fine."

"Do you have anyone you can call?" he asks. "I really think you should get in touch with your mother."

Johnny and I look at each other again. He knows who I want to call. He shakes his head slightly.

"What about Meredith?" Johnny asks.

"Listen, if I'm not going to Fest, you're going to need her. Let her sleep. Both of you, go sleep. The nurse is nice. I'll be fine. Nothing's really happening here."

They know I'm right. They all need sleep if they're going to pull off the event tomorrow – without my dad, or me, or Karl Bell.

After they leave, I go back to the ICU. I walk carefully through the hall to the nurse.

"Do you think I could get a blanket?" I'm regretting my choice of Umbros and a t-shirt with my Birkenstocks, but I hadn't been thinking clearly when I got dressed at three in the morning.

She seems overly excited to be able to get something for me. I suppose it's because most of her patients don't need anything so simple. She ducks into a closet and comes back with two blankets, a pillow and hospital socks with tread on the bottom.

"I'm Lisa," she says. "I can put a small chair next to his bed, if you want. But you may be more comfortable in the waiting room. I'll come get you if anything changes."

"What could change?" I hear panic in my own voice even though I don't feel it.

"Probably nothing. He's stable and we're keeping him sedated. Go get some rest. I'll check on you in a bit."

I set up camp on a plastic couch.

CHAPTER 36

Time moves in strange ways inside the hospital. Once it's "real" morning and not "god-awful-middle-of-the-night" morning, people start to filter in to visit the not-so-sick on the regular wards. The windows of the waiting room, which had been black holes of reflection when I first got here, give way to a view of Oakland I've never seen before. It's strange to be above the streets and bars I'm used to sneaking into late at night. I try to see all the way to Chris' place, but taller buildings block my view. I can see the hospital I was in as a kid. The hospital where we met Karl Bell.

When Meredith shows up, she's wearing a Fest shirt and carrying a bag of food from The O. I can smell it before I see her.

"How'd it go?" I ask.

"Fuck Fest," Meredith says loud enough for everyone in the waiting room to hear. "How are you?"

"I'm tired. Nothing's really changed. They're keeping him sedated so nothing really can change. You brought me O fries, I'm not sure if that's mean or nice."

"Yeah, well, Johnny was very clear. No food until you call your brother."

"I tried him already. No one answered. I didn't want to leave a message because what was I supposed to say? 'Call me at the hospital.' That would totally freak him out."

Meredith looks at me as if she doesn't believe me. She reaches into the bag, takes out a fry and eats it. "Try again."

I'm calculating the damage the fries can do to my arteries. I decide I don't give a shit.

"Since when do you care what Johnny says? Give me the food."

Meredith shakes her head.

"Try him again. Not because Johnny said to, but because it's the right thing to do. You can't be here alone. When's your mom even supposed to come back?"

"What day is it today?"

"Saturday."

"Tomorrow, I think."

At the pay phone, I punch in the string of numbers that make up my calling card and then the number to Nate's house. As I suspect, no one answers. It's kick-off time for Penn State's homecoming game. The whole town is at the stadium.

"See?" I say. "No answer. Please, can I have lunch? I'm starving."

"Promise you'll keep trying?" Meredith hands me the bag. It's still steaming hot. She also reaches into her pocket and hands me a few meal bars. "I grabbed these from your house."

I wish she hadn't. I put a handful of fries in my mouth.

"Did Karl Bell really steal your car?"

"That's what they told me."

"He's such a piece of shit."

"No arguments here."

I continue to stuff food in my mouth. The fries are warm and salty, meaty in their greasiness.

"Is your dad going to be ok?"

"As far as I know. I mean, he looks horrible, but they say most of the damage is superficial."

As I parrot Doug's words, I start to believe them.

"And you?" she asks.

"I'm fine. Chris didn't show up at Fest, did he?"

"No. Was he supposed to?"

"No, it's just ... I don't know, I called him a little while ago. He didn't pick up, and neither did the answering machine. I mean, that thing's a piece of crap, but at least it usually picks up … So really, how was Fest?"

"It was fine. But we missed you. Johnny missed you."

"That's nice of you to say."

"I can't just sit around here." Meredith's leg is bouncing. "Do you want me to drive to State College and find your mom?"

"No. I know you're not gonna believe me, but I'm actually fine. You don't need to hang out. I don't want to play Boggle." I nod to the family in the back corner who has been playing all morning. "I'm just here because I'm supposed to be. You don't have to stay."

"Thank god!" She reaches into her boho bag and hands me three issues of *Sassy*, a copy of *Rolling Stone*, a sweatshirt and a pair of very expensive jeans. "Here. My dad said hospitals are cold, so I brought these."

"Your dad said that?" It feels strange that Mr. May and Meredith have had a conversation about me, let alone a conversation about my level of comfort in a hospital waiting room.

"Yeah, he also said he's going to sue the shit out of Karl Bell. You're not going to need a lacrosse scholarship now. Karl Bell's gonna pay for college. You can go anywhere you want."

She says it matter-of-factly, like it's the inevitable conclusion to this whole situation. It makes me wonder if, in fact, my father has orchestrated the whole thing. Would he pick a fight he knew he'd lose just to be able to make Karl pay?

"Call me later?" she says as she heads for the elevator.

She has no idea she has inadvertently dropped a bomb in the waiting room. I've lost my appetite. I curl up on a plastic couch, too tired to even think about what all this might mean.

CHAPTER 37

When I wake up, I call Chris again, and there's no answer. I don't really think about what I'm doing. I just walk out of the hospital towards his place.

The air is cool and damp – a contrast to the dry chill of the hospital. The sun is starting to set behind hazy clouds, and the sky is turning purple – also a contrast from the stark whiteness I've been in all day.

When I get to Chris' I let myself in the front door and climb the stairs to his apartment. The stairs must have always been this steep, but they never strained my muscles like they do right now. I reach for the key above the doorjamb, but it isn't there. I'm looking around on the floor to see if it's been knocked off the ledge when I realize the door to the apartment is open. It isn't just unlocked, it's not even closed. Inside, there's a version of Chris' apartment that doesn't quite make sense. Am I imagining things due to sleep deprivation? I rub my eyes, but nothing changes. It's like a funhouse mirror in reverse. The furniture's still there, but nothing else is – no magazines, no clothes, no empty bottles or plastic cups on the floor left over from too many late nights. I go into each room looking for evidence anyone lives here, any proof I've spent too many Saturdays sleeping in the bed that's now stripped to a bare, stained mattress. There's no evidence a living, breathing person has ever lived here. As the understanding that Chris is gone breaks through my fuzzy brain, I'm also forced to accept I never knew the furniture wasn't his. I feel itchy and cheap, like I'm part of what's been rented with the furnished apartment. I make it to the disgusting bathroom before I throw up. With no towels to wipe my mouth, I splash my face with water and use Meredith's sweatshirt to dry my hands.

I consider closing the door to the bathroom – locking myself in and giving myself no way out, but I know that won't help. Other unhelpful thoughts enter my head. Was the whole summer, going back to the day my dad inexplicably came home with the RX-7, all in my head? Would it be better or worse if the last six months hadn't happened? It would be better if my dad weren't lying in a hospital bed. And it would be better if Karl hadn't come back to town. It would be better if I hadn't fucked Dylan. Would I give up the time I spent with Chris to erase everything else? It's a futile delusion fueled by stress, but I let my mind wander anyway. The short curls growing out from the pixie cut are proof I haven't made it all up, but still, I wish I could go back and do the whole summer over again.

Would I have the guts to stand up to Karl? To tell my parents what happened, knowing my mom wouldn't have her business, and I wouldn't have Frazer. Is it really my fault – or my boobs' fault – that my dad's in a coma, that Karl Bell has vanished with my car?

I didn't ask to look like this. I didn't ask to lose weight because my mom figured out some very specific chemical reaction that changed my metabolism, if that's even what happened. And who has a growth spurt at 16? No one asked me if I was ready to be looked at differently. What if I liked it better when no one was looking at all? But then there'd be no Chris. But there is no Chris.

The realization that he's gone settles in. I walk from room to room noticing what's been left behind: a bulletin board by the front door, a mirror over the dresser in his bedroom, the Formica kitchen table I adore with its metal sides and matching chairs, but there's no trace of Chris.

I should walk back to the hospital, but I can't bring myself to leave the apartment. Once I do, there will never be a reason to come back, and I can't face the future that starts the moment I walk out the door. I should be more upset about my dad than Chris' disappearance, but I'm not. I'm embarrassed by my priorities.

I drop into one of the heinous couches that I hate even more now that I know they aren't his. I don't know how long I've been asleep when I hear the familiar sound of Johnny and Tess talking intimately in the stairwell. From the landing, I look down at them as Johnny turns the key in his door.

"Oh shit," he says. "You scared me."

"Can you tell me what's going on?"

"You don't know?"

"Know what? Where is he? What's going on?"

Johnny and Tess climb the stairs, and we sit in the living room of what was once Chris Thompson's apartment. They sit on either side of me but don't say anything.

"Come on, I know he's gone. Just tell me where."

"He's going on tour," Tess says. "With Fifty-Seven Flights. In Australia. He's acting as the guitar tech for them and playing with that Australian band they're touring with: A Combustible Event? Their guitarist met a girl, and he wants to stay in the States with her, so Chris is joining the tour."

"But where is he *right now*?"

"He's flying out tomorrow. He took all his stuff to his parents' today."

I feel my body dissolve the way it does when I can't deal. When I didn't know where he was, I could tell myself I was jumping to horrible, inaccurate conclusions. But it couldn't get much worse than this.

"He's going to Australia without saying goodbye? Are you serious?" I turn to Johnny. "And you didn't tell me?"

"Don't yell at me," Johnny says. "He made me promise. He told me he was going to tell you, but I guess after last night, I don't know … He said he was going to handle it."

"Well he didn't handle it, and you should've told me!"

"This isn't about me, Alice."

"Oh luv, let her be mad at you," Tess says. "She needs to be mad at someone. She deserves to be mad at someone."

"How long have you known?!"

"His plan was always to stay through last night's show," Johnny says. "He made us promise not to tell you."

"Oh my god," I say to her. "What about you? What about your band? He's your pretty-boy frontman!"

"Actually, something really cool happened last night. There was a guy at the show who represents a band in London, and they're looking for … well … they're looking for me. I'm going home."

"What!? When?"

"End of the month?"

I turn to Johnny.

"Not me," he says. "You're stuck with me."

"Oh my god … so, like …" I'm choking back tears. "Everything's over?"

Light-headed, I fold over myself with my head on my knees. Johnny and Tess each put a hand on my back, and I let myself cry, holding nothing back.

"You fell in love with him, didn't you, luv?"

"I don't know."

"Just because you didn't say it doesn't mean –"

"No." I interrupt her. "No."

This will not be the story of my first love. Not if it ends like this.

"I told you not to do that," she says softly, ignoring my protests. "I told you this wouldn't end well."

"I know."

"I told you this wouldn't end well first!" Johnny chimes in.

"Shut up," Tess and I say in unison.

Johnny looks deflated, and suddenly I don't want to be here anymore. It's as if staying any longer in the emptied apartment will prevent me from remembering how it was before. If that's something I'll ever even want to do.

"I need to get back to the hospital."

"Do you want me to walk you up there?" Johnny asks. "Is your dad awake?"

"No. No change. I'm fine to go alone."

"Are you sure?"

"Do you want me to come?" Tess offers.

"No, really, I'm good."

I can't take their pity right now, because their pity means I'm someone to be pitied.

"You don't look ok," Johnny says.

I shoot a look at him.

"What? You don't. I mean, how could you? I'm just saying I'll walk with you."

"Thanks Johnny; I'm good."

"Here." Tess reaches into her pocket, lights a cigarette and hands it to me. "Take this."

"Thanks." I'm full of gratitude, if only because the cigarette gives my fingers something to do.

I take a long drag and one last look around the apartment. I remember all the cigarettes Tess passed to me here, and how I'd scan to the room to make sure Chris wasn't looking when I took a drag. Of course, he could always tell later, when we kissed after everyone left. But while I was doing it, smoking and staring at him across the room, I felt like I could get away with anything. I knew smoking was stupid. And I knew things with Chris would eventually end. But in those moments I felt so in control, like I was pulling one over on everyone – the girls at school who thought I was beneath them, the Summer Team coaches who cut me, my parents. And then there were the other moments, the moments I was deep in conversation with Tess about who-knows-what, and I'd catch Chris looking at me like I was his – a look of meaningful desire, void of need or desperation. But that's all over the minute I walk out of the apartment; I give up my shadow life and go back to just being me.

CHAPTER 38

It's later than I realize and dark outside. The smoke of the cigarette burns my lungs as I climb the hill to the hospital. When I get there, the waiting room is mostly empty. Part of me is disappointed my mother and brother haven't magically appeared, but another part of me knows my dad would prefer to wake up to me.

The blankets and pillow Lisa The Nurse had given to me are folded up on one of the couches, and, after checking on my dad (no change), I settle in for another nap. The dream comes quickly, but it's different this time. The weather is the same (the perfect crisp air, the wind in the trees, the blue of the sky), but instead of being at the top of the hill with everyone, I'm at the bottom, in the dip right before the street starts to rise up again to the main road. I'm alone. I reach up to feel my hair. It's short. I look down and see the shape of my breasts under my t-shirt. It's me now, at seventeen. I'm still marveling at my own body, my own age, when the boys start flying down the hill on their bikes in pairs, each coming to a skidding halt just beyond me. The speed is terrifying. The game is terrifying. I hadn't realized that when I was ten. And the main road is so big. A semi-truck rumbles past. That doesn't happen in real life; I've never seen anything bigger than a city bus on that road.

I'm still reeling from the vibrations of the truck when I turn back to look up the hill and see myself, age ten, flying down the street. The look on my own small face is pure joy. I remember feeling the wind whip around me. I remember being sure I was going to win. It was because I didn't know what it would take to stop. For a moment the 17-year-old me shares the 10-year-old me's joy, even though I know what's coming. But then now-me lunges towards then-me. Like Superman stopping a car in motion, I stand directly in my own path. Then-me first looks scared and then angry, but she doesn't change course. She comes right at me like she wants to bike through me. I reach out my arms and grab her handlebars. I feel super-human strength surge through my arms as I stop the bike in an upright position. Her feet can't touch the ground; they dangle like little pendulums. She looks at me with rage.

"I could have won!" she yells without opening her mouth, the way you can in dreams.

"It wouldn't feel the way you think it would feel," I say without opening mine.

I touch her hand, my hand, where the scar will be.

"Bitch!" She screams, and then hops off the bike and runs back up the hill.

Now-me is considering going after her when sleeping-me feels someone sit down on the couch. I wake to see Johnny at my feet. When I sit up, he hands me a large cup with a Burger King logo.

"Thanks." I take the cup without hesitation. I don't calculate the calories or the damage to my body. The gooey, cold, sugary strawberry oozes down my throat. I feel a chill and am thankful I've changed into Meredith's very expensive jeans. After a long sip, I hand the cup back to Johnny. He takes a sip and hands it back to me. I take another long sip. We sit silently as if we're each willing it to be four years ago when a Burger King shake meant it was a slow day at the station.

"I brought you something else." Johnny digs an envelope out of his pocket and hands it to me. It isn't sealed, and on the front, written in messy, unfamiliar handwriting, is "For Alice."

"What is this?"

"It was pushed under my door."

"It's from him?"

Johnny nods.

Aside from the time he gave me his number, I've never seen Chris Thompson's handwriting, which further reinforces the idea that I never really knew him.

"Did you read it?"

Johnny shakes his head. "I wanted to. But I didn't."

"Are you lying to me?"

"I don't lie to you."

From his other pocket, he pulls out a single cigarette and a pack of matches.

"Tess thought you might want this."

I smile through the tears that have started to roll down my face. She knew exactly what I would want in a situation I can't even process. And she's leaving, too.

"I'll stay here," Johnny says. "Take a walk."

After another long sip of the strawberry shake, I exchange it for the cigarette and matches.

Outside it's dark. In less than 24-hours in a hospital waiting room, day and night have become inverted. I'm sleeping and waking at strange intervals. Before lighting up in the smoking area, I accidentally make eye contact with a woman who looks like she's been on hospital time for a few weeks already. We both look away quickly.

Walking out of the parking lot, I turn the envelope over in my hand. There's a slim chance it can make everything ok, but the feeling in the pit of my stomach says otherwise. In the same way, I know my dad will eventually be ok – the way you can know things in dreams even if they don't make sense – I know Chris is gone, will likely never be back, and nothing he can put in an envelope is going to make it ok. I consider lighting it on fire with the cigarette, dumping it in the gutter and walking away like some hero in a dark action film. I wish for the strength to do it, but in the end, I open it, pull out a crumpled piece of paper and shove the envelope back into Meredith's jeans. I walk through the Oakland streets I'd once jogged with him. Each time I take a drag, I'm struck by the fire I feel in my lungs and how it's similar, yet completely different, from the heat I felt when Chris touched the small of my back or brushed my shoulder with his thumb.

Princess – By now someone must have told you about Australia. I'm sure you're pissed and I get it. I just needed to get outta here. You understand right? If you weren't really mad at me right now you'd be happy for me I think. I know I should have told you but I couldn't. I was going to tell you last night, but after everything that went down, I thought maybe I should just go. But I should have told you before. Anyway. I think things could have been way better between us (maybe one day?) but we had a lot of things working against us. I know some things I did or didn't do confused you. I just didn't want things to get out of control. And I figured you'd end up hating me anyway, so I just wanted to hang out for as long as possible and have you hate me when I'm not around. You probably thought I was a better person than that. I'm not. This sounded way better before I wrote it down. I don't know when I'll be back. If things go well I'll be gone for a while. I guess I hope you don't hate me forever. Dont hate me forever, ok? – CJT

I gasp audibly for air.
Don't hate me forever, ok?
I say it over and over again in my head as I face the uncomfortable fact that I don't hate him at all. I almost wish I could. I am mad. And hurt. But I don't blame him for getting out. I'd get out, too, if that were an option. He'll start over in Australia, and I'll start over wherever it is I end up.
Graduation can't come soon enough.

*   *   *   *   *

Back at the hospital, Johnny is pacing.
"Everything ok?" I ask.
"Nothing's changed here. Everything ok with you?"
"Define everything." I sit down next to him and pull the blanket up around me.
"You don't have to tell me what it said, just tell me you're ok. Are you ok?"
I take a heavy breath.
"Ok, obviously you're not ok. But you'll be ok, right? You're not, I don't know … God, Alice, I told you –"
"Don't," I say sternly. "Don't I-told-you-so me, Johnny. Not right

now. Not ever."

"I don't mean it like that. I just didn't want to see you hurt and now you're hurt. And I should have stopped it."

"It wasn't yours to stop. And no one's blaming you. This, like most things in life, is not about you."

"So you're going to be ok?"

"I don't have a choice. But right now I'd like to be alone. I promise I'm not mad at you. I just don't want to talk to anyone right now."

"I won't talk," he says. "I'll just sit here. I can do that."

"No you can't."

"You're right, I can't. You sure you want me to go?"

"I'm sure." I stand up, pull him off the couch and hug him goodbye. "I'll call you tomorrow."

"I feel like I've let you down."

"You haven't. But one more thing …"

"Yeah?" He's visibly excited he might be able to help in some way.

"You know how everyone thinks my dad is so crazy?"

"Yeah …?"

"Do you think …?" I can't put it into words. "Would he have …?"

"What Alice?"

"The fight …?"

Meredith's words are pounding at my head. Was my dad crazy enough, desperate enough, to bring this upon himself?

"We don't know why any of this happened. Your dad is wild, but so is Karl Bell. And when they drink? Forget it. This isn't your fault, and it's not yours to fix. Don't waste time on that."

He hugs me for a long time, and then I make him go.

Slumping back onto the hard plastic couch, I feel something crumple. I reach into the back pocket of Meredith's fancy jeans and pull out the envelope. I hadn't realized the note wasn't the only thing in it. I peel back the flap.

There's a photo. It's a picture of Tess and Johnny in Chris' living room. It's clearly a post-show night – I can tell by the pizza boxes and beer and full ashtrays on the steamer trunk. He has his arm flung over her; she's tucked into him. They're dancing, him reluctantly, her with abandon. I don't understand why a photo of the two of them is in the envelope, so I flip it over to see if anything's written on the back. "us 7/92" is scrawled in messy handwriting that could be the same as the note's but could be someone else's. Still confused, I flip the photo back over. Then I see it. In the bottom left corner of the frame, out of focus and in the distance, I can see Chris on one of the disgusting couches and me on the floor. My back is up against the couch, my shoulder inches from his knees. I can barely make out his hand resting on my shoulder. As if it's too much to see, as if I still might get caught, I quickly shove the picture back into my pocket. I look around the waiting room to see if anyone has observed my strange behavior. I'm alone, but I'm not. Something feels fuller, calmer, in my chest.

I gather my things and head back into the ICU thinking of all the questions I have for my dad and all the answers I'll have to wait for. I ask Lisa The Nurse for the chair next to my dad's bed she offered earlier. She says she thinks that's a good idea. As she moves things around to make room for a flimsy chair I'm certain won't hold my frame, I check my dad for signs of consciousness. The machine is still breathing for him, his chest rising and falling with its clank and hiss. I still feel, no, I know, he will be ok, eventually, which is the only reason I'm able to continue breathing myself. I stand next to my dad's head and start telling him about my college applications and the essay I need to write that I want him to proof for me. Eventually talking and getting no responses, save for the beeps of the machines, feels silly, so I fold myself into the chair and hold his hand.

ACKNOWLEDGEMENTS

I've dreamt of being a published author and writing a page like this for a long time. So let's get to it:

Thanks to my parents who have celebrated my writing since the beginning (which was in second grade). My mother, Susan, typed my drafts at the dining room table before I was old enough to type myself. My father, Neil, provided feedback (though never in red pen) and taught me what constructive criticism was.

Thanks to the following communities who have pushed me and supported me (in my writing and in my life): The Ellis School for Girls, Long Lake Creative Arts Camp, Pennsylvania Governor's School for the Arts (r.i.p.), George Mason University, the entire borough of Brooklyn (especially "group" and "the bar"), CUNY/Baruch, and most recently, my Lancaster community of writers, storytellers, and activists, especially Write Now Lancaster, Carla Wilson/Lancaster Story Slam, Anne Kirby/The Candy Factory, and Lancaster Against Pipelines.

Thanks to my 'Burgh FB Fam, who acted as my memory boost and army of fact checkers (while the book is fiction, I tried to stay true to the setting and only strayed when necessary to the story); my critique partners and beta readers (too numerous to name, but each one evident in the text); the writers who offered advice and support along the way (including those in my virtual spaces (#binders, #pitchwars and #1linewed)); and any editor who has ever published a piece of my poetry, fiction or nonfiction. Your stamp of approval kept me going when this journey got rough.

Thanks to YOU, the reader. This is the book I needed when I was sixteen. I hope it finds you when you need it. I'd love to hear from you. Please be in touch through www.JamieBethCohen.com.

Shout-outs and deep gratitude to: Rachel Smith, Jill Belanger, Andrew Cohen, Matt Cohen, Jo Ellen Smith, Erica Charpentier, KMay,

Lindsay Thompson, Rachel Terrace, Melissa Sutyak and her family, Eva Telesco and her family, Malinda Clatterbuck and her family, Kevin Ressler, Jeanne Elbicki, Squeaky Patty, Sue Stack, Gabby Taub, Leigh Shulman, Susan Minasian, Michael Resnick, Ed Aubry, Doug Woods, Jaime Levine, Emma Coax, Sakena Washington, Michelle Johnsen, Meghan Kenny, Genevieve Abravanel, Leah Thomas, Russ Smith, Billie Cohen, Amber Carlin Mishkin, Mel May, Andrea Kresge Phillips, Dave Hall, Michele Bacon, Heather Christie, Hannah Goodman, Dano, Lindsay Jill Roth, Aimee L. Salter, Gemma Roskam Baker, Kit Frick, Caren Lissner, Molly Pascal, Emily Popek, Melissa Ressler, Genevieve Miller Holt, Billy Bragg, Sassy Magazine, and most importantly, Bitter Delores.

This book would not exist without Michele Lombardo.

My children (N and J) and my husband Sam have made nearly as many sacrifices to bring this work into the world as I have. They didn't always sacrifice willingly (I don't blame them!), but the fact that you are holding this book in your hands is a testament to their support. I am eternally grateful for their love and honored beyond words to be a part of our family.

And a note to anyone who is being hurt: It's not your fault. Please don't try to solve the problem on your own. Tell someone what's happening and get help. RAINN's National Sexual Assault Telephone Hotline (800.656.HOPE) and Crisis Text Line (Text HOME to 741741 in the US) are good places to start.

ABOUT·THE·AUTHOR

Jamie Beth Cohen writes about difficult things, but her friends think she's funny. Her non-fiction has appeared in TeenVogue.com, The Washington Post/On Parenting, Salon, and several other outlets.

Although always a writer at heart, Jamie has done a number of other things in order to feed, clothe, and shelter herself and her family. Her favorite job was scooping ice cream in Pittsburgh, PA when she was sixteen years old. She thinks everything about sixteen was wonderful and amazing, except all the stuff that was horrible.

She lives in Lancaster, PA with her husband, their two children, and one cat. She has BA in English/Writing from George Mason University and an MSEd in Higher Education Administration from Baruch College/City University of New York. She is a proud graduate of the Pennsylvania Governor's School for the Arts ('92) and The Ellis School for Girls ('93).

Connect with her at www.JamieBethCohen.com and on Twitter (@Jamie_Beth_S). She would love to hear from you!

Thank you so much for reading one of our **Young Adult Fiction** novels.
If you enjoyed our book, please check out our recommended title for your
next great read!

What the Valley Knows by Heather Christie

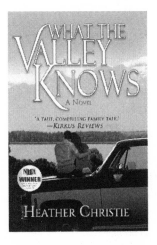

"A taut, compelling family tale." *–KIRKUS REVIEWS*

Made in the USA
Columbia, SC
10 November 2022